Can't Be That Other Woman

Can't Be That Other Woman

Ambria Davis

www.urbanbooks.net

Urban Books, LLC
300 Farmingdale Road, N.Y.-Route 109
Farmingdale, NY 11735

Can't Be That Other Woman

ISBN 13: 978-1-64556-389-1
ISBN 10: 1-64556-389-8

First Trade Paperback Printing August 2022
Printed in the United States of America

10 9 8 7 6 5 4 3 2 1

Distributed by Kensington Publishing Corp.
Submit Orders to:
Customer Service
400 Hahn Road
Westminster, MD 21157-4627
Phone: 1-800-733-3000
Fax: 1-800-659-2436

Can't Be That Other Woman

by

Ambria Davis

Dedication

This book, like every other one of my books, is dedicated to my beautiful daughter, Nevaeh H. Davis, and my handsome son, Kayson J. Weber.

I want to thank God for blessing me with the two of you. Y'all are the reason for my constant striving toward success. Without y'all, I honestly don't know where I'd be. The love I have for y'all is undeniable and unconditional. Don't ever let anyone tell y'all different. I do everything for you two. Always have and always will! Forever my babies. Mommy loves y'all with every fiber in her. Muah1 *143*

Acknowledgments

First and foremost, I want to give all thanks and praises to the man up above. Without him, none of this would even be possible.

To my parents: thanks for being so hard on me when I was a child. I now know why y'all were doing it. I love y'all.

To my sisters: this past year hasn't been easy, but thank God that we're still here. I love y'all and I thank God every day for y'all.

To my aunts: thank y'all for everything. I appreciate y'all, and even though I don't say it much, I love y'all.

To my cousins: I know we may fuss and fight a lot, but no matter what, we're always there for one another. We're not just fam(ily), we're best friends also. I love y'all. Never let no one tell y'all any different.

To my sissy Racquel: Words can't explain how much you mean to me. Thanks again for giving me a chance. I love ya, sis.

To my readers: Thanks to each and every one of you, because without y'all, I'd be nothing. I appreciate the support, and I'm highly grateful for everything. My readers rock!

Shout out to my Tigerville family.

Free Pat-Meat, Big Dog & Casimere 3rd

R.I.P Lynetta, Earline, Geanetta (Black Gal), Mark, Lil Adam, Teresa, Rowland Morris, Casimere Jr., Ralph, Juan, Gee Gee, Frank, and Leontine. Continue to watch over and smile down on us. We love and miss y'all.

Chapter One

Delaney

"Laney, Laney!" I heard someone calling my name repeatedly. It felt like that sleep was just getting good, only for them to come and fuck it up. Frustrated, I threw the covers over my head, looked at the clock, and noticed that it was a little after 7:00 in the morning. I was never able to sleep in on a Saturday morning. It was either I had to work early, or this shit was always happening. Lord knows I was beyond tired. I had closed the store the night before, and I did not get in until almost 12:30 because I ended up missing my bus home. Then, to top that off, when I did get inside, it was filthy. Therefore, I had to pick up everything and clean up. I would be lying if I said I was not tired of doing the same thing repeatedly, because I was, and it looked like the shit wasn't getting any better. Every day, I had to come from work or school and then clean up.

Bad thing was, my little sister, Daija, was 16 years old, so she knew better. Her little fast ass was too busy out there running those streets and chasing after those no-good-ass niggas to even care. She didn't even go to school anymore, and my mother was so tired of the people at the school calling her that she ended up giving them my cell phone number. Almost every day, I had to tell her something about not going to school, and she would always pretend that she was listening to me. Honestly, everything I was saying to her would just go through one ear and out the other. It was obvious that she was more grown than I was, so I had stopped wasting my time with her and decided to put more energy into my other three siblings. It made no sense to try to help someone when they didn't want help.

Throwing the covers back, I got out of the bed and went to answer the door for whoever was knocking. Opening the door, I was ready to cuss someone out; then I noticed who it was. I smiled at the sight of Dedrick, Derrick, and Dallas, my two brothers and little sister, all standing there in the pajamas that I had gotten for them last week.

"Laney, we're hungry," Dallas said, rubbing her eyes. I smiled at her batting those long eyelashes of hers, which immediately melted my heart. Baby girl was my heart. All of my siblings were, but Dallas and I had this deeper bond. She was a loving and caring person for someone so little, and she would always listen the first time I told her to do something, unlike my little brothers, who I'm pretty sure had woke her up and made her do this. They knew Dallas was my weakness. I tried my best to give her anything her little heart wanted. She was my baby, and I had her spoiled.

At a young age, I could tell that Dallas was destined for greatness. She wasn't like the rest of us. I only hoped that she would be the one to get up out of here one day and make something out of her life. I hoped that she would go to college, get a degree and a well-paying job, and have a wonderful family—all of the things that I would like to do, but I could not because of my situation.

Maybe she can be the one to break the cycle in this family, I thought.

"Let me wash my face and mask my breath. Then I will come and cook you all some breakfast," I told them.

They immediately began dancing and cheering all at once, like I had just told them I was taking them to Chuck E. Cheese or something.

"But first, tell me if y'all brushed y'all teeth or not."

They instantly stopped dancing and stood there staring at each other, which let me know that they hadn't. I almost busted out laughing at how scared they were now looking.

"How about y'all go brush those teeth first, and I'll go get breakfast started."

"Yay!" they all yelled at once before they took off running toward the bathroom. Shaking my head, I headed to the kitchen.

On my way to the kitchen, I stopped by Daija's room. When I had gotten in from work the night before, I noticed that she wasn't there, and when I finished cleaning up, she still hadn't made it home. Therefore, there was no telling what time she had come in that morning. Peeking through the door, I noticed her sound asleep under the covers.

I wonder what kind of trouble she got into last night, I thought as I continued to watch her sleep.

Although she was heading down the wrong path and making bad decisions already, Daija was a very pretty girl. She stood a few inches shorter than I was, at five foot three inches. She weighed in at about 140 to 150 pounds, with a perky set of 38-C cups and an all-right booty. To me, her body made her look much older than her true age, which was why niggas were always up in her face. I could only wish she would be smart enough to know better, but I knew she wasn't. Daija was a rebel. She would do anything to cause trouble. That's how she demanded attention. Unfortunately, I knew she wasn't a virgin, which saddened me, because had she just looked around at everything and seen the bigger picture, things could've probably been different.

"So, are you going to just stand there and stare, or are you going to say something?" Daija asked, scaring the shit out of me. I hadn't even noticed that she was up. Hell, her eyes were still closed. How did she know I was even there?

"Umm, I came to tell you that breakfast will be ready in twenty minutes."

"Well, you wasted your time, because I'm not hungry. Now get out of my room and close my door behind you," she said, pulling the covers over her head.

I didn't miss the attitude she had either. Shaking my head, I stepped back, getting ready to close the door, but then I stopped. I was tired of her and that flip-ass mouth of hers.

"You know what, Daija? That little attitude you catching, you can keep. Know that I will never kiss anyone's ass, I don't care who it is. You getting an attitude for nothing, but that's cool and all. I only came up here to let you know so you can put something in your stomach, and here you want to bitch. Just remember when your little ungrateful ass comes to me and ask for something, my answer is no!" I yelled back at her. I was sick and tired of her ass playing with me as if she were so fucking grown. If she were fucking grown, she wouldn't be out here making those silly-ass mistakes she keeps making and take her stupid ass to school.

"I don't care, Delaney. I don't need you. I can go out there and get my own shit. You don't have to do shit for me. You're not my momma. Sonya McGuff is," she yelled, hopping out of the bed. She walked—more like ran—to the door. She stood only a few feet away from me, rolling her eyes with her arms folded across her chest.

I don't know if she thought she was intimidating me, but just to be spiteful, I folded my arms across my chest and began rolling my eyes back at her. I wanted to see if her bite was half as big as her bark.

"You're so dumb. You don't even know better, and I feel sorry for you. I know that I'm not your mother, and I'm not trying to be. I'm just your sister, who's actually trying to look out for your little stupid ass, but all of that ends today. Since you're so grown, make sure your ass fends for yourself. Pads, tampons, food, clothes, shoes, hair needs, and everything else. Make sure you take care of that shit on your own. When you're out there being fast and carrying on like you don't have the sense God gave a billy goat, make sure you call on somebody else when the police have you. Do not call my phone for anything, because I won't be helping you. You don't need me, and I'm not trying to help anyone who obviously doesn't want my help. So, since you're grown, stay grown!" With that said, I left the room and headed straight to the kitchen to get breakfast started. I didn't have any more of my time to waste on Daija. She was on her own from now on.

It took me a total of thirty minutes to finish cooking breakfast. Since I still needed to take care of my hygiene, I decided to do that first. When I was done, I walked into the living room, where the kids were sitting down, watching their Saturday morning cartoons.

"Come on, y'all. Let's go eat before the food gets cold," I said to them. My brothers took off running for the kitchen. "Hey, y'all walk now, and don't touch nothing. I'll be there in a second."

"Come on, Laney. Let's go eat," Dallas said in an innocent little voice that melted my heart. She grabbed my hand with hers as we began walking to the kitchen. Once we made it to the kitchen, she released my hand and took her seat, which was always next to the chair that I would sit in. Again, I smiled at her before I went about the task of fixing their plates. There was a little bit of everything, from grits, eggs and bacon, to sausage, ham, toast, and waffles. I wanted to make sure that they were nice and full until it was lunchtime.

Once I finished fixing their plates, I fixed one for myself and sat down with them. We prayed and gave God thanks for our food before we dug in. As we sat there and ate our breakfast, we talked about day-to-day things, like what was going on in school, the kids' grades, cartoon shows, things that were happening around the neighborhood. and what the kids wanted to be when they grew up. I wasn't surprised when Dedrick and Derrick said they wanted to be professional football players. Hell, they ran around the neighborhood playing football almost every day. I knew that by the time they grew up, they were going to be awesome football players. Dallas, on the other hand, said she wanted to be a doctor, which came as no surprise to me, because she was always trying to help others.

Once we were finished eating, I ushered the kids into the living room, while I went to clean the kitchen. After I was finished washing the dishes and putting them away, I went to throw out the trash and get the mail.

Walking back into the house, I threw the mail on the counter and went back into the kitchen. I was about to sweep and mop the floor when my mother walked into the kitchen. I immediately became disgusted at the sight of her. She stood there in a dingy white T-shirt that actually looked like it hadn't been washed in days. She had on a pair of sweatpants, which were too big for her, with her hair all over her head. I'm pretty sure that her breath was stank because she hadn't used either one of the toothbrushes that I'd bought her. Nor had she used anything else I gave her to take care of herself.

"Why didn't you wake me for breakfast?" she asked, walking over to the now empty stove.

Rolling my eyes, I didn't even answer her. *Why the fuck would I feed you when you're always leaving us hungry?* I thought as I began filling the mop bucket with water.

"Delaney, I know you hear me. Make me slap the fuck out of you, hear?"

Stopping what I was doing, I stood there, and I just looked at her. I hated when she started trying to play momma all of a sudden. Where the hell was all this motherly shit when we needed it, like when we didn't have any food to eat, or soap to take a bath? Where was the mothering when she let the light people come and turn off our lights? I could think of a few other times when we needed her to act all motherly, but right now was definitely not one of those moments.

"What? You got something to say, Delaney? Well, go on 'head and say it." She posed with her hands now on her frail hips. She was moving so much that I was afraid she was going to break them.

Opening my mouth, I immediately closed it back when no words came out. Who was I kidding? Even though my mother wasn't shit, I still loved her, and no matter how much she didn't do right by my siblings and me, she was still my mother. No matter what she said to me, I wasn't going to disrespect her, so instead of telling her anything, I simply walked off to my room.

As soon as I walked through the door, my phone started to ring. Walking over to the dresser where it was, I picked it up and noticed that it was the number to my job. *But today is my off day*, I thought as I debated whether I should answer. After a few seconds of debating and the phone still ringing, I decided to answer it.

"Hello," I said, taking a seat on the bed.

"Good morning, Delaney. It's the assistant manager at the store. I know today is your off day, and I'm sorry to be calling you, but Leila wasn't able to make it to work today. I was calling to see if you could come in and work her shift."

"Well, what time does it start?" I asked, a little annoyed. I had made plans to chill with my friends that day, but now it seemed like I would have to cancel.

"It starts at eleven this morning," Christina, the assistant store manager, replied.

I looked at the clock and noticed that it was almost ten, which meant that I would have to hurry if I wanted to be there on time.

"Okay, I'll be there," I told her.

"Oh, thank you so much, Delaney. I already called two other employees who weren't able to come in, so this really means a lot. Saturday is our busiest day. I couldn't fathom being here by myself all day," she said, sounding relieved.

"Okay, I'll see you in a minute, Christina."

"Okay, and thanks again," she said, hanging up the phone.

I sat there for a few minutes after getting off the phone with Christina. I was still tired from the night before, but Lord knows I needed all of the money that I could get. I knew my friends were going to be mad with me, but the money came before anything, so they were going to have to wait. I could hang out with them some other time. Right now, I was about to head to the money.

Unlocking my phone, I went straight to my contact list. Once I found the name that I was looking for, I clicked on it and hit CALL. Placing the phone to my ear, I began getting my things ready for work as I waited for my friend to answer the phone.

"Hello," she said, answering the phone and sounding as if she had been asleep.

"Damn, it took you long enough to answer the phone. I bet your ass was still sleeping, huh?" I said before I busted out laughing.

"And you know this, which is why I don't see why you called me this early," she said in between yawns.

"Actually, I called to tell you that I won't be able to hang out with you guys today."

"Damn, Delaney. Why you can't come now?" she asked, sounding a bit sad. "You know we were really looking forward to spending some time with you. Shit, we haven't seen you outside of school in forever."

"I know, and I'm sorry, Tracy, but my manager just called asking if I could come in today. You know how hard things are right now. I just couldn't turn down extra money to hang out."

"I know, and I feel you on that, which is why I'm not mad this time. But you know Kaleb is going to be disappointed, right? He was really looking forward to seeing you."

"Girl, whatever. He will just have to wait until next time," I said, not even worrying my nerves about Kaleb. "But, umm, can you come take me to work? I have to be there at eleven, and it's almost ten o'clock. By the time I take a fifteen-minute shower, do whatever I have to do, and try to make it to work by the bus, I'll be past late. I can't wait until I can buy me a car."

"Delaney, I'm still in bed," she began whining. I felt for her if times were ever to get hard on her. She was so spoiled that she barely knew the word *struggle*.

"Please! I promise I'll let you use my employee discount on a pair of sneakers next time you stop by the store," I said, practically begging.

She sat there for a few seconds in silence. I knew she was going to say yeah. Her being silent was only to make me sweat.

"Okay, but you better be ready by the time I get there, or else you won't have a ride to work," she said, hanging up the phone.

Jumping off the bed, I grabbed my work clothes and made a dash for the bathroom. Turning on the shower, I waited for the water to warm up and then got in. I didn't have time to do the things I'd normally do, so I grabbed the washcloth and soap and immediately got down to business. Once I made sure that I had washed every inch of my body, I rinsed off and repeated the process. When I was done, I turned the shower off and got out. Moving fast, I dried off, applied a little bit of lotion to my body, and got dressed.

Once I was finished, I headed to my room. After putting my shoes on, I brushed my hair into a ponytail just as Tracy started blowing outside. Grabbing my purse and phone, I headed into the living room, making sure to lock my door behind me. Before leaving, I gave Dedrick, Derrick, and Dallas each five dollars for something to eat, gave them a kiss, and left. I was going to miss my babies, but we needed the money, so I would just have to see them when I got back home.

When I arrived at work, the place was already packed with people. I noticed the minute I walked through the door how much Christina's face had relaxed. I guess she thought I wasn't going to make it. I couldn't blame her, though. The way the store was packed, I couldn't imagine being there alone either. I only had about ten minutes to get myself together, so I headed to the back to clock in.

"Thank God you made it here. I really thought I was going to have to be here by myself today," she said the minute I came back to the front of the store.

"I told you I was coming. I don't know why you would worry yourself. When I say that I'm going to do something, I always do it," I said, placing my nametag on. I didn't wait for her to reply before I walked on the floor and started helping the many people that were in there. I just prayed that I didn't get grumpy, being that I didn't get enough sleep.

It was about two o'clock that afternoon when I finally realized that I hadn't had a break, or lunch for that matter. The store was super busy, and time just seemed to fly on by. I was on my way to look for Christina when Tracy texted me, saying that they were waiting on me at the food court. Lord knows I wasn't trying to mess with their asses. I was almost to the register when someone stopped me.

"Excuse me, miss, but can I get some help, please?" a voice said from behind me.

"I'm sorry, but I'm about to head to lunch. Let me grab the manager, and she will help you. Don't go anywhere," I said without even taking a glance at whoever it was. By now, my stomach was talking to me, and all I could think about was putting food in it.

"Come on, pretty lady. I promise it won't be long," he replied in this sexy voice that I finally noticed.

When I looked up, I almost fainted. Never in all my seventeen years of being on earth had I ever seen a man this fine. I mean, dude was so fine he made my stomach do flip-flops. This man was a stallion, and all I wanted was a ride. Standing at what looked to be six feet two inches, this man was definitely that nigga. His skin was a smooth caramel in color, his body was covered in tattoos, and he had a pair of big brown eyes that would make any woman drool at the sight of him.

As I watched his mouth move, I stood there staring at him. I didn't hear a word he was saying because he had me in a trance. I had never been with a man physically, but I surely wanted to change all of that with him.

"You okay, ma?" he asked, waving his hand in front of my face.

"Umm, y–yeah. I'm good," I replied, embarrassed. I couldn't believe I got caught staring. "What can I help you with?"

"I was wondering if you had this in a size thirteen?" he asked, holding up a pair of black leather Air Max 90s.

"Uh, I don't know, but I can go check in the back for you," I said, grabbing the shoes out of his hand. For a brief second, our hands touched, sending this shockwave through my body.

I looked up, trying to see if he had felt it. I could tell from the surprised way he was looking that he felt it too. I quickly pulled my hand back before forcefully swallowing the lump that had formed in my throat

"Umm, 1–let me go look for those shoes for you," I replied, stuttering. I damn near knocked over a barrel of socks trying to get my ass up out of there. I was moving like my ass was on fire. I don't know what it was, but this man really had knocked me off my square.

The moment I got to the back where all of the shoes were, I released the breath that I'd had no idea I was holding. I took a moment to calm down the beat of my heart. I didn't know what this man was doing to me, but I was glad this would be my first and last time seeing him.

After getting myself together, I prepared to look for the shoes. I was happy when I did find the size he was looking for, which meant that he really didn't have to come back looking for them. The shoes were high on the shelf, and my little ass could barely reach them, so I had to fish the ladder out of the utility closet. After getting the shoes from their spot, I went back to the front of the store.

"I'm sorry it took me so long. I had to get the shoes from a high spot, and as you can see, I'm really short," I said once I reached him. I really hoped he wasn't mad that I took a minute.

"It's okay, ma. You should've came and got me, and I would've helped you out." He smiled.

The minute he showed his perfectly white teeth, I felt myself getting moist. *I got to get the hell away from him,* I thought.

"Would that be all you need today, sir?" I asked, trying to hurry his ass out of there.

"Yes, that would be all," he said, flashing that smile again.

"Okay, follow me, and I'll check you out," I said, heading straight to the register.

"Oh, Delaney, I've been looking for you, my dear. It's time for you to take your lunch," Christina said, walking over to me.

"I know. I'm going as soon as I finish ringing this gentleman up," I told her.

Once she noticed whom I was talking about, she damn near showed all thirty-two of her teeth.

"You know, I can do it if you want me to," she offered. I knew the bitch really was doing that because she wanted him. She never did shit like that any other time.

"No, I got it," I said with a little attitude. I couldn't believe I was getting jealous over a man who actually wasn't mine. Hell, I did not know him at all. The only thing I knew was that he was fine as wine, and I had a crush on him.

"Okay," she said before she took one last look at him and left.

"So, your name is Delaney, huh?" he asked as I rang up his shoes.

"Yeah, that's my name," I replied just as I got through ringing up the transaction. I placed the shoes in a bag and proceeded to tell him his total.

"My name is Onijae," he said before he handed me a hundred-dollar bill. When I reached back to give him his change, he stopped me.

"Nah, ma, you can keep it," he said, grabbing his bag off the counter.

"I can't do that, Onijae," I responded. I was trying my best not to let Christina hear or see this. "I could get fired for this. I can't take your money."

"You're not taking it. I'm giving it to you. Now, go take your lunch, pretty woman. I'll see you later, Ms. Delaney," he said, turning around and leaving the store.

I made sure that Christina was nowhere around before I placed the money in my pocket and went on my lunch break.

I missed Onijae already. I knew it was wishful thinking, but I wished that I could run into Onijae again. I knew I most likely wouldn't, but that didn't stop me from wanting it to happen. Whom was I kidding? I knew for sure that this man was older than I was, so what would he want to do with me? He probably had a woman and kids at home, while my little hot ass was lusting over something that could never be.

Just forget about him, girl.

As I made my way to the food court, I pulled my phone out to text Tracy. I wanted her to know I was on my way in case she was still looking for me. Immediately, she texted back and said that they were still there, which I was happy for. I told her I would be there in a minute, and as I placed my phone in my pocket, I bumped into someone from behind.

"I'm so sorry. I was totally not paying attention to where I was going," I said as I scrambled to help them pick up their bags.

"It's okay, ma," the voice said, causing me to freeze in place. Even though I'd just met him, I knew his voice.

When I looked up into those big brown eyes, I wasn't surprised when I noticed that it was Onijae.

"So, we meet again," he said.

"It seems so," I said, handing him the bags that I had picked up from the floor.

"Thank you. So, where are you so in a rush to go to?" he asked as he gestured for me to start walking.

"To the food court. In case you've forgotten, I haven't had any lunch, and my stomach is talking in tongues now," I said, rubbing my stomach. Just the thought of food had my stomach crying and begging for food.

"Can I join you?" he asked, shocking me.

I could feel my heart rate speeding up. I wanted so badly for him to join me, but I remembered that I was meeting my friends. "I'm actually about to meet my friends," I said, a little disappointed, wishing like hell that wasn't the case.

"It's okay, ma. Maybe we can do it some other time. It was nice meeting you, pretty lady."

"You too," I said before we parted ways.

As I continued to walk to the food court, I couldn't help but look back. When I spotted him staring at me, I waved before turning back around. I damn near ran off. I didn't know if or when I was going to see him again, but I surely hoped it would be sometime soon.

Chapter Two

Onijae

I had no intentions of going in there and flirting. Hell, I really had no intentions on going there at all that day actually. Once I got to the shop and finished the few heads that I did have that day, I didn't have anything else to do, so I decided to go to the mall. I was only going to pick up a pair of tennis shoes to wear to our annual barbecue, which my company was throwing for the community the next week. Not only would there be free food, but we would also be giving free haircuts, raffling off gifts and a few other things. There would also be a bouncy house and a water slide since it was kind of hot outside.

The moment I saw shorty, I couldn't help but to step to her. I mean, I'd never in my life seen someone so perfect and sweet. I couldn't leave the store without at least speaking to her.

The minute she opened her mouth to speak, my heart melted. She had this innocence about herself that I absolutely just loved. I knew I was wrong for even thinking about another woman while I was with Bianca, but I couldn't help it. Besides, lately something had been up with her, and I just couldn't put my finger on it. I still loved my girl, but it was just that things had been different lately.

As I stood there watching shorty walk away, my mind was telling me to go after her. I'd never felt this way about another female since the day that I first met Bianca back in high school, and that was a long time ago. I knew nothing could possibly come out of this, and yet I still wanted to get her number.

Fuck it, I thought as I began walking back toward the food court.

I was halfway there when my phone began to ring. Looking at the screen, I noticed that it was Bianca calling. I wanted to ignore her and get at shorty, but I didn't. Something was telling me not to. I noticed there was a bench to the left of me, so I took a seat on it.

"Hello," I answered on the third ring.

"Hey, baby, what are you up to?" she asked, sounding rather jolly.

"I'm actually in the mall right now. What's up?"

"Oh, nothing. I was just calling to see what you were doing," she responded, confusing me. Bianca never called to check up on me. Sure, we would send a text here and there, but never a call, unless it was important.

"Oh. How's your day going?" I asked.

"It's going. I'm about to go shopping with my sister. Then I'm going to grab a late lunch. You want to join?"

"Nah, baby, I can't. I'm swamped. I have to go to back to the shop and to the car wash."

"Okay, well, I'll see you later," she said, sounding a little upset.

"See you soon, bae," I said and hung up.

I continued sitting on the bench for a few more minutes. I really didn't know what was going on between Bianca and me. I had no idea why things were so strained, and I had no desire to figure it out. I mean, I loved her, and I still wanted to be with her, but shit wasn't the same anymore for us. I hoped that we could get it together before things fell all the way apart.

Instead of going back to the shop as I had planned to, I decided to drop through on my parents. I hadn't seen my mother in a few days, and I was missing the shit out of her. I knew for sure that she was going to curse me out the minute I strolled through the door, but I was prepared for that. I hoped my little sister was there to soften the blow, though.

Pulling up to my parents' house, I shut the engine off and sat there. I mentally prepared myself for the backlash that I knew I was going to get. If there was one thing that I knew for sure, my mother was going to chew me a new asshole. She hated when we went numerous days without talking to her. Hell, she hated when we went one day without talking to her, so I knew for sure that this wasn't going to ride.

Pulling out my phone, I decided to call my brother, Omari. I knew for sure that if I hadn't been there, his ass hadn't been there either. He was worse than I was, and that was why my mother and father stayed getting on him about it.

"'Sup, li'l nigga? To what do I owe the pleasure of this call?" he said once he answered the phone.

"Shut up, nigga! I'm over here at our parents' house, and I was wondering if you wanted to spin through," I asked him.

"Nah, nigga, you mean you want me to come through so they could fuss at both of us instead of getting you by yourself?" he said, already knowing the deal.

"Nigga, you know just like I know that you haven't been here in a minute, just like my ass," I said, cutting straight to the chase.

He knew just as well as I knew how our parents were. He could act as if he weren't worrying about it, but he and I both knew that this shit was getting to his ass too.

"Yeah, yeah, yeah, whatever. I'll be there in a few minutes. See you later," he said, hanging up the phone in my face.

After sitting there for a few more minutes, I opened the door and got out. *Time to face the music*, I thought as I straightened out my clothes.

I took my time as I walked up the driveway to the house. I hadn't even made it to the door before it came swinging open. I paused immediately and began laughing. Standing there with a broom in her hand and her hair in some rollers was my mother. I should've known better. I hadn't expected her to come at me like this, but I should've expected her to do something.

Lillian Love was a woman who didn't play or take shit from anyone. At forty-six years old, my mother didn't even look her age. She could've easily passed for a woman being in her early thirties. She'd been married to our father, Omari Love, Sr., for twenty-five years, but they'd been together for a total of thirty years. Together, they produced three kids. Omari was the oldest of the three. I was the middle child, and then there was my little sister, Tracy.

Back in the day, my father worked at a local warehouse. He worked hard, day and night, to provide for his family. He later became a lead man. Being one to think beyond the point, he invested his money in a couple of local businesses that later made him more money than we could spend, and life for us was kind of peachy.

Since he was the man of the house and could easily provide for his family, he wanted my mother to be a stay-at-home wife and mother to his kids. She told him hell no and cursed his ass out for even bringing that shit up to her. In her words, she wasn't going to be like them other women. She had my brother when she was nineteen years old and me when she turned twenty-two, and she still managed to get through school. She became a schoolteacher, and then she later had Tracy at twenty-nine. By the time she turned forty-two, she was retired and enjoying her money.

My pops later retired and handed his businesses down to my brother and me. He was waiting until my little sister turned twenty-one so she could get what was rightfully hers. Our parents were hardworking, and they made sure that all three of their kids assumed their roles and had their work ethics.

"I should beat your ass with this damn broom, Onijae," was the first thing she said out of her mouth.

"Now, why would you want to do that to your baby boy?" I asked, laughing at how serious she was.

"Hell yeah, I would," she said, standing firm. She stood in the door with the broom clutched in her hand, refusing to let me inside. "What the hell do you want? You weren't worrying about coming up to see me all of those other days, so why the hell are you coming up here now?"

"Ma, I'm sorry. I've just been busy with the shops and shit," I said, defending myself.

"Watch your damn mouth when you talk to me, boy. Now, bring your ass in here before I whack your ass upside the head with this damn broomstick," she said, moving to the side so that I could walk inside.

"I love you too, Ma," I said, walking straight to the kitchen. I went to the refrigerator, grabbed a beer, and took a seat on one of the bar stools. I could hear her saying some shit behind me, but I didn't pay her ass any mind. For her ass to be only four foot eight, she had a mouthpiece on her. I could see where Tracy got that shit from.

"Where's your dumb-ass brother?" she asked, walking into the kitchen.

"I don't know. When I called him, he said that he was on his way over here," I said, taking a sip from my beer.

"I should've known that y'all asses would've appeared together. I got a good mind to beat both of y'all asses with my belt when he gets here," she fussed. "You hungry?"

"Nah, I'm straight. I had some McDonald's earlier when I left the mall," I told her. The minute I saw her face, I knew I shouldn't have told her that.

"That little girl still has you eating fast food, I see," she said as she started to fix me a plate of food anyway.

"Ma, I really don't have time for this right now," I said, turning the bottle up. My mother wasn't a fan of Bianca. She never had been. To her, Bianca was a gold digger, a leech. She thought that she only wanted me for what I had, but I knew different.

Bianca had been there for me through everything, and in return, I give her whatever she wanted. She was only working because she wanted to. I had already made it clear that she did not have to.

"I didn't say anything, Jae," she said, placing the plate in front of me.

"Where's Dad?" I asked, changing the subject.

"He was in the bathtub last time I checked. I'll go upstairs and get him for you," she said, disappearing out of the kitchen.

I sat there thinking about what had just happened. I didn't expect my mother to be a fan of Bianca, and I didn't blame her. My brother and sister weren't fans of hers either. The only one who showed her a little respect was my father.

About two and a half years ago, I had caught Bianca cheating on me with a dude she worked with. The fucked-up thing about it was that it happened in our house. She didn't even have the decency to get a fucking hotel room or anything. She brought him in the home that we both shared, and the shit fucked me up pretty bad. Had I not gone home that day, I probably wouldn't have ever found out about it.

Of course, I kicked her ass to the curb, but that didn't last long, because I really loved her. She was my heart, my soul, and my life, so I took her back. Of course, my family thought that was a bad idea, but I didn't care. It was my decision, my life, and my choice. Unfortunately, things hadn't been the same since then, but we were working on it. At least, that's what I kept telling myself.

"Is it safe for me to come in here?" my brother asked, peeking his head into the kitchen.

"Hell no, it's not. Now, bring your ass on so I can beat you with this broomstick," my mother said, walking over to him with the broom in her hand like before. I hadn't even noticed when she got back in the kitchen.

"Come on, Ma. You know I'm too old to be getting beat with a broom," he said with his hands up.

"Yeah, you can keep telling yourself that. As long as you're on this earth and I'm your mother, you'll never be too old for an ass whooping," she said, popping him upside his head. "Now, take a seat next to your brother while I fix you a plate."

"Yes, ma'am."

"Ma, where is Tracy?" I asked her. I hadn't seen or heard her anywhere in the house.

"Child, she's at the mall with her friends. You know that child is never home."

"Her ass better not be up to no good out there," Omari said with a sour expression on his face.

"Unlike you and your brother, my daughter knows the home training I taught her. She especially knows not to go too long without talking to her mother," she said, giving both Omari and me the evil eye.

"That's because she still lives in the same house as you."

"Nah, that's because she loves her mother," she said, pretending to be offended. She placed Omari's plate in front of him and took a seat at the table with us.

"Ma, you know we love you. We just be busy, that's all," Omari said.

"I know, but you know y'all are my babies. I worry when I don't hear from y'all in a few hours, so y'all should know better than to ignore me for more than twenty-four hours." She started chastising us as if we were little boys.

"We're sorry, Ma, and we promised not to do it again," I said, trying to make her stop talking about it.

"Uh-huh, I'll believe it when I see it."

For the next hour, my brother, my mother, and I sat around the table, chatting about what was going on in our lives. It was mostly about our business and a few other things. When my little sister showed up, it was like a little reunion. We pulled out a deck of cards and a few board games and got everything rolling. Once my father heard all of the noise, he came down as well, and the party was in full swing.

Bianca

I was beyond happy when Onijae said he didn't want to meet with me. It only made it easier for me to do what I had to do. What he didn't know was that I was actually not about to go shopping for me. Well, at least not right now. I had other plans, which didn't include clothes or any such thing else.

Please allow me to formally introduce myself. My name is Bianca Janae Harris, RN. I am one of the baddest bitches ever to grace the state of Texas. In my eyes, there isn't another bitch who can touch me. I work at Parkland Hospital in Dallas, Texas, where I am a head nurse. I drive a 2009 Bentley Continental GT, which I paid for myself, and live in a spacious five-bedroom, three-and-a-half-bathroom house. I don't need anyone to tell me that I'm the shit because I already know that.

At twenty-five years old, I stand at an even five feet. I'm a redbone, and a cute one at that. I sport a shoulder-length, honey blonde bob, which I keep laced in a thirty-inch weave that is always styled to perfection. My body is so perfect that one would think God himself made me. I have a perfect set of breasts that are plump and firm. My stomach is flat as a board, and my ass is a nice size. It isn't too big or too small, so I am thankful. I'm a high-end bitch, who likes the finer things in life. Whatever I want, I get—no, ifs, ands, or buts about it.

My boyfriend, Onijae, was definitely one of a kind. We'd been together for a total of eight years, and I was glad to be able to call him mine. I wanted nothing more than to be able to call him my husband, but he wasn't going for that. To him, it was too soon to get married, but I begged to differ. I mean, we'd been together for almost ten damn years. How was that too soon?

I didn't know what it was, but I was kind of feeling like he was distancing himself from me. I tried to pretend as if I was not noticing it, but I did. Things hadn't been the same with us lately, and I was wishing like hell that we could get back to our safe place. I was not trying to lose my man. We'd come too far to part ways now. I was going to do whatever was in my power to keep my man, and I had a great way to start things off.

After getting off the phone with Onijae, I called up my sister, Candice. I had many things to do before Onijae came home that night. I knew damn well that I couldn't do it all by myself. Therefore, she was the perfect person to come in and help me with this situation. It also helped that she was a party planner, so this was going to be right up her alley. This was going to be a day well spent.

An hour later, I pulled up to North Park Center shopping mall on a mission. I wasted no time finding a parking spot, grabbing my purse, and getting out. I was already late, and I knew more than likely that my sister was going to be mad as hell with me. I was practically running into the building. I didn't need her to be bitching. This wasn't my cup of tea, so I needed her for this.

"It's about time your ass got here. I was just about to leave," she yelled the minute she saw me.

I rolled my eyes because I knew that this was only going to be the first of many complaints that I would be getting from her.

"How long have you been here?" I asked, even though I really wasn't trying to hear the answer because I knew she would just try to complain some more.

"For over an hour and some change. That's why I was getting my ass up to leave."

"Candice, please don't leave me. I need you to help me. I promise that I'm going to make it worth your while," I said, begging her. She was lucky that I wanted to do something good for my man, because if I didn't, her ass could've walked right out the fucking door for all I cared.

"Uh-huh, you better. Now come on, because I'm going out tonight, and I'm not trying to be up in here all day fooling with you," she said, walking off.

Instead of responding, I silently sent a prayer to the man upstairs, asking him for strength and patience. I knew Candice was my big sister, but sometimes she acted like a bitch. She forever had this attitude as if somebody was supposed to jump every time she said so. That shit was a bad habit, but I never told her anything about it. Just by her attitude, I knew today was going to be one of those days.

Three hours, twelve stores, and twenty-something bags later, we were finally leaving the mall. I was exhausted and in need of a good bath, but unfortunately for me, my night was just getting started and wasn't about to end any time soon.

After parting ways with my sister, with plans of hooking up with her next week, I hopped in my car and headed to the grocery store. I needed to pick up a few things before I made it home. Just thinking about all of the things that I had planned, I got excited. Onijae's ass was going to be in for a good surprise the minute he walked through the door. I hoped that he liked it. Shit, I had skipped a whole day of work to do something special for him, so his ass better like it, or else I'd be cursing his ass out.

Pulling into the parking lot of the grocery store, I quickly found a spot, grabbed my purse, and got out. I made sure to lock my door and turn on my alarm system, because I didn't trust anybody in Dallas. All people around there did was steal, and I couldn't wait until we moved from around there.

I was thankful that the store wasn't packed. Instead of playing around, I grabbed a basket and went about my business. Since I really didn't have any time to spare, I headed straight for the vegetables. I grabbed a few carrots, some potatoes, and parsnips. Once I had that, I went to the meat department and grabbed a nice roast before getting the rest of the things I would need to help me prepare the food. Since I really didn't have time to stop anywhere else, I grabbed a bottle of red wine and a six-pack of Heineken to go with it.

I was happy when I got home and didn't see Onijae's car. Since it was Saturday, I wasn't expecting him to be home for another three to four hours. The timing would be perfect, because it would provide me with more than enough time to get everything cooked and set up for that night.

Pulling into the garage, I happily bounced out of the car and proceeded to bring in all of the bags. It took me a few minutes to carry everything inside, but I did it.

As soon as I had gotten myself together, I took all of the bags from the grocery store and brought them into the kitchen. Without missing a beat, I washed my hands, rolled up my sleeves, and began the task of cooking. I began cutting up the vegetables and potatoes first. When I was through, I seasoned them, placed them in the pot, and set them on the stove to simmer. Removing the roast from its pack, I placed it in the sink and washed it off before I seasoned it and placed it in the pan and threw it in the oven. I would wait until everything was almost done to pop the rolls in the oven. Since I bought a cake from the store, I didn't have to prepare dessert, but I did remove it from its box and place it in the glass cake stand that was on the table. I then set up the table with candles.

Once I had everything going, I grabbed the bags from the foyer and headed upstairs to get the bedroom ready. After remaking the bed and spreading candles throughout the room, I pulled out the two bags of roses and started a trail from the door to the bed. I then took the rose petals and made a heart in the middle of the bed. Once I was done, I grabbed the black box that contained the watch I'd just bought from Macy's and placed it in the middle of the heart.

Satisfied with the outcome, I headed back downstairs to check on the food. That shit had the whole house smelling good. After I placed the food on a low fire, I headed back upstairs to prepare myself for the night.

It was almost nine o'clock that night when everything was finally done. I had Nicki Minaj's "Feeling Myself" blaring through the speakers of my phone, and I can honestly say that I was indeed feeling myself. I stood in front of the mirror, admiring the way I was looking. I was dressed in a bare-all Chantilly lace plunge teddy that I had gotten from Victoria's Secret. On my feet, I had a pair of black patent leather, peep-toe platform heels. I placed my hair into a ponytail with some Chinese bangs. Since I was already pretty, I only applied a little makeup to my face with some black MAC lipstick.

Picking up my phone and Bluetooth pill speaker, I headed downstairs. I was placing the speaker on the table when my phone began ringing. Looking at the screen, I noticed that it was my sister calling. Rolling my eyes, I had a good mind to let her call roll to voicemail after the shit she had put me through that day. I didn't know how long it was going to take me to get over that shit, but her ass couldn't get a damn thing from me anytime soon. Going against my better judgement, I answered anyway.

"Hello," I answered with a bit of an attitude.

"Bitch, you can lose the attitude, because you know I don't give a shit no way," she said, unbothered. I should've known that the shit wasn't going to faze her. She didn't care about anything. She had a carefree attitude that most people hated, including me. If a bitch was mad at her, they were most definitely mad by themselves, because she didn't let anything get to her. She was the type of chick who would sit next to the bitch that she knew for sure didn't like her and be like, "Hey, girl," because that's the type of shit she did.

"What you want, Candice?" I asked her.

"I'm calling to see how everything is going. Onijae done came home yet?"

"You think I would be answering the phone if he was?" I told her.

"Point taken," she said, laughing. "So, how is everything? You did it just like I told you to, huh?"

"Yes, and everything is fine. If I wasn't running around like a chicken with my head cut off, I'd send you a picture," I said, pulling the string up out of my ass. That's why I rarely wore shit like this.

"No need to. If you did everything I told you to, I already know how it looks," she boasted.

"Ol' cocky ass," I told her, laughing. I was about to say something when I heard the garage door opening. "Oh, bitch, I have to go. My man is home!"

"Okay now, don't go making any babies tonight. I'm too young to be an aunt," she said, laughing.

"Girl, shut your ass up. I'll talk to you tomorrow."

"All right now. Have fun and make sure you do everything I tell you to," she said before I hung up on her.

I didn't know why, but I was a ball of nerves. It was funny how I'd been with this man for years and yet I still got butterflies whenever he was around.

Quickly moving, I hurried up and scrolled to my music and chose R. Kelly's *12 Play* album before I plugged the phone up to my speaker. I then grabbed the single rose, placed it in my mouth, and sat down with my legs open. I couldn't wait to see the expression on his face when he walked through the door. I hoped he likes this, because I planned to do something good to him later on.

Chapter Three

Onijae

It was almost nine o'clock at night when I pulled up to my house. I had no intention of staying over at my parents' house that long, but once we started having fun, the time just flew by. In fact, if my parents didn't have to wake up for church in the morning, we'd probably still be sitting at the table, clowning and having a good time. Shit, I almost didn't want to leave, but I knew I had to go home to Bianca.

After parking the car into the garage, I grabbed the plate that my father had sent over for her and got out. I noticed that the house was a bit dark, so most likely, she was in there sleeping. I hoped she wouldn't be too mad about me coming home late.

Opening the door, I was momentarily frozen at the sight before me. Sitting on the table was a candlelight dinner, set for two. Even though I wasn't hungry, whatever she had cooked smelled good as fuck. Placing the plate on a table in the hallway, I began walking into the kitchen. When I rounded the corner, I was stunned the moment my eyes landed on Bianca. She was sitting in a chair, at the kitchen table, with a single rose in her mouth and her legs wide open. She looked so different that I almost didn't recognize her.

"What's all this about?" I asked her.

"I just wanted to do something special for my man," she said, getting up from the chair. She then walked over to me and handed me the rose. "I love you, Onijae."

"I love you too, baby," I said, placing a kiss on her lips. Her lips tasted so good that I pulled her in to deepen the kiss.

"Slow your roll. We'll have enough time to do that later on. Come on and follow me," she said, pulling back. Grabbing my hand, she led me over to a seat by the table. "You can sit down while I go get your plate from the kitchen."

She disappeared into the kitchen. I took a seat and waited for her to come back. A few minutes later, she returned with a plate in her hand and a bottle in another. She set the plate and bottle in front of me and walked back into the kitchen. A few seconds later, she returned with a plate of her own and sat across from me.

I couldn't lie and say that I wasn't stuck, because I was. I had no idea why she was suddenly doing this for me. Maybe she felt what I had been feeling these past few years. Maybe I wasn't the only one who knew that there was a strain on our relationship, and maybe this was her attempt to try to fix it.

Or maybe she's trying to kill your ass, I thought.

For the next few minutes, we sat there in silence while we ate. The sound of R. Kelly's voice and the forks hitting against our plates were the only noise in the room. To be honest, I hadn't even taken as much as five bites from my plate.

"All right. Enough of this," she said, pushing her plate away from her. "I know you're confused as to why I'm even doing this, because I can see the look on your face. Not only that, but you're barely eating your food. I'm guessing you think I did something to it, but I haven't. I told you that I'm doing this because I wanted to do something special.

"Onijae, things haven't been the same between us since
... well ... since that thing happened, and all I want is for
us at least to try to work it out. I mean, you wouldn't have
taken me back if you didn't love me and want to work it
out, right?"

She waited for me to answer, but when I didn't, she
started talking again.

"You don't have to say anything, Onijae. At least try. I
know I was the one who messed things up between us. I
can't tell you enough times how sorry I am for doing so,
but please don't hold this over my head too long. I really
am sorry, and I want more than anything to be able to
make this work, but I can't be the only one trying. If you
don't want this to be anymore, then tell me. I won't be
mad about it. Hurt, yes, but I'll never be mad, because
like I said, I brought this upon myself."

"Bianca, I love you, and yes, I want to make things work
with you, but it's still hard for me to trust you. You don't
know how fucked up it was when I saw you having sex
with that dude in our bed. That shit had broken me. It
fucked me up and caused me to lose any trust that I've
ever had for you," I said, looking up at her. I had never
really told her how I felt, but I guess right now was the
perfect time to tell her. "It's going to take us a while to get
back to where we once were, but I'm willing to try. I don't
want you to go anywhere because I love you more than
life itself. You're just going to have to give me the time to
do so."

"That's all I ask for. As long as I know that you're
willing to try, then I'm good," she said, getting up from
her seat. She walked over to me and sat on my lap, so
that she was facing me. We sat there staring at each other
without saying a word. I could see the love that Bianca
had in her eyes for me, but as I said, I needed to be able
to trust her again.

Before I knew it, her lips were on mine. It caught me by surprise, but I returned her kiss. Only the good Lord knows that this was long overdue. Bianca and I hadn't had a sexual relationship in months. That's how much we had grown apart. Yeah, I know most men would've probably started cheating or maybe even left, but I wasn't like most men. Sex wasn't everything in a relationship. When I wanted someone, I wanted to give them my full, undivided attention, no matter if we were having sex or not.

In my case, I wasn't getting that same spark with her anymore. Every time I saw her naked or we would even attempt to go there, all I could think about was her and that nigga Carlos. It was sad, because that was years ago, and I still hadn't gotten over that.

"Come on. Let's head to the bedroom," she said, getting off my lap. She blew out the candles before she grabbed my hand and led me up the stairs.

Again, I was shocked when we made it up the stairs. There were rose petals leading from our bedroom door all the way into the room. The bed was covered in rose petals and everything. I guess she really wasn't playing.

"You want to hop in the shower with me right quick?" I asked her.

"Nah, you go ahead and do you. I'll be waiting for you when you get out."

"Okay," I said before I headed into the bathroom.

I was only trying to take a quick shower, so I stripped out of my clothes and hopped in. I wasted no time grabbing the soap to wash every inch of my body, rinsed off, and repeated the process. I grabbed a towel and dried off, then grabbed another one and tied it around my waist before I headed back into the bedroom.

"It took you long enough," Bianca said the moment I entered the room. She was now lying on the bed as naked as the day she was born. What caught my eyes was the fact that she had her legs spread wide open and was playing with herself, causing my other head to begin twitching.

Walking over to the bed, I immediately dropped the towel that was wrapped around my waist. Taking my dick into my hand, I stood there stroking it as I continued to watch her. After a few minutes of stroking myself, I dropped down to my knees and crawled closer to her. Removing her finger, I replaced it with mine and began to work it in and out of her. I got excited when I pulled it out and it was covered in her juices.

Reaching up, I tried placing the finger in her mouth, but she turned her head. The shit rather pissed me off, but I didn't say anything. I wasn't even about to give her head for that shit. Since I was already hard and needed a release, I got up and walked over to the nightstand and pulled out a condom.

"Really, Onijae?" she asked once she noticed what it was that I was doing.

I ignored her and walked back over to the bed. I became annoyed when I noticed her sitting up on the bed.

"Are we going to do this or not?" I asked with my dick in my hand.

"You're really going to use a condom with me, Onijae?"

"You already know the answer to that, so I don't know why you're even asking," I told her. I don't know why she was trying to act as if this shit was new to her. Ever since I'd taken her back, we'd been using condoms during sex. I had even made her go to the clinic to get tested. Shit, as I said before, it was going to be hard for her to gain my trust again.

"But you just said that we were going to try and make things right with us again, Onijae."

"I know what I said, and this is me doing it," I told her.

"But that doesn't make any sense. We shouldn't have to use a condom. You're the only man I've been dealing with since that happened."

"That may be true or not, but until I'm comfortable enough again and we're back where we used to be, I'll be using these," I told her. I could see the hurt lying within her eyes, but I wasn't trying to see that. I was comfortable this way, and until then, we were going to do it my way, whether she liked it or not.

"Fuck this shit!" she said, jumping up from the bed. "I'm tired of you treating me like a first-class whore. I've told you repeatedly that I'm not cheating on you, but you won't believe me. Just because I've made one little mistake doesn't mean that I will continue to do so. You don't know how hard it was for me when you found out. When you threw my ass to the curb, I thought I had lost you for good. Trust me when I say that I'm not trying to lose you, but I see that you're still stuck in the past."

"What the fuck you expect me to do? I treated you with the utmost respect, gave you everything your heart desired, took you places we've both never been before, but most of all, I confessed my true love for you. I was going to ask you to be my wife. I wanted you to be the mother of my kids, but you know what happened? You ended up doing a nigga dirty. You cheated on me, played me for a fool, and you expect me to be cool with the shit?" I yelled, heated.

Yeah, I know that was in the past, but the shit was still fresh to me. I honestly didn't know how I was going to get over the shit. I know some may think that I was wrong for the way I was acting toward Bianca, but to me, I was not. Love these days is hard to find, and so are faithful people. When I loved, I loved hard, and I expected the same in return. I would have never done the shit to her that she'd done to me. She was lucky that I even took her back. Had she been in my shoes and I had been the one to cheat on her, she probably would've left me and never looked back. Now, because the shoe is on the other foot, she wanted to act as if it was no big deal. Well, she had another thing coming.

"I don't know how many times you expect me to apologize for the shit, but again, I'm sorry! If I could've taken it all back, I swear to the man upstairs, I would. I never meant to hurt you, Onijae, but I can't keep apologizing repeatedly for the same shit," she said before she broke out crying. "I'm tired of you holding this shit over my head. If you don't want to be with me, then say that. I have no problem walking out of the door."

I walked over to her and held her. I felt bad for the things that I had just said to her, but I was only being honest. Either she had to accept that and give me time, or she would have to leave me. It was just that simple.

It was safe to say that our night didn't go the way it was supposed to go. She couldn't rush me to give her my trust back. That shit had to be earned.

Tracy

"Mama, can my friend come over for dinner today?" I asked my mother as we sat at the table, eating the last of our breakfast.

It was Sunday, which meant that it was the Lord's Day, as well as family day. Every Sunday after church, both of my brothers would come back home to our parents' house for dinner. Since they hadn't been there two Sundays in a row, Mama made sure to let them know that they had better be there that day, or else she would beat them with her broom for real this time. My mother had been up since five o' clock this morning cooking her Sunday meal, so if they knew like me, they would show up, or else Mama was going to show out.

Not only were my brothers coming, but my aunts and uncles were probably coming too. Not to mention that my brother was probably bringing his girlfriend, and I hated her ass. I really didn't see why he was even with her. The bitch cheated on him, and he had the nerve to take her ho ass back. I don't know what he was thinking, but I lost mad respect when he pulled that move. I loved my brother to death, but he was as dumb as a bird when it came to that broad. He gave the chick whatever she wanted. She didn't even have to work, and she cheated on a man like that. She knew I didn't like her, and I never tried to hide it. If it weren't for my brother, I would've whooped her ass a long time ago.

"Girl, I'm not trying to be looking into none of your little friend's faces. Let them spend Sunday with their own parents," Mama said, taking her pies out of the oven.

"But Ma, Delaney's my best friend. I want you to finally meet her," I told her. "Besides, her parents don't be around enough for them to hang out on Sundays. She takes care of her little sister and brothers. It's because of me that she's even going to church. Ma, please let her come. I promise to do the dishes for a whole week if you do."

"I don't know, T. You're going to have to ask your father. You know he loves having family time on Sundays," she said.

Before she could even turn around to look at me, I was halfway up the stairs. I was happy she said that because I was a daddy's girl. Whatever I wanted, my daddy made sure that I had it. I knew that when I asked, he was going to say yes, which was why I practically ran to my parents' bedroom.

I hoped my daddy was dressed because I didn't even bother to knock. I just busted right on in.

"Daddy!" I yelled once I didn't see him in the room.

"Good morning, princess. What are you hollering for so early this morning?" he asked, walking into the room with his face full of shaving cream and a razor in his hand. I walked over to him and placed a kiss on his cheek before I proceeded to walk in the bathroom.

"Daddy, can my friend come over for dinner after church? I already asked Mama, and she told me to ask you," I said, taking a seat on the toilet. I watched as he walked back over to the sink and continued shaving his face.

"So she sent you up here to me, huh?" he said, laughing.

"You know she always does that. But can I? Daddy, I promise that she's nothing like my other friends. She doesn't get into any trouble. She's on the honor roll, she takes care of her sister and brothers, and she has a job. She doesn't be hanging in the street, which is why she's my best friend. And she doesn't steal, so you don't have to worry about anything going missing from out of here."

"Uh-huh, and why are we just now getting to meet your best friend?" he asked, looking at me through the mirror.

"Because like I said, she takes care of her siblings, and she has a job. If she's not doing that, then she has her head in her books. She doesn't do anything else other than those three things. Shit, we barely have time to hang out now," I said.

When I noticed his face, I realized that I had cursed. "I'm sorry, Daddy. Now, what's it going to be? And before you answer, I promise to do the dishes for a week."

"Well, what about her parents? Where are they?" he asked.

Instantly, I felt bad. I knew that he would want to know about her parents, but I was just happy that he had asked me instead of asking her. I began to tell him about her parents and everything that went on into her life.

I could tell from his facial expression that he felt sorry for her, but he didn't need to. Just looking at her, one would never know that she was going through all of that. Delaney was seventeen and as strong as ever. She was also shy and embarrassed, which was why every time I'd invite her over to the house, she would always come up with some sort of excuse. I knew it was only because she was embarrassed, but as I told her, she was my friend, and she had nothing to be embarrassed about. I didn't care about what she had or what she didn't have. Material shit didn't matter to me. She was my friend because of the person she was. Delaney wasn't rich, but she would give someone the shirt off her back if she had to. Even though she was going through her own problems, she was always trying to help others. That's what had drawn me to her.

"Well, since you said that, then yeah, but don't forget about doing the dishes, or else I'm going to extend it to a full two weeks."

"Thank you so much, Daddy," I said, running over to hug him.

"Hey, hey, hey, you're going to make me cut myself," he said, pulling the razor from his face.

"I'm sorry, Daddy," I said, laughing.

He turned around and placed a kiss on my forehead before ushering me out of the room so that he could finish getting ready for church. I ran full speed out of the bathroom before he could come up with something else.

Once I made it to my room, I called up Delaney and invited her over to my house. Of course, she tried to come up with some excuse about not being about to come because she had her siblings, but I told her she could bring them along too. I was sure my parents wouldn't mind.

It was going to be hard for me to keep up my end of the bargain, but I was going to try. I couldn't wait for my parents to meet Delaney. Not only that, but I was happy that I was going to have someone to talk to that day. I knew they were going to love her because she was such a loving and caring person.

I was happy when church let out earlier than I expected it to. Normally, it would last for about two hours, but I guess the pastor had other thangs going on. After paying our tithes and doing the usual handshakes and hugs with the other members, we were out of there. I wasn't surprised when my brothers didn't show up. I just hoped that they showed up for dinner, though.

Since I drove my own car, I hugged my parents and told them that I would meet them back at the house. Once I got in my car, I threw my purse in the back, hopped in, and went to pick up Delaney and her siblings. I couldn't wait to see her little sister, Dallas. Baby girl was as cute as a button and the sweetest. She was well mannered, and Delaney kept her dressed nice. She was also smart as hell in school.

Pulling out my phone, I dialed Delaney's number. I needed to make sure that she was ready when I got there.

"Hello," she said, answering the phone.

"What are you doing, heffa?" I asked her.

"I'm over here finishing Dallas's hair."

"Delaney, I hope when I pull up that y'all be ready. I can't be late, or else my mother is going to flip," I told her.

"Chill out, Tracy. You're not going to be late. We'll be ready when you get here."

"You better be, or else I'm going to be mad with you. I already promised my father that I was going to do the dishes for a week if he let you come," I confessed.

"I know you didn't," she said, laughing. "You doing the dishes? I would love to see that."

"Well, bitch, be late, and you'll be doing more than watching. You're going to be right beside me helping."

"Uh-huh . . . whatever. Now, let me go and get dressed before you be washing dishes forever," she said, laughing hysterically.

"Yeah, whatever, trick. Bye."

"All right girl, bye," she said and hung up.

I was praying that she'd be ready when I got there, because I wasn't playing. My mother would trip if I was late, and my father would too.

Chapter Four

Delaney

I stood in front of the mirror, combing my hair for the fourth time that morning. I'd changed my clothes three times already, and I was seriously thinking about changing them again. I had on a black knee-length skirt, red-and-black dressy blouse, and some flat black shoes. My hair was flat-ironed straight, with a part straight in the middle. I didn't have on much makeup. I only had on some lip-gloss and a little bit of eye shadow.

"How does this look, Dally?" I asked Dallas.

"You look pretty, Laney," she said, bouncing up and down on the bed. She had said the same thing the first three times.

"Dallas, get down before you start to sweat and smell like a pig," I said, walking over to the bed. She stopped jumping and got down. "Come here. Let me straighten your clothes out."

She was dressed in a yellow-and-white sundress with her white dress shoes. I had combed her hair in four plaits with two yellow bows and two white bows. Her baby bang was laid down to perfection. She had on the jewelry I had gotten her for her sixth birthday. She was dressed the way a little girl was supposed to be dressed, and I was happy.

"Come on. Let me spray on a little of my perfume. Then we can take a mirror pic before Tracy pulls up," I told her.

After spraying perfume on both her and me, we headed over to my full-length mirror and took a few pictures. Of course, all of them were cute. I had the hardest time choosing just one for my profile picture on Facebook. Instead, I made a collage of all of them and then set the new profile picture.

We were heading to the living room when I heard Tracy's car horn. I hurried back into the room to grab Dallas's sweater and mine. Before leaving, I stopped in the room to check on my brothers. They were playing their games and didn't want to come, so for that, I was happy.

"I've already cooked for you guys. All Dedrick has to do is fix the food and warm it up in the microwave. We'll be back in a few hours," I told them.

I wasn't surprised when they didn't answer me, so I walked over and got in the front of the TV to be sure that I had their undivided attention.

"Y'all heard what I said?"

"Yes, now move out of the way so we can finish playing our game," Dedrick said.

I gladly handed him back his remote and walked out of the room. Grabbing Dallas's hand, I locked the door before we headed out. When we made it to the car, I opened the door for Dallas to hop in. Once I made sure that she was buckled safely inside, I hopped in the front seat, and Tracy pulled off.

"You look cute, boo," she said, looking over at me.

"Thank you," I replied with a nervous chuckle. "I changed so many times. I was about to cancel on you."

"And I would've dragged your ass out of that house." She looked back at Dallas. "Hey, Deedy, you're looking as cute as always."

"Thank you, Tee Tracy," she said, laughing a girlish giggle.

"Girl, I can't wait for you to meet my parents. They're going to love you, and you're going to love them too," she said. I didn't reply. Hell, I was too nervous to say anything. I'd never met Tracy's parents, but she did tell me a lot about them already. I knew they were wealthy people from the way they kept her. That was why I always made up excuses when she would invite me over to her house. I knew I wasn't in her league, which was why I never uderstood why she still wanted to be friends with me.

I'll admit, though, that my assumptions of her were all wrong. She wasn't like most of the rich girls that went to our school. She was cool and down to earth. She never judged me, even after I told her about my parents and everything that I was going through. She vowed that she was going to be there for me, and so far, she'd kept that promise. I was grateful for her. If it wasn't for her, I don't know what I'd do or how I would be able to make it.

"We're here," she said, interrupting my thoughts.

I looked up and almost fainted. The house she pulled up to must have belonged to a famous person.

"Oh my God, Trace. Girl, y'all house is beautiful." I gasped as I admired the view. Immediately, I began fidgeting with my clothes, trying to make sure that they were straight.

"Calm down, Delaney. I already told you that you look wonderful, so don't go acting that way. My family is not like that. We're still black. We don't put people down because they don't have anything. Instead, we help them. We don't see dollar signs, and we're not bougie either. Now, come on, because you look like you're getting ready to run on down the street," she said, laughing as we made our way toward the house.

"Oh, good. My brother's here. Hopefully my other brother will come, so you'll get to meet my whole family today," she said.

I didn't reply. I just grabbed Dallas's hand as we followed behind her. The minute she opened the door, I was taken aback. Of course, there was no butler or anything like that, but the inside of the house was as beautiful as the outside. The carpet was so clean that I was afraid to walk on it in fear of getting it dirty.

"Come on. Let's head to my room. I need to change first," she said as she directed me toward some stairs. We followed her up the stairs and into her room, which was bigger than our entire apartment. Just like when we first walked in, I was scared to move or sit down, in fear that I would mess something up.

"Oh, Laney, look," Dallas said, running toward Tracy's bed, where there was a whole bunch of stuffed animals sitting on it. When she got up on it, I almost had a heart attack.

"Dallas Ranae McGuff, get your tail from off that bed. You know better than that," I said, giving her the mad face. She looked at me and got down before she walked over to Tracy.

"Delaney, I told you to chill. That girl wasn't doing anything wrong," Tracy said, walking over to me. She gave me a look of her own before she and Dallas disappeared into her huge walk-in closet. Moments later, they came out, with Tracy now dressed in a floor-length sundress with silver sandals.

"Lay-Lay, can you put my hair in a messy bun like you always do?" she asked, handing me her comb and brush.

"Girl, come on," I said, walking over to the vanity Tracy had in the corner of her room.

Within no time, we got straight to it. Thirty minutes and many re-dos later, she was finally satisfied with the way her hair looked. She even let me cut a bang in the front of her head. Yeah, I knew how to do hair, but that didn't mean that I liked doing it. I only used my skill on Dallas, Tracy, and my own hair. I didn't have time to be doing anyone else's hair. Shit, I had enough on my plate as it already was.

"Come on before my mother come up here and embarrasses us," she said, quickly straightening out her room.

I decided to help her since my nerves were once again on edge. I couldn't believe that I was finally about to meet her parents. I really hoped that they didn't look at me as if I were beneath them. I mean, just because Tracy took to me didn't mean that they were going to do the same. I didn't care how much she said they were nice. I still felt shy and embarrassed. Hell, I hoped they weren't going to watch me all night, because I knew that my clumsy ass would be bound to mess up or something.

"Come on, scary," she said, dragging me by the arms.

We left her room and made our way down the stairs. The whole way there, my heart was beating like a drum. The minute we reached the last step and I heard voices, I thought for sure that I was going to pass out. We reached the kitchen door, then we suddenly stopped.

"I was just about to come upstairs and get you all," an older version of Tracy said, walking over to us. She hugged Tracy before she noticed Dallas and me. "Hello, sweetheart. My name is Lillian. I'm Tracy's mother."

"Um, I'm Delaney," I managed to get out of my suddenly dry mouth. I swallowed the lump that had formed in my throat before placing a smile on my face. "It's nice to meet you, ma'am."

"Honey, you can cut it out with that *ma'am* stuff. You can just call me Lilly," she said, hugging me. Surprisingly, I wasn't shy or embarrassed anymore, so I hugged her back. "And who may this little cutie be?"

"My name is Dallas. It's nice to meet you, Ms. Lilly," she said happily. She took us all by surprise when she ran over to Ms. Lillian and hugged her as if she knew her.

"Aww, it's nice to meet you too, sugar," she said, picking her up. I was about to protest when Tracy gave me the eye and shook her head. "Come on. Let's go ahead and get you fed, baby. They can go ahead and starve if they want, but you won't."

Without another word to Tracy or me, Ms. Lillian took off with Dallas on her hips. I wanted to tell her that Dallas was six and perfectly capable of walking, but instead, I kept my mouth closed. By the way her eyes lit up when she saw Dallas, I could tell that she loved kids.

"Don't tell her nothing about Dallas. In fact, don't even try to chastise or whoop Dallas in her presence, because she will not like it. Yes, I know that's cheeky of her, but my mother loves kids, and it looks like she has a soft spot for Dallas," Tracy whispered to me as we began walking into the kitchen.

I didn't have a problem with Ms. Lillian being attached to Dallas. My baby sister had that kind of effect on people. She would walk into a room and make everyone fall in love with her. She did that with Tracy, and it looked like she was about to do the same thing with her mother.

After meeting both of Tracy's parents and her oldest brother, we took a seat at the table in the dining room. Soon, everyone began engaging in a conversation. Ms. Lillian was waiting for her other son to come, so that we could begin eating. I could see what Tracy was saying about her mother, because ever since we'd been here, she'd had Dallas glued to her hip, and she let her do whatever she wanted.

We sat there waiting on her son for a few more minutes, until she got the phone and called him. After calling and cursing him out two times, he finally said that he was outside. She then asked both Tracy and me to come help her with the dishes. We had to make two trips because of all of the food that she had cooked.

We were almost in the kitchen when I heard a voice that I thought I recognized. Shaking my head, I thought I had to be tripping, because I knew the world wasn't that small—or at least that's what I thought.

Walking into the kitchen, I spotted this cute little red chick sitting at the table. I could tell that she was stuck up and uptight from the way she was looking at me, but I decided not to let that deter me. Instead, I spoke to her and kept it pushing. I wasn't surprised when she didn't speak back. She looked like one of those people who thought the sun rose and set on her ass. What bothered me the most, though, was the way she kept staring at me.

I was two seconds away from asking her what the hell she was looking at when Tracy tapped me on my leg. "I see you over here ready to go off and shit," she whispered, trying to stifle a laugh. "Don't let that bitch get to you. Trust me when I tell you that she's all bark and no bite."

"I'm not worrying about her, but what I do want to know is why she clocking me so fucking hard," I said, still looking at ol' girl, who was still looking at me.

"She's probably intimidated, that's all. She does that every time someone new comes around. What she needs to be concerned with is herself. I don't know why my brother is still with her cheating ass anyway."

"So, she cheated and around here acting like she was the one who was cheated on?" I asked, not believing the shit.

"Yup, and my dumb-ass brother took her ho ass back. Now her ho ass be on that stalking shit. If she knows like I do, she wouldn't jump stupid. It's only because of my brother that I haven't whooped her ass, but she better not fuck around, or else I'm going to show her stupid ass," she said, just as her mother called everyone's attention.

They began fixing everyone's plate before they prayed over the food. When I opened my eyes after saying "Amen," I got the shock of a lifetime.

"Do you want something to drink, Delaney?" Tracy had asked me. I heard her, but I didn't. I was too busy trying to figure out why the dude I had met in the mall was sitting across from me at Ms. Lillian's dinner table. "Delaney, you okay?"

"Umm, I'm fine, boo," I said, finally tearing my eyes away from him. I turned to Tracy, who was staring at me. I leaned in closer to her because I didn't want anyone to hear me. "Umm, Trace, who that dude sitting across from us, next to the chick who was staring at me earlier?"

"Oh, girl, that's my other brother Onijae," she said, nonchalantly shrugging.

"Oh, okay," I said, trying to play the shit off. On the inside, I was screaming, though. I couldn't believe the dude I had a crush on and thought I'd never see again was my best friend's brother.

Never in a million years would I think that I'd be seeing him again, especially not sitting across from me at my friend's dinner table. When I looked back across the table, he was staring at me. I immediately put my head down, grabbed my fork, and began eating. I could already tell that this dinner was going to be eventful.

Onijae

I don't know if it was fate or a mere coincidence that the girl I'd been thinking about was sitting across from me at my mother's dinner table. At first, I thought I was tripping, but I closed my eyes a few times, only to still see her sitting there. I had no idea that she and my little sister even knew each other, let alone that they were best friends. If that wasn't the good Lord sending me another sign, then the stars must have been in alignment. I damn sure didn't think that I was going to be seeing her in my parents' house. I couldn't wait until I was able to pull Tracy's ass to the side. I needed to know how and why she didn't tell me she had a friend this damn fine, and why this was the first time she'd come around.

I didn't mean to, but I found myself sitting at the table, staring at her. Shorty was so beautiful and perfect to me. When she smiled, she showed off a cute set of dimples that I hadn't noticed the first time. My heart swelled once her little sister hopped off my mother's lap and went to sit on hers. I could tell that they had this tight bond.

She and my sister were so engrossed in whatever my mother was saying that she didn't even bother to glance my way. I decided to redirect my vision somewhere else, and when I turned my head, I found Bianca staring at me. I tried to play the shit off, but I could tell that I was in deep shit. I was caught red-handed.

I didn't even sit there worrying my nerves. When I spotted my little sister getting up, I got up and followed behind her. Bianca was just going to have to wait until later to bitch and moan.

"What's up, Tracy?" I asked, as I followed her to the living room.

"What do you want, Onijae? I'm sure your little girl-friend is probably looking for you," she said, sounding as if she had a bad taste in her mouth.

My little sister didn't like my girlfriend and vice versa. That was no secret. That was why I made sure never to leave them in each other's presence. I didn't need shit popping off. I already knew how my little sister could get, and it's sad to say, but Bianca wasn't fucking with that. Tracy would straight fuck her up, because my brother and I made sure that Tracy could defend herself.

"I'm not worrying about her ass," I said, waving her off. "What I'm more worried about is why you didn't tell me you had a friend as fine and cute as the one you got sitting at Ma's dinner table."

"I didn't know I was supposed to be telling you about my friends," she said, rolling her eyes.

"I didn't say all that, with your smart ass. I said, why you didn't tell me you had a friend as fine as Delaney is?"

"Nigga, how do you know her name? And don't act like we didn't see you staring at her at the table either. You need to watch the shit before your girlfriend starts popping off at the mouth and we have to beat her ass in here."

"Chill out, T street," I said, calling her by the nickname we'd given her when she was a child.

"Boy, don't be calling me that shit," she said, frowning her face up. "Now, tell me what you want, because you really blocking me right now."

"Blocking you? The fuck I'm blocking you from? Tracy, don't fuck around and get fucked up. I'm still your big brother. Remember that shit!" I said, immediately flying off the handle. I didn't know who she thought she was talking to, but she needed to remember just who the fuck I was.

"Boy, bye. Ain't nobody got time for that shit! Was you thinking about me being your sister when I told you not to take that skeezer back?" she clapped back.

I didn't say shit because I knew what she was talking about. If my sister had it her way, Bianca would've been gone.

"Yeah, that's what I thought," she said, pushing past me.

"Wait, wait," I said, pulling her back. I could tell that she was frustrated, but I didn't care. "Aye, give me ya girl's number."

"Oh, hell no. That's what you came all the way back here for?" she asked, calling me out.

I didn't say shit. I just stared at her because that was, in fact, the only reason I had gone back there.

"Nah, Onijae, I'm not about to let you play on my girl, especially not while you're fucking with miss want-to-be Barbie. No, sir. I don't need her trying my friend, because I swear, I'm not going to be sparing her any ass whooping if she fucks with her."

"Chill out. I just want to ask her about the shoes I bought at her store the other day," I said, not even believing the shit that was coming out of my own mouth.

"Well, if that's the case, why don't you go back to the store where you got them from?" Then she remembered something. "Oh, hell no. You were the dude she kept talking about!"

"She was talking about me?" I asked, ignoring the faces she was making.

"Yeah, and my answer is still no. My friend doesn't need all of what you're trying to bring into her life. She's a good girl who already has a lot going on in her life right now. She doesn't need some temporary fixture coming in to fuck shit up, and she especially doesn't need a man who already has a woman," she said, giving it to me raw.

Had I not been the one trying to get with her friend, I would've applauded her little speech. The shit she said was moving, but it didn't move me much. I still wanted Delaney, and nothing was going to stop me from getting her.

"So, I take it that I have to get her number on my own, huh?"

"Look, let me give you a little lesson on women, especially this one. No woman wants a man who already has a woman attached to him," she said, tapping me on my shoulder and pointing behind me.

I turned around to see Bianca heading in our direction. "Fuck," I mumbled under my breath.

"My biggest advice to you—don't put yourself in a new situation while you're already in a complicated one. She's out of your league, a good girl. So, I'm telling you to leave her alone," she said, just as Bianca reached us.

"I'm ready to go," she said, looking at Tracy and rolling her eyes. I watched as Tracy smiled and then looked back at me.

"On another note, I'll text that to you," she said, smirking. She walked off, but then stopped when she got a few feet away. "You better get this *Bride of Chucky*–looking bitch out of here, because if she rolls her eyes at me one more time, I'm going to poke her in them."

"Bitch, you got me fucked up, so don't think for one minute think I'm scared of your little ass!" Bianca retorted before I could respond.

I didn't know how she did it, but Tracy was back in front of us in two seconds flat.

"And don't think that my little ass is scared of you either," she said, putting her hand in Bianca's face.

I was praying that Bianca would just let it go, but unfortunately, God wasn't hearing me that day.

"Bitch, you better keep your hands out of my face before I—"

Bianca's words were cut off when Tracy's fist kept connecting with her mouth.

"Before you what? Huh, bitch?" Tracy asked as she began pouncing on her.

I don't know how or why, but I stood there stuck. I always knew this day was going to come, but I didn't know it would come like this.

"You got me fucked up, little girl. Now I'm going to whoop your little ass like your mother should've," Bianca said, hitting Tracy with a two-piece combo to her face, which only seemed to make her even madder.

Just as we'd taught her, Tracy shook that shit off and countered that with a jab to Bianca's nose. She then started raining blows to her face. It was only when I saw blood and heard Bianca screaming that I finally came to my senses and broke them up.

Grabbing Tracy, I pulled her off Bianca and held her tight around her waist, which was a big mistake. Bianca got up from the floor and started swinging on her. She even caught me with a few licks.

"Let me go, Onijae! That hoe's hitting me, and you're letting her!" Tracy yelled to me, kicking the shit out of me.

No matter how hard those kicks were, I was not about to let her little ass down.

"I'm going to handle it, Tracy, but I'm not letting you go," I told her as I walked with her into the living room.

"What the hell is going on?" I heard my brother say from behind us. He looked from Tracy to Bianca, whose hair was all over her head. I thought for sure that he was going to try to help me defuse this situation, but I was wrong.

"Oh, shit, Ma!" he yelled, running out of the room like a big-ass kid. What he didn't know was that he made shit a whole lot worse. A few minutes later, he returned with both of my parents and Tracy's friend.

"Onijae, put my damn child down," Mom was hollering and walking over to where we were standing.

I did as I was told and stepped to the side because I knew she was about to get real.

"Now, somebody tell me what the hell is going on in here!"

I stood there as my little sister started telling her everything that was going on—and when I say *everything*, I mean she told them everything. What I was stuck on was the fact that she called me out. She told everybody in the room how I came at her to get Delaney's number. I knew she only said that because she didn't like Bianca and that she thought I was helping her, but I was going to fuck her little ass up. She should have known better than that.

I wasn't shocked when Bianca gave me a look of disdain. Hearing that her man was asking for another woman's number was something that she definitely wasn't trying to hear.

From out the corner of my eye, I spotted Delaney placing her hair into a ponytail. She then removed her jewelry and placed it on one of the living room tables. She then turned to her little sister and whispered in her ear. A few seconds later, the little girl went running out of the room.

"I'm sorry, Mr. and Mrs. Love, but if anybody knows anything about me, I don't play when it comes down to that," she said before she nodded her head toward Tracy.

Before anyone knew what was going on, she ran up on Bianca and started beating the dog shit out of her. Shorty threw them hands as if she were a professional boxer or something. Bianca wasn't even able to get a lick in. Delaney straight tore through her ass within a matter of minutes.

"Somebody get this bitch off of me!" Bianca yelled out.

I know someone was going to say that I was wrong, but this time, I chose to stand in place. I wasn't getting in this, so instead, I allowed my brother and father to break them up. I didn't want anyone to think that I was choosing sides or anything.

"Onijae, you know that I love you, but I'm going to ask you nicely to get and escort your girlfriend off of my premises," I heard my mother say from behind me.

I turned, giving her a look, asking if she was serious. She folded her arms across her chest and gave me a look that said, *sure the fuck is.*

"All right," I said, walking over to Bianca. "Get your shit and come on. If your ass isn't outside by the time I get back, then I'm leaving your ass, and you'll be walking home."

I wasn't mad with my mother. Hell, I halfway expected her to go straight dumb, so for her just to put us out was cool with me. I didn't even say another word. I left Bianca's stupid ass standing there. If she knew like I did, she would want to hurry up and bust a move. Not only was I not playing about leaving her ass, but my mother could just change her mind and decide to fuck her up. It was bad enough that they didn't like her before. Now I was more than sure that they disliked her ass even more after this, and I couldn't say that I blamed them neither.

When I made it to the car, I hopped in and started it up. No more than two minutes later, I spotted Bianca walking to the car. She opened the door and hopped in without saying a word, which I was glad for, because I really wasn't in the mood to talk to her. Only thing I really wanted to do was get home and go straight to bed, which was why I ended up doing 80 miles per hour the whole ride to our house. I turned a one-hour trip into a twenty-minute trip, tops.

When I pulled up to the house, instead of pulling my car into the garage as I would normally do, I left it in the driveway. I turned the car off and got out without saying a word to her ass. I was so busy trying to get out of the car that I didn't even put it in park. I just turned it off. That's how bad I was trying to get away from this bitch.

"You don't have to break your neck," she said, following behind me.

"Bianca, if you knew like me, you would really leave me alone right now," I said, opening the door. I headed straight for the stairs, taking them two at a time.

When I made it to the bedroom, I went over to the dresser to get my pajamas. Once I had everything I needed, I headed to take a quick shower. After my shower, I dressed and headed back into the room, where I found a now sobbing Bianca sitting on the bed. Ignoring her, I exited the room and headed to one of the spare bedrooms. I was not going to entertain her shenanigans anymore. If she wanted to act like that, then that was on her.

I was just about to get in the bed when my phone chimed, indicating that I had a new message. Walking over to where my phone was, I picked it up and noticed that it was Tracy. I placed the phone back on the dresser because I didn't have a damn thing to say to her. I was still mad about her ratting me out.

I walked back over to the bed and got in. I must have lay there for ten minutes, staring up at the ceiling, when my phone chimed again. Knowing that it was my sister, I ignored her yet again. I was going to make her sweat. She needed to see what I was feeling.

Deciding to call it a night, I reached over and cut off the lamp. My phone chimed again. Getting up, I knew that if I didn't answer her, my phone would be ringing all night long.

Unlocking the screen, I scrolled to my messages.

Tracy: Did you make it home okay?

Ignoring that one, I went to the next one.

Tracy: please answer!

Just like the one before that, I ignored it. The third was explaining how she was.

Tracy: I'm sorry about calling you out, but when you were holding me, I thought that you were intentionally letting that bitch hit me.

Immediately, I realized that I had hurt my kid sister's feelings, and I saw how she could feel that way, since I grabbed her instead of Bianca.

Jae: I'm sorry. I would never deliberately allow anyone to put their hands on you.

Tracy: I understand ♥
Jae: I'll see you soon, good night.

After texting her, I placed the phone back on the dresser and headed back to bed. The minute I laid down, my phone chimed again. *Fuck*! I thought, getting up yet again.

"I'm going to cut this fucking phone off tonight!" I huffed as I made my way back over to the dresser. It was my little sister again, but this time she sent me a phone number. I was about to ask her whose number it was when she sent another text saying that it was Delaney's number. To say I was surprised and yet happy was an understatement. I thanked her before saving Delaney's number. I then powered my phone off and got back in the bed.

It was definitely an eventful day, but overall, I was a happy man. I couldn't wait until it was the right time for me to use this number. I was going to make shorty mine. I just had to wait until the right time to do so, and I hoped that would be sooner, not later.

Delaney

A whole week had passed since the shit that went down at Tracy's house, and I still felt like shit. I couldn't believe that I actually went off and had a fight in those people's house. I mean, I knew they would understand and forgive Tracy for fighting, but I was a different story. I should've left well enough alone and minded my own business, but I couldn't, because Tracy was my best friend. I wasn't about to let anyone mess with her, and I knew she wouldn't let anyone mess with me.

I stood in the school hallway, getting ready to head to my locker. I only had one class left, and then I was free to go home. I was thankful that it was Friday because Lord knows I was tired. I had to work all day that week, and then I went straight home to take care of my siblings. I couldn't wait to get home because I was going to dive straight in my bed, where I was planning to stay until the next day.

I was about to head into class when I heard my name being called. I turned around just in time to see Tracy speed-walking toward me.

"What's up, boo?" I asked her.

"Why haven't you been answering my damn calls and texts?" she asked, sounding a bit upset.

"My bad, Tee. I've been so busy with school, work, and my siblings that I haven't had time to do anything," I told her.

"I know your scary ass is lying, Delaney. You need to get up off that shit. You're just worried about what my parents might say, huh?" she asked me.

"Honestly, yes," I answered, feeling like a fool yet again.

"I thought so. Girl, my parents aren't tripping on that. I told you my people aren't like that. If anything, they're happy that I have a friend like you. At least they know you're going to have my back whenever I need you," she said, erasing my worries. "With your little scary ass."

"Girl, fuck you. Shit, I thought your people were going to tell my ass not to step back into their house," I told her truthfully.

"Trust me, Delaney. If they didn't want you to step foot back into their house, they would've put your ass out the minute they made Onijae escort his bitch-ass ol' lady out."

"Oh, okay." I felt relieved.

"Oh, I actually came here for a reason," she said, grabbing my arm.

"What's up?"

"My mother was wondering if you would let Dallas come over today. I told her that I would have to ask you, since you've never allowed her to leave out of your sight, other than school. So she insisted that you guys spend the night, if you guys aren't busy."

"I see Dallas has gotten somebody else to fall in love with her tail," I replied, laughing.

"Girl, I'm saying. The other day she went shopping, right? When she got home, she came in with two hands full of bags. Crazy thing is, the clothes were from a children's boutique. Now, I know I'm too old to even fit them, and none of my brothers have kids, so I asked her who they were for. She shocked me when she said they were for Dallas. I mean, she bought clothes, shoes, bows, and barrettes. I know she loves kids, but she took things to a whole new level. I'm like, how do you even know that you'll be seeing her again? She was like, 'Because your friend will bring her back whenever she comes.' She told me to tell you if you don't bring her back, then don't even try to knock on her door. She even told me that if I didn't get her to come to our house tonight, for me not to come home. Ain't that some shit? Tell Dallas she's going to have me competing with her for my own mother," she said, laughing.

I laughed too because Mrs. Love most definitely was crazy. I couldn't believe she fell in love with Dallas after just one visit. Then she had the nerve to go out shopping for her and stuff. That was crazy, but Tracy had one thing right, though. Dallas wasn't going nowhere without me, especially not with people I didn't know. I mean, I figured that they were good people, but I still had to get a feel for them. Until then, the only way my little sister was going over there was if I was there with her.

"Girl, your mother is a trip, but we don't have any plans. So, yes, we'll come over," I told her.

"Good, now I can breathe easily. Meet me at my car once class is over. We need to go to the mall before we head home to get y'all stuff."

"Why do we need to go to the mall?" I asked, frustrated. I hated going to the store with her because she didn't know how to stop shopping. She would go into every store, sometimes more than one time. Lord knows I didn't have time for that.

"Because we have somewhere to be tomorrow, and we have to be on point because there's going to be a lot of people there," she said, walking off. She knew what she was doing when she did that shit.

"Tracy, I'm not about to play with you in them people store, especially not on a Friday evening. I'm going home. You can pick me up when you're through shopping."

"Girl, whatever. You better be at my car when the bell rings, or I'm telling my brother that you don't want to see him," she said, looking at me and laughing.

"Girl, I'm not worrying about your brother," I said, blushing so much that my cheeks began to hurt. "Besides, he has a girlfriend already."

"Girl, ain't nobody worrying about Bianca's stupid ass. But you're right. We can't have you being no nigga's other woman, even if that nigga is my brother. So, in that case, we're going to have to find you a nigga tomorrow, which means that we have to go to the mall for the perfect outfit. Make sure you be at my car, okay?" she said, poking her tongue at me. Before I could open my mouth to anything else, she took off running to her class.

I couldn't do shit but laugh at her ass. She would do anything just to get me to go shopping with her. What she didn't know was that she made my mind start twirling the minute she mentioned her brother. It was no secret that I had the biggest crush on him. Dude was too fine for any girl not to. Only thing was that he had a girlfriend, so my crush was going to remain just that, a childish crush. With any luck, I'd get over it soon and find someone in my league.

"Tracy, can you please slow down?" I gasped, sounding as if I was about to run out of breath. We were currently in the mall getting an outfit for her brother's company barbecue the next day, and I was beat. The minute she told me that was where we were going, I tried backing out, but she damn near threatened to cut me if I did. She made some noise about me being there, in case Bianca tried to start something, but I knew she didn't need me. She only wanted me to be there for what, I don't know. So here we were, running through the mall like two damn fools, looking for an outfit.

"Come on, Delaney. Let's just go in this one store, and I swear we're going to leave right after," she said, looking at me. I looked at her sideways because she had said that about the last few stores we had visited. "I tell you what. I'll buy you something if you come. Deal?"

"Deal." I quickly accepted. Who was I to turn down her offer to buy me something?

"That's a damn shame," she said, shaking her head. "And here I thought you were my friend."

"I am your friend. Your best friend, at that. I just can't pass up the opportunity to get something new. You know my money ain't long like yours."

"Delaney, chill out with that, okay? I already told you that as long as I got, you got. So don't be tripping on all of that shit," she said as we made our way into Neiman Marcus.

After spending twenty minutes in the store and not buying a damn thing, we finally left. Tracy tried going back into a store that she had already come out of, but I straight up told her no. She even tried bribing me again, but I wasn't taking that shit. I was tired and ready to go, so we left.

Before we headed over to her house, we had to stop at my house first. When I opened the door, the house was exceptionally quiet. What surprised me the most was that the house was clean. I mean, I halfway expected to walk into a noisy, dirty living room, but it wasn't. I then walked to the kitchen to see that it, too, was clean, with pots on the stove. Walking over to the stove, I removed the lids off the pots to find food in them. I thought my eyes were playing tricks on me, so I placed the lid back on them and checked again. Just like before, there was food in them, which meant that someone had already cooked and cleaned. The question was, who?

Leaving the kitchen, I headed toward my brothers' and sister's room. When I passed by Daija's room, I noticed the light on. Remembering how things had gone down the last time I stepped in her room, I decided not to go in. Once I made it to the kids' room, I was surprised to find them already in their pajamas, watching TV.

"Hey, y'all," I sang from the doorway.

"Hey, Laney," Dedrick and Derrick both said, running over to me and giving me a hug.

"Where's Dallas?" I asked once I noticed she wasn't in the room.

"She's in the room with Daija."

"How was y'all day? Y'all was good at school or what?" I asked them.

"We had a good day," Derrick said.

"Yeah, and I had a test today and passed it with flying colors," Dedrick chimed in.

"That's good. I brought y'all something from GameStop today," I said, holding up the bag that I had hidden behind my back. They immediately started smiling and dancing. I pulled the two video games that I had bought them out of the bag and handed the games to them.

"Oh, Laney brought us a new game!" they yelled happily before they hugged me again.

"Thanks, sis!"

"Y'all welcome, but aye, Dallas and I are about to go sleep at Tee Tracy's house. We're coming back tomorrow. So, I want y'all to be good until then, okay?" I told them.

"Okay," they said, not really paying me any mind. They were too busy pulling their PS4 out of the box to go and play it. I walked over to them and stood directly in front of them, so they could hear me.

"I'm not playing now. Don't let them tell me that you guys were bad, or I'm going to take them games back, okay?"

"We won't. We're going to be good. We promise," they told me.

"Okay," I said, smiling. I then placed a kiss on their foreheads before making my way back to the door. "If something goes wrong or y'all need something, don't hesitate to call my phone."

"Okay. Bye, Delaney."

I told them bye before I left and made my way to Daija's room. I stood at the door for a good minute before I finally knocked. A few seconds later, Dallas opened the door. When she saw me, she ran straight in my arms and hugged me as if she hadn't seen me in a million years.

"I'm happy to see you too," I said, smiling.

"Laney, look," she said, stepping back to show me how she looked. Daija had put her hair in some curls, and they looked as if they were playing dress up. She had eye shadow and red lipstick on. "Daija and I were having fun. You want to join us?"

"I see, but I came to get you. We're going to Tee Tracy's house," I told her. I noticed the way her eyes lit up when I told her that.

"Yeah, we're going by Ms. Lillian?" she asked, jumping up and down. She was so happy that it made me happy too.

"Come on, li'l bit. Tracy's outside waiting, and we don't need her blowing the horn like a fruit man," I said, grabbing her hand.

I was about to leave when Daija called my name. I turned around to see her getting up from the bed.

"What's up?" I asked her. Instead of answering me, she stood there twiddling her thumbs. She wasn't even looking at me because her eyes were down to the floor. "Is something wrong, Daija?"

"No, there's nothing wrong," she said, finally bringing her eyes up to mine.

"Well, what is it? Because I have to go," I told her. I hoped she wasn't trying to ask me for anything, because I was going to hurt her little feelings and remind her of what she told me.

"Look, Delaney, I just wanted to tell you that I was sorry about everything I said to you. I know everything you told me was nothing but the truth, but I didn't want to hear it. The truth is, I try to be like you, but I can't. I'm not as smart as you are, I'm not as pretty as you are, and I'm not independent either. If it weren't for you buying me the things that I do have, I wouldn't have anything. I know I sounded ungrateful, and again, I'm sorry for that. Please forgive me," she said with tears rolling down her face.

"It's okay, Daija. I forgive you, sis," I said, pulling her into a hug. What warmed my heart was when she hugged me tighter, as if she was afraid she was going to lose me. "I have to go, but we'll talk some more when I get back, okay?"

"You promise?" she asked like a little child.

"Yes, I promise," I told her, pulling back. "If you need me, call me, okay?"

"Okay," she said, nodding her head.

I looked at her once more before I left and headed to my room. As soon as I stepped foot in the room, my phone started ringing.

"What's taking you so long, Delaney?" Tracy asked once I answered the phone.

"I'm coming. I just had to get the kids straight first," I told her as I grabbed my overnight bag.

"Okay, but hurry up. My mother just called looking for us."

"All right," I said before I ended the call.

Grabbing the bag, I went to the drawer where I kept Dallas's nightclothes and mine and placed a few items in our bag. I then went to the bathroom to grab our toothbrushes before I headed back into the room.

"Come on, Dallas. We have to go," I said, grabbing her shoes and sweater and helping her put them on. Once I made sure that we had everything that we needed, I closed and locked my room door and headed out of the house with Dallas in tow. After getting our stuff into the car, I got in.

"Damn, it's about time. I was starting to think you weren't going to come," Tracy joked once I got in the car.

"Girl, whatever," I said.

She looked at me and shook her head before she pulled off. I couldn't wait until we made it to her house. I was going to take a bath and head straight to bed. I was burnt out, and the next day, I was definitely going to need all of my energy. I only hoped and prayed that Onijae's little girlfriend wasn't going to be on the bullshit, or else we were most definitely going to fuck her ass up again.

Chapter Five

Onijae

It was the day of my shop's annual barbecue, and I was running around like a chicken with my head cut off. I'd been up since six o'clock that morning, trying to get everything in order, and it was already nine. The event didn't start until twelve that afternoon, so I still had a little while to go.

As usual, the shop would be closed that day, but there was going to be a spot set up out where we would be giving away free haircuts, as well as prizes like bikes, a couple of TVs, money, etc. I also had to get the spacewalks and slides set up. Then I had to go and set up the tables and chairs, as well as get the games together. I was happy that my mother was cooking the food, or else I would've really been losing my mind.

I was on my way to the park to hook everything up when my phone began ringing. Reaching it out of the cup holder, I noticed that it was Bianca calling.

What the fuck does she want now? I thought as I placed the phone back in its previous spot. I had given her the job of bringing the gifts to the park, and this was her fifth time calling me. If I had known her ass would be this damn aggravating, I would've gotten my brother to do it for me. Speaking of him, I was about to call his ass up to come and help me set the rest of the stuff up.

"Hello," he answered on the third ring.

"Damn, nigga, let me found out you been out tricking last night," I joked. He sounded like he was still asleep, which disappointed me, because I really did need him at that moment.

"Nah, nigga, I was chilling. What's up with you, though?"

"Nigga, I need you to meet me at Klyde Warren Park, so you can help me set up and shit."

"Bruh, I'm still in the bed. Give me some time to get up and brush my teeth and shit," he huffed.

"Yeah, and don't be trying to take an hour. You only live ten minutes from the park, so don't make me come over there and get you."

He did that shit the last time, and I had to do everything by my damn self, but his hungry ass came and ate up all of the food.

"You do remember that I am the big brother, right?" he said.

"Nigga, I didn't say all that. Just meet me in thirty minutes, damn," I said, hanging up on his ass. He was always trying to talk major shit that I didn't have time for.

After hanging up the phone with him, I decided to call Bianca's ass back. It had been a week since that shit went down between her, my little sister, and Delaney, and she was still feeling some type of way. I already told her that I wasn't trying to have any shit out of her today. I really hoped she listened, because I wasn't about to let her put her hands on my little sister again, girlfriend or not.

"Yeah?" I asked once she answered the phone.

"Oh, so now you decided to call me back?" she said smartly.

"Look, if you called to piss me off, you might as well just hang up the phone. I don't have time for your shit today," I told her straight. I really wasn't trying to hear her shit, nor did I have the time to.

"Look, it really doesn't have to be all of that right there. I was just calling to tell you that I was still in the salon."

"The fuck you mean?" I asked, not believing what the fuck I was hearing. All I asked her to do was to get the shit out of the spare room and bring it to the park. You think she did what the fuck I asked her to? That's why we were always going at it. She never did what the fuck I asked her to do, but she was always trying to tell me what to do. "Please tell me you're bullshitting right now."

"You heard me, Onijae, and no, I'm not bullshitting. I'm still in the salon. I haven't even gotten in the chair yet—"

I hung up the phone before I said something that I would later regret. This bitch really knew how to piss me off. Now I knew for sure that I was going to be late.

When I arrived at the park, I was pleased with what I saw. The spacewalks, slides, and barbecue grills were already set up. I was thankful because now all I had left to do was set up the tables and chairs, which gave me enough time to run and get the shit Bianca had left at home.

I had just gotten out of the truck when I spotted my mother's and sister's cars pulling up.

"What's up, boss? You need some help?" Jamar and Devin asked, walking over to me. They were two of the five barbers that worked with me in the shop.

"Y'all niggas did this shit?" I asked, pointing toward the things that were already set up.

"Yeah, we remembered what happened last year, so we decided to come out and help you set everything up before everything starts," Jamar said, laughing.

"Good looking out," I said, dapping them off. "Well, in that case, y'all can start unloading the tables and chairs from the back of the truck too. I'm going see what's up with my mom and sister."

"Damn, who is that fine shorty there?" Devin asked me.

I turned to see Delaney walking behind my mother and sister with an aluminum pan in her hand.

"That's my little sister's best friend," I said, giving them the side eye. Them niggas were staring a bit too hard for my taste.

"Damn, does shorty have a man?" Jamar asked while licking his lips.

I was about to tell them, "Yeah, me, so keep y'all hands and eyes off," but I thought otherwise. After all, I was still with Bianca, so I really couldn't do anything with her.

"Hey, baby," my mother said, placing a kiss on my cheek.

"What's up, ladies?" I asked them.

"What's up is this heavy-ass pan in my hand. Could you please do me a favor and grab it before I drop it?" Tracy said, bouncing from one foot to the next.

"You better watch your mouth, little lady."

"I'm sorry, Ma, but this pan is really heavy," she whined like the spoiled brat that she was.

"I got it," Jamar said, walking over and taking the pan from her.

"It wouldn't have been heavy if you and Delaney weren't trying to cook everything in our kitchen," my mother said, smiling. "Thanks to them, I didn't have to lift not a finger."

"So they cooked all of this food?" I asked, pointing to the pans in their hands.

"No, it was really Delaney who did everything, but I helped a little," Tracy said, smiling.

I looked over to Delaney, who was blushing so hard her cheeks were red.

"Hey, I helped too," I heard Delaney's little sister pipe in. I hadn't even noticed she was standing there.

"Well, thank you, little lady," I said, grabbing her into a big hug and placing a kiss on her cheek. I then did the same to my mother, little sister, and Delaney. "Thanks. I don't know what I would've done if y'all hadn't come through. I still gotta go back home and get the prizes because Bianca's dumb ass is still in the salon."

"Now you see why I can't stand your girlfriend," Tracy said, shaking her head. "Give me the keys to your truck. Delaney and I will do it. We're just going to have to get dressed early."

"Nah, I'm straight. I don't need y'all going over there and tearing my shit up," I said, laughing at her.

"Boy, ain't nobody trying to tear shit up," she said, mushing me in the head. "Now, give me the keys before I change my mind."

"And what am I going to ride in?" I asked her.

"Here," she said, handing me the keys to her car. "Onijae, I swear, if you even so much as bring my baby back with a scratch on it, I want a whole 'nother car."

"Girl, go sit your little ass down. Mama and Daddy got your ass too damn spoiled," I said, yanking the keys out of her hand.

"Don't try to act like y'all didn't help create that monster. Now, come on and get the rest of these pans out of my car. Dallas and I have to go home and get cute," Mom said, walking off.

"Oh yeah, and there's some on my back seat and in the trunk of my car too," Tracy said as she and Delaney headed to my truck.

"Aye, y'all know y'all wrong for this shit, right?" I told all of them.

"Yeah, whatever," Tracy said, throwing up her middle finger.

"And you better not be speeding in my damn truck neither, Tracy!" I yelled at her, but she ignored me.

"Aye, y'all come help me get the food and shit out of these cars, man," I said to Jamar and Devin.

Together, we headed over to my mother's and sister's cars. It took us some time, but after about six trips between the three of us, we finally had everything up and ready. Now the only thing to do was wait for the people to come. I was hoping it turned out as good as it had the year before, because we spent a lot of time and money on this event.

Delaney

"Come on, Delaney," Tracy said, walking up behind me. "Girl, Onijae's going to kill us. We were supposed to be at the park an hour ago."

"Girl, I'm coming," I said as I stood in front of the mirror, giving myself a once over. I had on an all-black, crossover-neck two-piece. I was trying to decide if I wanted to wear some shorts or just wear the sheer cover that I'd bought to go with it.

"Oh, bitch, you look hot!" Tracy said, walking over to me.

"Thanks, and so do you," I told her. She had on a bathing suit like mine, except it was gray.

"You think I should wear the shorts or the cover?"

"Honestly, I don't think you should wear anything. You too fine to be covered up all the damn time. If I had an ass like yours, I'd be trying to flash that bitch every chance I got."

"Girl, please," I said, shaking my head. "I will not be the only one out there half naked. You're putting on shorts, though."

"That's only because I have to. Trust me, if my parents and brothers weren't out there, I'd be wearing my shit as is," she said, flashing me a smile.

"I know you would be," I said, laughing.

My friend wasn't a ho—truth be told, she was still a virgin—but that didn't stop her from liking all eyes on her everywhere she went. Even at school, she just had to have all the attention. I didn't know what she got out of the shit, because I hated it when people looked at me too long.

"I'll just wear the cover up,'" I said, putting it on. Looking at her through the mirror, I noticed the look on her face. "What? It's see-through, so they'll be about to catch a slight glimpse of what I'm working with."

"Whatever. Just hurry the hell up. I'm about to head down to the car. Make sure you lock the door behind you," she said, leaving the room, closing the door behind her.

Once I was pleased with how I looked, I walked back over to the bed to put on my shoes. Tracy had tried to get me to put on wedges, but I quickly objected. I was not going out there like that. Instead, I brought a pair of black sandals.

I'd just buckled my shoes when I heard the door opening.

"I'm coming right now, girl. Damn," I said without looking up.

"You don't have to hurry up. She already left," I heard a deep voice say.

I looked up to see Onijae standing in the doorway, looking at me.

"Where'd she go?" I asked him, confused. "I know her ass didn't leave me here."

"Nah, I sent her to the park to drop the stuff off. I told her you could ride with me," he said like it was nothing.

"What you mean? Why she didn't come up here and get me? I would've finished getting dressed in the car," I told him with a bit of an attitude.

"Because she said you wasn't finished, and I didn't want you to rush." He said it as if that was going to make shit better, but it didn't. "Be cool, li'l mama. I'm about to hop in the shower right quick. I won't be long. So you can finish getting dressed."

"Yeah, whatever," I said, waving his ass off. I couldn't wait until I got to Tracy's ass. I was going to give her a piece of my mind.

Oh, well, I thought. *I might as well make myself comfortable, because it looks like I'm going to be here longer than I intended to.*

I was picking up my clothes when I felt someone behind me. Turning around, I came face-to-face with Onijae—well, more like face-to-chest. I opened my mouth to ask him what he wanted, but my throat went dry. Closing my mouth, I forced down the lump that had formed in my throat.

"Wh—what are you doing?" I stammered.

"You know I want you, right?" he asked, ignoring my question.

"I can't be with you, Onijae," I told him straight up.

"Why can't you?"

"Because you got a woman, and I'm not trying to be no man's other woman."

"I know that, but I still want you," he said as if he hadn't heard a damn thing I just said.

"I can't, Onijae," I said, shaking my head.

"Just try with me, ma. I promise I won't treat you any different than I do her," he told me.

Before I could open my mouth to protest or say something, his lips came crashing onto mine. I wasn't expecting it, but I quickly reacted. I didn't know much about anything, so when he stuck his tongue in my mouth, I got a bit afraid. When I tried to pull back, he pulled me closer.

"Don't run from me, ma," he said, sticking his tongue back in my mouth.

I was surprised when his hand went underneath my bathing suit cover and palmed my breast. I was prepared to stop him if he tried to take things a bit further, but he stopped before then.

"Your lips are so soft, ma. Let me go ahead and hop in the shower before things get too heated."

"Okay," I said, catching my breath. "I need to go to the bathroom anyways."

"There's one down the hall. You can head into the living room when you're done. I won't be longer than fifteen minutes," he said, giving me a quick peck before he left out the door.

I stood there trying to get myself together. I'd never been that close with a man before. Yeah, sure, I kissed a dude in my high school, but this was a grown-ass man— with a woman, at that. I knew I shouldn't be getting myself involved with him, but I couldn't help it. I wanted to see just how far this thing was actually going to go with us. Lord, I hoped I wasn't getting myself into something I couldn't handle.

"Wake up, sleepyhead," I heard someone say as I felt my body being shaken.

"Huh?" I asked, sitting up on the bed. Once I noticed Onijae standing there, I got confused. "What are you doing here?"

"What do you mean? You're at my house, remember?" He started laughing.

I looked around the room and noticed that he was right. Then I remembered earlier and got up.

"Damn, you fall asleep fast."

"Shut up," I said, playfully punching him in the chest. "I wouldn't have fallen asleep if your ass hadn't taken too long. Tracy's going to kill my ass."

"Nah, she already called. I told her that you were waiting on me. That was after she cursed my ass out for taking too long," he said, laughing. I shook my head and laughed also, because knowing Tracy, her ass had done just that.

"Well, come on then. I need to go see about my little sister. She's probably worried to death about me," I said, turning around to grab my bag and phone.

"Is it her or you who's worried to death?" he asked, pulling me to him from behind. He brushed his lips against my neck, causing me to shudder. "I want you so fucking bad, ma."

"I want you too." The words left my lips before I could fully process anything.

"Oh, you're going to get me. It just won't be right now," he said, letting me go. "Come on, let's get out of here."

"Okay," I said as I began following him out of the room and down the stairs.

I waited as he locked the door behind us before we proceeded to Tracy's car. I was impressed when he walked over to my side and opened and closed the door for me. Doing what I'd seen on a few movies, I reached over and opened his from the inside.

"Thank you, beautiful," he said, placing a kiss on my lips. "You know you're mine now, right?"

"What do you mean?" I asked, even though I already knew what he was talking about.

"I mean you belong to me. You're my girl now, so don't let me catch no other nigga up in your face," he said, sounding stupid as hell.

"Uh-huh, whatever," I said, waving his ass off. I couldn't believe his ass was trying to jump claim on me already.

"Whatever, huh? Make me fuck your little pretty ass up," he said, starting the car.

I didn't say shit as he backed out of the driveway and pulled off. I was not paying his ass any kind of attention, so he might as well cut that shit out. As far as I knew it, I was single and game to fuck with whomever I wanted. What he needed to be worried about was his ol' lady, not me.

Bianca

I hauled ass out of the shop the minute Tameka finished doing my hair. I knew Onijae was going to flip the minute I showed my face. I hadn't intended to arrive at the barbecue late, but here I was, late as could be. It was a good thing that I had brought my clothes along with me, or else I would've really been late, and I knew for sure that my man would've flipped his wig.

Pulling up to the park, I had to admit that it was packed out there. It looked like everybody who stayed in Dallas was in attendance. Parking my car, I looked around for my man, but I didn't see him anywhere. I turned the engine off and got out, about to go looking for him, when I spotted him getting out of his little sister's car.

"Damn," I said as I watched him. Even dressed down in a wife beater, some basketball shorts, and a pair of J's, my man was still fine. I moved in his direction, but then I noticed the passenger door of the car opening. I got heated when I noticed Tracy's little friend getting out.

I know this nigga ain't fucking playing with me! I thought. I marched my ass over to them. He was showing all of his thirty-twos, until his eyes landed on my ass. "So, this how we doing shit now, Onijae? So, you fucking with other bitches now?"

"Bianca, it's not even what you think it is," he said, walking over to me.

"Not what I think?" I asked, looking at him sideways. "What I think it is, is that you playing on me with these bitches."

"I don't care what goes on between you and your nigga, but I'm not going to be too many more bitches!" the little bitch had the nerve to say.

"Bitch, I wasn't talking to you. I was talking to my nigga, so if your little stupid ass doesn't mind, please be gone," I told her.

"Onijae, since your ol' lady feeling a bit froggy today, and I'm really not in the mood, please tell her to keep that shit over there, or else I'm going to fuck her up just off GP," she said as if she thought I'd give a fuck.

"Bitch, please. Don't let that little shit that happened a week ago give you too much courage because I'll slide your ass with the quickest," I said, stepping in her direction.

"Don't let that little girl shit fool you. I'll beat you like the dude you look like, bitch!" she replied, bucking.

"Nah, there's not going to be none of that shit out here," Onijae finally said. "Bianca, like I said, it's not what you think. I already told your ass not to come out here with that bullshit. I done put too much shit into this to let you come out here and fuck it up."

"So, do we have a problem over here or nah?" his ugly-ass little sister said, walking up, followed by his father and brother. I didn't even acknowledge them. Instead, I kept my focus on his ass.

"So, you really trying to play me for a bitch who still has Similac on her breath?" I asked. My feelings were seriously hurt.

"You know what? I'm not even about to entertain you. Unlike you, I have class, and I know when and when not to do something," she said, walking off.

I didn't miss the look she gave Onijae before she left, neither. I didn't know what was up with them, but I had better not find out he was on some shady shit.

"Come here. Let me holler at you right quick," Onijae said, walking off before I could object.

I looked at his father and brother, hoping they were going to say something, but they didn't. Instead, they walked off without saying a word to me. I expected that from Omari Jr., but I didn't expect that from Mr. Love. He was always the one in my corner, but I guess he wasn't that day. I watched them walk away before I finally got up the courage to go and talk to Onijae.

"What took you so long?" he asked the minute I walked up to him.

"What's up?" I asked, ignoring his obvious attitude.

"What's your problem, ma?"

"What do you mean?" I asked, which only seemed to piss him off more.

"I specifically asked you not to come here today with that bullshit, and here you are, bringing that bullshit!" He sounded heated.

"I didn't come nowhere with nothing. That bitch came at me the wrong way!" I yelled, getting in his face.

"First of all, lower your fucking voice because I'm not yelling at you. Secondly, you started that bullshit, so come with something else."

"Well, explain to me why that bitch was getting out of the car with you." This nigga obviously had me fucked up. "As a matter of fact, explain to me how y'all ended up riding in the same car alone anyways."

"First of all, I'm a grown-ass man, and I don't have time to be explaining shit to no damn body. Second, she came help me get the stuff *you* were supposed to be dropping off at the park. Lastly, if you wanted to be insecure and think that I might cheat on you, you should've never cheated on me in the first place!" He stormed off, leaving me standing there with my mouth wide open.

I stood there, feeling like the fool that I knew I was. Here I had put this man through enough and yet, I was always the one tripping. I couldn't help it, though. I was a firm believer in karma, and I knew that what goes around comes back around.

I couldn't fathom losing my man, especially to a chick that was still in high school. I wasn't about to let it go down like that. If she wanted *my* man, she had another thing coming to her, because I was not them little chicks she played with in the streets. I was going to make shit complicated for both of them. I was going to show them not to play with me. Onijae thought that I was tripping now, but just let me find out he was fucking with that girl, and I'd be ten times worse. All he had to do was try me and see.

After standing there for a few seconds longer, I started making my way toward the barbecue. I was halfway there when I stopped and turned back around. Instead of staying there to be treated like an outcast, I decided to leave and go home. It didn't make much sense to stay when I knew I'd probably be going off again. I was almost sure that Onijae wasn't going to miss me anyway.

Once I made it to my car, I started it up and drove off and drove home. When I pulled up into the driveway, I cut the car off, but I didn't get out. Lord knows I wasn't trying to go home to an empty house, but there I was. I loved Onijae with everything in me, and I just couldn't seem to see where things started going wrong. Sure, I had cheated on him, I knew that, but that was years ago. We should've been past that by now, but obviously, he wasn't.

I hadn't realized that I was crying until I felt the tears rolling down my face. I had no idea if I was crying because I was sad, or because I was truly frustrated with everything. Things were becoming a bit overwhelming, and I had no idea how to fix them.

Without thinking twice, I started the car and pulled back out of the driveway. Once I made it onto the main highway, I pulled out my phone and dialed the last number I intended to call.

"Hello?" He answered the phone, sounding surprised as hell.

"You busy?" I asked him

"Nah, I'm just chilling. What's going on?"

"Meet me at the spot in twenty minutes."

"All right," he said, causing me to smile.

"Okay, I'll see you later," I said, hanging up. I didn't have any second thoughts as I drove my car in the direction of the hotel. I didn't intend to do anything other than vent. Lord knew I had a lot of shit that I needed to get off my chest.

"Oh my Goooooood . . ." I moaned loud enough for the people in the next room to hear.

Carlos's face was buried deep between my legs, where it had been for the past thirty minutes. He was really putting some work in with that tongue, and I was damn near ready to start climbing the walls. I'd already busted all over his face twice, and I was just getting ready to catch another one. I almost went crazy when he stuck his tongue in me. I mean, my boy was licking and sucking as if it was going out of style. What sent me over the edge was when I felt him making a path toward my ass. When his tongue graced it, I thought I was going to have an instant heart attack.

"Bring that ass here, girl," he said as he pulled me back down. Once he had me where he wanted, he locked his arms around my thighs and dove headfirst back between my thighs, attacking my already sensitive kitty. I thought I was about to pass out.

"Oh . . . I'm 'bouta cum!" I yelled, grinding on his tongue. I could feel that shit coming, which caused me to move a little bit faster.

Just as I was getting ready to cum, he stopped.

"What the hell do you thinking you're do—" was all I got out before he shoved all ten inches of his thick dick inside of me, halting my words.

"Now, what was that you were saying?" he asked with a smirk on his face.

I wanted to answer, but the way he was sending them strokes had me confused. Yeah, that's right. His dick had me speechless, and I was enjoying every bit of it.

"Now, turn around."

He pulled out of me and waited as I got on all fours. I made sure to arch my back perfectly as I anticipated what was next to come. A few seconds went by, and nothing happened. When I looked back, he was sitting there, just staring.

"You better come on before you make me fuck you up!" I said, turning around. To give him a little motivation, I placed a finger inside me, which he immediately slapped away.

"I see I'ma have to teach you a lesson," he said with a sneaky grin on his face.

Placing his dick at my entrance, he fed me maybe an inch or two before he pulled back out. I became frustrated when he began rubbing the head against my slippery lips. My pussy was on fire, and I desperately needed him to put it out.

"Oh shit, Carlos!" I cried aloud as he plunged deep inside of me.

Seeing what he wanted, he wasted no time going straight to work. He began pounding my pussy as if my shit owed him something. My eyes felt like they were about to roll in the back of my head.

"Yeah, that's right. Take this dick!" He growled, causing my body to shiver. Something about the way he talked shit while beating my pussy up gave me an even better feeling. That nigga was hitting my spot so good I felt like I should pray or something.

"Oh, babe, wait. No, yeah, oh, right there. Right therr-rre . . ." I said, throwing it back.

"Do you still love me, Bianca?" he asked, pulling my hair.

In my head, I was saying yes, but not a word was coming out of my mouth. I was too busy focusing on the nut that was about to explode out of me.

"Answer my fucking question, girl!" he said, getting a bit aggressive, which didn't help at all. He pulled my head back, so that his lips were to my ear. "Tell me you love me."

"Y—yes, I fucking love you, Carlos!" I screamed as my body began shaking violently.

"Good. I love you, too," he panted before he placed a kiss on my neck and busted his nut inside of me.

We both collapsed on the bed, barely able to catch our breath. A few minutes later, he got up, headed to the bathroom, and got in the shower. Seconds later, he was back in the room.

"Come on. Let's go take a shower so we can go," he said, pulling my arm, but I refused to move.

"Go on. I'ma get in when you get out." Yawning, I reached up and grabbed a pillow so I could lie down a bit longer. Before I knew it, I was out like a light.

I was having the best dream of a lifetime when I felt someone tapping on my leg. Waking up, I was a bit confused, until I saw Carlos standing there fully dressed, with his phone in his hand.

"Damn. How long have I been out?" I asked, sitting up. When I looked out of the window, I noticed that it was already dark outside. I grabbed my phone to see if I had any missed calls from Onijae, but I didn't have any.

"You've only been sleeping for an hour, maybe," he said, looking at his watch.

"Oh, okay. Where are you going?"

"I have to go home and get ready for work. I got called in for a late shift. What time do you plan on leaving?"

"After I hop in the shower, I guess," I said, getting up from the bed. When I let the sheet go, I stood there completely naked in front of him.

"You sure you can't come back to bed?" I asked, grabbing his third leg.

"As much as I would love to, I can't. Let me get out of here before I'm late," he said, picking up his bag and walking away. When he reached the door, he turned back around to me. "Should I be expecting you to call me like before?"

"Carlos, I honestly don't know," I told him. "I just needed to vent, but apparently I needed more than that. I can't and won't promise you that we'll continue to have sex, but we'll always remain friends as before."

"Okay, I can respect that. Just call me when you make it home," he said, sounding a bit disappointed. "See you later, ma."

"See you later, baby," I said to his back.

After he left, I couldn't help but to sit there and think of the history Carlos and I had. He and I had been messing around for a year and a half prior to the time Onijae caught us having sex. He was cool people and gave me whatever I wanted. Onijae thought I was the one banking on my car, but it was Carlos who was actually paying for it. However, I couldn't give him what he wanted, which was my heart, because it belonged to my man. Now, had we met before Onijae, then yeah, he would've been the one. Unfortunately for Carlos, Onijae was my one true love, and I wasn't about to leave my man for nothing and no one. Being his friend was as far as we could go. Someday, I hoped he'd meet a woman who would love and be there for him.

Chapter Six

Delaney

"So, when am I going to see you again?" Onijae asked me. He'd brought Dallas and me home from the park. We'd stayed back to help him, and I was honestly beat.

"You just saw me all day today," I told him.

"I'm talking about one on one, with no one else around, Lay Lay," he said, calling me by the nickname he'd given me. I thought it was cute, and every time he called me that, I got a funny feeling inside.

"I don't know. You know I'm still in school. I also have to work and take care of my brothers and sister. So, I guess whenever I get free time."

"I hope it's sooner rather than later," he said, placing his hand over mine. I swear every time that man touched me, it felt like magic.

"I'll see," I said, looking out of the window. We were parked in front of my house. I honestly wasn't ready to leave him, but I had to get Dallas inside. "Well, I guess I'll see you around."

"You can bet that, li'l mama," he said, getting out of the truck.

He came around and opened my door for me. I thought he was going to move and let me out, but he didn't. He turned my body toward him and stood between my legs. For a minute, he only looked at me, licking those juicy lips of his. Instead of waiting for him, I pulled him closer and placed my lips to his. He parted my lips with his tongue as the kiss deepened. I was on a natural high as our tongues danced to their own music. I'd forgotten about where we were, until I heard Dallas cry out in her sleep.

"I should probably get her inside," I said, pulling back.

He looked at me before he nodded his head and went to open the back door. I got out, prepared to get my little sister, but he already had her.

"G'on, girl. I got her," he said, flashing me a quick smile.

I shook my head and laughed at him because he was definitely a fool, but a fine one. After getting the rest of the things from the back seat, I followed them to the door. Once I opened it, I told him to follow me to my room.

"This is a nice spot here," he said, shaking his head. He was talking about my room, which was decorated in all black with just a hint of purple. I was a neat freak, so I wasn't worried about him seeing dirt anywhere.

"Thank you," I said, placing my bag and purse on the floor by my closet. "Come follow me, so you can lay her down in her room."

We left the room and headed down the hallway. When I got to Daija's room, I thought I heard a few sniffles, but I wasn't too sure. I didn't want to bother her, so I didn't knock on the door. Once we made it to the kids' room, Onijae carefully placed Dallas in her bed, and we left.

"Come on so I can show you out," I said as I prepared to head to the door, but he pulled me back once I tried to pass my room. "What are you doing, Onijae?"

"I'm not going anywhere. I'm spending the night with you."

"Boy, you better cut it out," I said, moving out of his arms. I walked over to the dresser, where I began getting ready to go and take my shower. I didn't have the time to play with him.

"I'm serious, Lay Lay," he said, smiling a sinister grin.

"You already know where the door is. I'm gonna take a shower," I told him before I headed out of the room.

Only the Lord knew how much I really did want him to stay, but I knew that he couldn't. I was sure that he had to go run home to his girlfriend, which was the reason why I wasn't trying to get my hopes up high. If only things could've been different, though.

After taking a quick fifteen-minute shower, I brushed my teeth and tied my scarf around my head. I then cleaned up my mess. Before going to my room, I headed to check on Daija. Her light was still on, so I knocked on the door and waited for her to answer. A few seconds later, she came to the door, looking like a zombie.

"Hey, sis," she said, forcing a smile. I was caught off guard when she pulled me in for a hug.

"What's wrong, Daija?" I asked her. Daija was never like this. I knew something was wrong just by the way that she was talking.

"Nothing. I'm just feeling bad. I think I caught a bug or something," she said, shrugging her shoulders.

"Oh. Well, what did you do today?"

"Actually, I didn't do anything. I stayed in the house all day and watched TV."

"Oh, okay. How were the boys?"

"They were fine. They barely came out of the room. They played that game all day."

"I figured that," I said before we both became silent.

I stood there looking at my little sister. Something was indeed wrong with Daija. She looked pale, considering her natural complexion, and her clothes looked much too big. "Are you sure that you're okay? You know you can tell me anything, Daija. Look at me, Dai. I'm your big sister, and I'm always here for you, baby girl."

She looked as if she wanted to say something, but she didn't. I noticed her eyes were wet and her lips were trembling, but I decided not to speak on it, since she didn't want to. I'm sure when and if she wanted me to know, then she was going to tell me. Until then, I was going to leave her be.

"Okay. Well, I'll be in my room if you need me," I said, yawning. I looked at her one last time before I left and headed to my room.

When I walked in my room, the lights were off. The only light showing was the little light from the TV. *I knew his ass wasn't staying*, I thought as I removed my nightgown and walked over to the bed. I pulled back the covers and attempted to get in.

"Let me find out you doing all of this for me," Onijae said, causing me to jump.

"Damn, you scared the shit out of me!" I said, holding my chest. "Why are you still here?"

"What you mean?" he asked, sitting up. "I told you I was staying the night with you."

"Yeah, but I didn't think that you were actually serious, Onijae," I said, walking over to cut on the light.

"Damn!" he exclaimed the minute the lights came on.

I saw the lust in his eyes and then noticed that I was still in my panties and bra. I immediately grabbed my gown to put it back on.

"You don't have to act like that. I won't bite you unless you want me to." He flashed his killer smile.

"Boy, shut up," I said, laughing.

"Now, come on, so I can get some sleep. I'm tired as hell. They really wore my ass out today," he said, lying back in the bed.

Turning around, I turned the lights off and proceeded back over to the bed.

"You can take your gown off. I won't do anything to you. I promise."

"Okay," I said before taking the gown off again. Then I hopped in the bed, making sure to stay a few feet away from him.

"Stop running from me," he said, pulling me closer to him.

"I'm not running from you, Onijae. I'm just trying to give you some space, that's all," I lied. I was indeed running from him.

"Uh-huh. You can tell that lie to yourself, but I know what's up." He chuckled and pulled me closer.

"Whatever, boo," I said before it became quiet.

A few minutes later, I was met by the sound of him snoring lightly. Even though I didn't want to admit it, I smiled, knowing that he was actually there with me. I knew he had a girlfriend, but right then, none of that really mattered, because he was there with me.

After lying there staring into space for a few minutes, I became exhausted. Turning around toward him, I placed my head on his chest and eventually dozed off.

The next morning came faster than I had anticipated it would. I was all giddy and ready to play the devoted girlfriend, until I turned around and noticed that the side that Onijae once occupied was now empty. Sitting up, I looked around the room to see if he was anywhere else, but he wasn't. I then pulled back the covers and prepared to get up.

I noticed my phone flashing a new message. Grabbing it, I unlocked it and noticed that it was a message from him, telling me that he had to go, but he would see me soon. I started to text him back but then thought differently. I didn't know why I was fooling myself. I was certain that he had to go running home to his girl, which pissed me off. The nigga didn't even have the decency to wake me and tell me goodbye. Instead, he played my ass, and I was hurt behind that shit.

"Oh, well," I said, powering my phone off.

My whole day was completely ruined, and I didn't want to be bothered with anyone. I'd had plans to get up and make everyone breakfast, but I guess they'd have to eat cereal. I was in my bed, and that's where I planned to stay for the rest of the day. I didn't have time to be playing with him because I had exams the next day and for the next two weeks. Graduation was only a few weeks away, and I wasn't going to let anything or anyone stop me from walking across that stage.

Tracy

The next few weeks came around faster than I wanted. I'd been so busy studying and taking exams that I barely had time to do anything. The only things I did was study at night, go to school the next day to take my exams, then come home and study some more. I couldn't even spend time with Delaney, and we went to the same school. I couldn't wait until it was time for graduation, though. I was going to be on the first thing smoking to college.

Yes, things had indeed been a hassle, but overall, it had been great as well. One thing good about the past few weeks was that my mother and family had a chance to meet my best friend. That almost went off without a hitch. And I'd met my new boo.

Just thinking about him, I couldn't wait until we could chill again. He was caring, attentive, and funny as hell. He made sure to treat me right, and never once did he try to disrespect me. I only hoped that it stayed that way because I really wanted us to work out. I was tired of trusting dudes and not getting further than three weeks with them. I hoped he played his cards right because I damn sure wanted him to stick around for a while.

"What are you over there thinking about?" Delaney asked, breaking me from my thoughts.

"Girl, nothing," I said, smiling a girlish grin. I couldn't help it because I was definitely feeling an awesome type of way.

"Nah, bitch. What happened? I know damn well you ain't all damn happy because today was our last day of school," she said, getting a bit closer to me.

We were sitting at a table in Chick-fil-A, waiting on our order. Since we had early release and it was the last day for seniors, we decided to hang out before Delaney was scheduled to go to work at four.

"If I tell you, you better not tell my brother either, bitch," I said, looking around to make sure no one I knew was there and could hear me.

"Bitch, please. When have I ever told anyone anything you've told me? As a matter of fact, bitch, fuck you. I don't even want to know anymore, since you pulling a bitch card like that," she said, getting up from our table.

She walked over to the counter and grabbed our bags before walking back over to me and handing me mine. I thought she was going to sit down, but she didn't. She took her food and headed straight for the car.

Oh, shit, I thought as I got up and followed her out to the car. When I got in the car, I sat there, not even trying to start the car. I was looking at her, but she had her head down, looking at her phone, so I reached over and took it out of her hand.

"Tracy, give me my phone back. I'm not playing with you!" she said with an attitude. I looked at her and rolled my eyes before placing the phone in my purse and setting it on the passenger-side floor.

"You really need to lose the attitude. I only said that because the dude I'm messing with works in my brother's shop. I didn't want you to accidently spill the beans when y'all together or whatever," I said, explaining myself to her. I couldn't believe she had gotten mad in the first place, but I couldn't let her stay mad, especially over some bullshit like this.

"Well, bitch, that's all you had to say. You were playing me like I was a bitch who runs her mouth all the time," she said, seeming a bit relaxed now.

"Yeah, yeah, whatever. You shouldn't have gotten all amped up anyways," I said as I started the car.

"Wait, which one is it?" she asked as I backed out of the parking spot.

"Girl, it's Devin."

"You talking about the light-skinned cutie with the braids?"

"Yeah, that's him."

"Oh, girl, I wouldn't blame you. If you hadn't banked that, I surely was going to," she said, laughing.

"Bitch, please. Like my brother would even allow it," I told her. If she didn't know that Onijae was territorial, she was surely about to learn it.

"I'm tired of telling you that I don't run to Onijae's beat, and I damn sure don't care about how he feels. If you don't know, you already have a sister-in-law. Your brother just wants me to be the other woman," she said, sounding a little sad.

"When was the last time you talked to him?" I asked her.

"I haven't talked to him since the day of the barbecue," she said, looking down.

I could tell that he had her feeling some type of way, but I didn't say anything. I couldn't wait until I saw his ass because I was going to give him a piece of my mind.

I grabbed my phone out of my purse, preparing to make a call, when it began ringing. I got all happy-go-lucky when My Booskie, with emoji faces, flashed across the screen. I didn't want him to know that I was happy, so I took a few seconds longer to answer the phone than usual.

"Hello," I said, answering the phone.

"Damn, shorty, why you took so long to answer the phone? Let me find out you done kicked a nigga to the curb already."

"Boy, shut up. I was getting my food," I said, smiling like a schoolgirl.

"From where? You didn't go to school today? Don't be missing school before you make me tell your brother on you."

"Boy, please. For your information, we had a half a day today. For your information, today was our last day of school, and you can tell my brother whatever you want. I'm seventeen years old, and he ain't my damn daddy," I said, snapping on him. "Besides, how will you explain to my brother about knowing I didn't go to school anyway?"

"Damn, li'l mama. I was just fucking with you. You don't have to jump down a nigga's throat."

"I wasn't jumping down your throat. I was just letting you know. Anyways, what are you doing?" I asked, changing the subject.

"I'm just chilling, that's all," he replied, sounding high or some shit.

"Where are you, Devin?"

"I'm at the shop, why?"

"Nothing. I just asked. You miss me?"

"You already know I miss you. I wish I could see your ass right now."

"I wish I could see you too," I said sadly, and then I thought of something. "Where my brother at?"

"He up in the back room. Why?"

"Nothing. Let me call you right back," I said, hanging up the phone before he could say anything. I immediately called my brother's phone to see what was up with him.

"To what do I owe the pleasure of this call?" he asked, answering the phone on the first ring.

"Boy, bye. What are you doing?" I asked him.

"I'm doing what I do every day all day. Now, what do you want?"

"Well, if you insist on cutting straight to the point, I saw this dress I wanted for my graduation party, and I was wondering if you wanted to buy it," I said, coming up with the first lie that popped up in my head. I knew damn well that I didn't see or find a dress, and I damn sure wasn't buying one this early. Besides, I wanted to shop in Miami for a dress anyway.

"I knew damn well you weren't calling me just to call me. Your ass always wants something," he said, fussing as usual.

I rolled my eyes because he wasn't doing nothing but wasting his breath. Just like Omari, he was going to give me anything I wanted. That was the perk of being the last child, and especially being the one and only daughter.

"Whatever, Onijae. Are you going to buy the dress for me or nah?" I said, cutting him off. I really wasn't trying to hear his mouth. I was only using his ass to get to see my baby anyway.

"Don't get smart with me, Tracy. How much is it?"

"Five hundred dollars," I said, lying through my teeth again.

"Girl, you better go ahead somewhere. I'm not giving you five hundred dollars for no damn dress. I'll give you two hundred and fifty dollars, but that's about it. You better get Mama and Daddy or Omari to give your ass the rest."

"But, Nijae, Daddy's going to make me clean up or something. You know I can't be doing none of that," I said, practically crying like a baby. I was really giving him everything.

"Yeah, and that's good. Your ass isn't too good to be cleaning up. They have your ass spoiled like that. That's why you don't like doing shit now. Come get the money, and your ass better hurry up before I change my damn mind," he said and hung up.

"Bitch-ass nigga!" I screamed at the phone. I turned to see Delaney laughing at me. "What the hell you laughing at?"

"Your spoiled ass. I pray for the man who has to deal with you after all of this. You gon' break the man's pocket and run him dry."

"Bitch, shut up. I had plans on splitting the money with you, but I changed my mind now," I said, poking my tongue out at her. The look on her face was priceless.

"You gon' do me like that?" she asked, faking as if she was actually hurt.

"Nah, you know you my boo. We gon' go shopping tomorrow, but for now, let me go see my nigga," I said, heading toward my brother's shop.

I was so excited to see Devin. I hoped like hell that I could contain myself because I wasn't trying to get us busted, especially not this early in the game.

When I arrived at the shop, I pulled around into the parking lot that was reserved for customers, but I didn't get out right away. Instead, I cut the car off and sat there. I pulled down the visor to check my makeup before adding a little lip-gloss to my lips. Once I was pleased with how I looked, I got out and waited for Delaney.

A few minutes later, we were walking up to the door as if we owned the place. I mean, I know I was. I was trying to make my man see me before I entered the building.

When we opened the door, I didn't expect the whole barbershop full of niggas, who were now looking at both Delaney and me. I tried playing it off as if it was nothing, but then a light-skinned dude pulled me by my arm.

"Say, li'l mama, what's your name?" he asked me.

"First of all, don't be pulling on me like that, and secondly, my name damn sure ain't little mama. So leave me be," I said, scrunching my nose up while pulling my arm out of his hold.

"Damn, little mama, you cold. Make me have to tame you."

"Nigga, I ain't no animal. You better go home and try that shit on yo' mama," I said, getting in his face. I didn't care if he was a man. He wasn't about to play with me like that.

"What did you just say?" he asked, getting up from his seat. The nigga had to be six feet plus, but still that didn't scare me, nor did it make me back down.

"Nigga, you heard what the fuck I said. Don't think I'm scared of your ass," I said again. I wanted him to know how much he didn't scare me one bit.

"Yo, what's good?" I heard from behind me. I turned to see Devin standing there with this ill mug on his face.

"Nigga, you don't have shit to do with this. This between me and shorty, who apparently can't keep her mouth closed," he told Devin with a mug of his own.

"Apparently, you don't know who this is, or else you wouldn't be talking to her like that. You see I'm making the shit easy on you. Now, if I go call my boy Jae out the back, your ass will most definitely be grass," Devin said calmly with his arms folded across his chest. If you asked me, the nigga was a little too calm for me.

Right on cue, I spotted the door to the back part of the shop open. I watched as Onijae came swaggering out of there with a smile on his face. I became disgusted when

I noticed Bianca following behind him. I looked over to Delaney, who had this look on her face that I couldn't read.

It took him a while, but once Onijae spotted us standing there, the smile he once had was gone. He was not looking at me, and also refusing to look at Delaney. I knew he knew he was fucked, which was why I didn't say anything.

"Call me when you get home, baby," Bianca said, giving my brother a kiss on his cheek.

She looked at both Delaney and me before she smirked and walked out the door. I wanted to run behind her and smack the fuck out of her for being a stupid bitch, but I thought about it and decided that I was going to get both her and my brother back. They didn't know it now, but Delaney and I were going to be laughing in the end.

"What's going on here?" he asked, referring to Devin and the dude who was engaged in a stare-off battle.

"Why don't you let ol' boy tell you?" Devin said, nodding his head toward the dude.

"Talk to me," Onijae said, giving dude his attention.

"Nigga, you too sensitive for me, but check it out. I was chilling when I spotted these two ladies walking through the door. I thought for sure that today was my lucky day, and you know me, I couldn't let them pass by without speaking. I grabbed shorty and tried to holler at her, but she got all ignorant and started acting all crazy and shit. Taking 'bout my mama and shit. Then this nigga come in here, trying to play captain save-a-ho," he said, ranting and raving.

He was so busy explaining himself to Onijae that he didn't see when Devin cocked his fist back. Before he could get another word out of his mouth, Devin punched him in it.

"Bitch-ass nigga!" Devin yelled as he continued to attack him.

I felt so bad for dude because he didn't get a chance to get a lick in. Devin was really putting it on him. All I, as well as everyone else in the shop, could do was look on. They were all over the shop, making a complete mess and fucking shit up.

"Help me break this shit up!" Onijae yelled to a few dudes standing a few feet away from them. On cue, they ran over and helped him separate both Devin and the dude.

"Get that nigga the fuck up out of here!" Devin yelled, out of breath, before Onijae and some other dude pulled him to the back of the shop.

We stood there and watched as the rest of the dudes pulled ol' boy to the front of the shop and put him out. When everyone was cleared out, I looked at the shop, which was now a mess.

"Where are the brooms?" Delaney asked. I guess she was thinking the same thing I was thinking.

I walked over to the utility closet and grabbed both of us a broom and dustpan before I walked back over to her. She was already picking up things, so I decided to help her. It took us a minute, but we finally had picked up everything. Since we had no idea where anything went, we just placed them on the receptionist's desk. Once we were through, we began to sweep the floor, and when we were done, everything looked straight. The shop was damn near empty, and the guys were finally walking from the back of the shop.

"Damn, nigga, you look bad," I joked at Devin, who was holding a bag of ice to his busted lip.

"Girl, yo' ass. I should've let that nigga whooped yo' ass," he said, poking his tongue out at me.

"And we just would've been fighting too. Now, let me see," I said, walking over to him.

I peeped how Onijae was just standing there looking at us, but he never said anything.

"What the hell you looking at?" I asked.

"Nothing," he said, shaking his head.

"Onijae, I'm about to go grab me some lunch. Y'all want something?" Trice, the girl who braided hair in the shop, said.

"Nah, I'm straight. You want something, Dev?" he asked, looking at Devin.

"Nah, I'm good. Besides, I think Tracy owes me lunch, since I took one for her ass," he said, mushing my head.

"Yeah, well, you gon' be waiting on that lunch for a while then," I told him. I busted out laughing at the way he was looking at me. "Oh, stop looking at me that way. I'll take you to lunch since you insist on holding this over my head."

"All right. Let me go change my shirt and shit. I'll be back in a minute," he said before he disappeared to the back of the shop.

I took a seat in the chair as I waited on him to come back. When I looked up, I noticed Onijae was staring, but it wasn't at me. When I followed the line of his vision, I found Delaney sitting in a chair, playing with her phone. He looked at me and nodded his head toward her, but I shook my head before flipping him the bird and pulling my phone out as well. There were two other dudes in there, with the exception of another barber.

I was about to say something when the door to the shop opened and in walked this handsome, dark-skinned dude. When I said dude was *fine*, he was just that. He had to be an even six feet and rocked a head full of hair. Dude's hair was so long that I was beginning to think he had a weave in his head or something.

"Excuse me," he spoke out to get our attention. I couldn't help but to notice the accent he had. It sounded like he was from Jamaica or something.

"What's up? I'm Onijae, and I'm the owner. How can I help you?" Onijae asked, walking over to him.

"Hi, my name is Aqura. I'm looking for someone to wash and someone to braid my hair."

"Well, the girl who does the braids isn't here right now. She just went to lunch, and she won't be back here for an hour and a half," he explained to dude.

"Oh, okay," Aqura said, turning around.

I looked over to Delaney, who was still playing on her phone, and thought of something.

"Hold up, wait!" I said, stopping him in his tracks. "I know someone who could do his hair."

"Yeah, who?" Onijae asked with a confused face.

"Delaney," I shouted out, louder than I had anticipated.

"Say what now?" she asked, finally pulling her eyes from her phone.

I got up and walked toward her.

"Why did you say my name?"

"I just told my brother how I knew someone who could braid hair."

"Well, I don't know why you did that, because I'm not putting my hands in nobody's head," she said, looking at him and rolling her eyes. I know she was doing that because of what had happened earlier. What she didn't know was that I was doing this for her.

"It's not for him. It's for . . ." I said, already forgetting dude's name. "What's your name again?"

"Aqura," the dude stepped up and said.

The minute her eyes landed on him, I noticed the change in her body. She was seeing exactly what I was seeing, and that was how fine and cute this man was.

"Like I said, Aqura here needs his hair braided, and I was just telling my brother how I knew someone who could braid hair. Especially since Trice is gone and every-thing," I said, looking at Onijae, who had a screwed-up look on his face. I wanted so badly to bust out and laugh, but I didn't.

"Okay, well, if your brother doesn't mind, then of course, I'll braid his hair," she said, looking at Onijae, who really looked like he wanted to curse us out, but he didn't.

"Yeah, go ahead. I'll be in the back of the shop. The prices for braids are on the wall," he said. He didn't say another word. Instead, he just looked at Delaney once more before he left the room.

Once he was gone, I let out the laugh that I had held in before I walked over to Delaney.

"You know my brother is pissed, right?"

"Girl, I don't give a damn about how he feels. That man is not about to have me feeling the side effects of being a side bitch. To hell with what he thinks," she said, obviously pissed also.

"Anyways, the washbowl and shampoo are in the back of the shop," I said, pointing to the area. I spotted Devin walking my way with a huge smile on his face. "I'm 'bouta take my man to get some lunch. I'll see you when I get back."

"Bitch, I know you ain't trying to leave me in here with your brother," she said, pulling my arm.

"Nah, I'm trying to leave you in here with Aqura. I saw the way you were looking at him, and he most definitely was looking at you too. So, stop being a coward. My brother won't start shit because he doesn't want Bianca to find out. Do you and get this nigga number, please," I told her. Delaney was definitely naïve and a Miss Goody Two Shoes, but she needed to loosen up a bit. I was hoping that Aqura would do that for her.

"You better hurry up, too," she said, walking off. She walked over to Aqura and whispered something to him before they took off walking toward the washbowl.

Shaking my head, I turned and headed toward Devin, who was waiting by the door for me.

As we made our way toward the car, I only had one thing on my mind. Well, not so much a thought, but a wish, and that was that my brother and Delaney would behave while I was gone.

Chapter Seven

Delaney

I don't know what Tracy thought she was doing, but I was going to run with it for now. I knew my friend had my best interest at heart, which was why she did most of the things that she did.

I couldn't lie and say I wasn't hurt when we first got in there and I spotted Onijae and his old lady coming out of the back office. No wonder the nigga had been ignoring me. He talked all that shit, but no matter what, I would always have to come after his main lady. It didn't take a rocket scientist to figure out just what had been going on in that back office, but I wasn't tripping. At least, that's what I kept telling myself. The nigga didn't even speak to me. He just looked at me. Yeah, I saw him. I looked him dead in his eyes, rolled mine, and went to playing on my phone. Since he acted as if I didn't exist, I didn't have a damn thing to say to him then.

As always, Tracy was trying to broadcast my talent. I didn't know why she liked to tell people I could do hair when I barely did it. Besides, the only people's hair I did from time to time was hers, Dallas's, Daija's, and mine. I used to do my mother's hair, but she didn't let me anymore. That was a conversation for later on, though. Now, here I was, about to braid some nigga's hair. She was lucky that it actually wasn't something for her brother, and since I saw how much it actually got under his skin, I decided to do it.

After washing Aqura's hair twice, I took him over to one of the stations. I hoped like hell the person who this station belonged to didn't catch an attitude because I really wasn't in the mood. All I was trying to do was braid this man's hair and get out of there once Tracy returned.

"So, how do you want your hair braided?" I asked dude after I had finished blow-drying it.

"It really doesn't matter. You could just do you. I just need something done to it and shit," he replied. I didn't know why, but when he licked his lips, my midsection started to feel funny.

"Okay," I said as I began parting his hair down the middle. Since he had so much hair, regular, straight back braids weren't going to do it any justice. I decided to do some train tracks. I was going to do all type of designs I'd been dying to do in a man's head. I had wanted to do them in Dallas's head, but I knew it would make her look like a tomboy, which she hated.

I was in my zone as I worked on the left side of his head. I wasn't a slow braider, so it was no surprise when I was quickly done with that side. I made my way to the right side before he finally decided to speak.

"So, what's your name?" he asked me.

"My name is Delaney," I replied, a little scared. I didn't know why I did that, but every time I talked to a boy, I became nervous.

"That's a pretty name for such a pretty lady. You got a man, Ms. Delaney?"

"No, I'm single like a dollar bill. You got a woman?" I threw back at him, which made him laugh.

"No, ma'am. I'm actually single myself," he said, laughing again.

"Yeah, well, how old are you?"

"I'm twenty-two. I'll be making twenty-three in May. How old are you?"

"Dang, I at least thought you were a little older than that, but I'm seventeen. I'll be making eighteen in May also," I told him.

He moved his head and looked back at me with unreadable eyes.

"Why are you looking at me like that?" I asked, a bit nervous.

"Because I thought you was in your twenties. I had no idea that you were seventeen years old."

"Well, it looks like we both thought wrong," I said, folding my arms across my chest.

"You feisty, too. I like that." He laughed before he turned back around so that I could finish his hair.

"Mm-hmm," was all I said as I went back to doing his hair.

Thirty minutes later, I was putting the finishing touches on his head when Trice, Tracy, Devin, and the rest of the crew started returning to the shop.

"Damn, bitch, them braids are sick as fuck. No offense, Trice, but Delaney, my brother needs you up in his shop too," Tracy said, causing everyone to walk over to her.

"Shit, after seeing this, I'm thinking about going back to school to perfect my craft. Baby girl, you did the damn thing," Trice said, pulling me in for a hug.

"Thanks, boo," I replied, feeling a bit embarrassed.

"Bitch, please. I hate when you do that shit," Tracy said, already calling me on my shit. "You did the damn thing. There's nothing wrong with receiving compliments, Delaney, so let that shit go."

"Okay," I said as I spotted Onijae emerging from the back of the shop. Our eyes briefly met before I felt a pair of arms on my shoulder. I turned to see Aqura standing there, looking like a tall glass of hot chocolate.

"Come take that walk with me outside right quick," he said, taking my hand before I could object.

I looked at Tracy, who wore a smile of acceptance. She winked at me before I exited the door.

"Here," he said, handing me three hundred-dollar bills.

"Nah. That style wasn't nothing but a few dollars. You giving me two-sixty too much," I said, pushing his hand back.

"Come on, man. Take the money. You got my hair braided to perfection. You deserve it, baby," he said, but I still continued to shake my head no. "Look, shorty wants you in the window," he said, causing me to turn around.

I felt him stick something in my back pocket, so I pulled it out. I turned to give it back to him, but he was now in his car, flashing me this million-dollar smile. I shook my head at him before finally giving in.

"Okay, I'll keep it," I told him.

He started his car and rolled down the window a bit. "That's more like it," he said, blowing me a kiss. "But since you don't have a man, is it okay if I take you out?"

"I don't know you. For all I know, you could be a killer, so why would I let you take me out?" I asked, bullshitting with him.

"I'm no killer, baby. I'm sweet as can be, unless someone tests me," he said, getting a little more serious.

"I feel that." I agreed with what he was saying.

"So, are you going to let me take you out or not?"

"I don't know," I said, hunching my shoulder like a little girl.

"It's a yes or no answer. I won't be mad if you say no, baby. At least I know I tried," he said, making me laugh.

I stood there for a minute, contemplating my answer. Before I could open my mouth, my phone began buzzing. I looked to see a message from Tracy. When I opened it, I laughed at what it said. Turning around toward the shop, I spotted her looking at me. I winked at her before turning back around to Aqura.

"Looks like we got an audience," he said, getting out and nodding toward the shop.

"Yes, that's my best friend. So, about you taking me out, my answer is yes," I said, barely able to get the words out right. My chest was pounding, and I could hear my heart beating through my ears.

"All right, that's cool. Let me get your number, then," he said.

I called out my number to him, and a few seconds later, my phone began ringing.

"That's my number, beautiful. Make sure you use it."

"All right, boo. I gotcha."

"All right. I'll be calling you in a few days, so you better answer that phone," he said before he pulled me in for a hug. It was unexpected, but I hugged him back.

"Okay, I'll be waiting," I said, pulling back.

He winked before getting in his car and pulling off. He wasn't down the street good before Tracy's ass came strolling out of the shop

"I hope like hell that you got that nigga's number. Shit, especially how long your ass been out here," she said, butting in as usual.

"For your information, I actually did get his number," I said, turning my phone so that she could see it.

"That's good. Now my brother can see that he can't have his fucking cake and eat it too. His ass was watching y'all the whole fucking time." She started laughing as if that shit was straight comical or something.

"Bitch, you need your ass whooped."

"I don't need shit," she said. She looked at me and smiled before walking back into the shop.

I turned to watch what was going on in the streets, when I heard the bell ring behind me again.

"You better be ready to go, since you're out here stalking me and shit," I said before I turned around. I was shocked when I turned around and saw Onijae standing there, not Tracy.

"So what, the cat's got your tongue?" he asked, flashing a quick smile before it disappeared behind a grin.

"What do you want?" I asked, rolling my eyes at him. I really couldn't believe he had the audacity to try to question me about any damn thing.

"You know what I want, Lay Lay. Why are you out here playing on me like that?" he asked, stepping a little closer so that no one could hear us.

"I don't have time to play games with you, Onijae. I don't hear from you in weeks, then when I do see you, you and your old lady all lovey-dovey. I'm not that stupid. I know when someone's trying to play with me, so come with something better than that. I told you that I'm no one's fool," I said, looking him straight in the eyes.

"I had to play things cool. When I went home that morning, she knew exactly where I was. The crazy bitch tracked my GPS on my truck. The only thing she didn't know was that you were the one who lived in that house. I spent the last few weeks trying to get things right, in order, so I can be with you, Delaney," he had the nerve to say.

"Cut the bullshit, Onijae. You didn't spend the last few weeks doing shit for nobody but your damn self. You were the only one benefitting from that shit. I tried texting you and calling you, but I got nothing, so I stopped fucking trying. I'm only seventeen. I've barely had my heart broken. I'm not about to let it be by a man who has a woman that he's attached to."

"I told you that this won't be like that. I won't treat you like the rest of them niggas treat the females they sleep with. I actually want you, Delaney."

"If you want me like you say you do, then tell me why the hell you're still with Bianca then, Onijae?" I asked, raising my voice a little.

"Lower your voice before people hear you," he said, looking around us. Once he saw that no one was paying us any mind, he continued. "If I could get rid of her today, I would."

"Well, what's stopping you then?" I asked, pissed off by the shit he was saying.

"I still love her. I mean, I'm not in love with her, but I still love her."

"Well, if you love her, then you should do right by her then," I told him.

I looked at him, waiting on him to respond, but he didn't say anything at all. I left him standing right there, feeling whatever way he was feeling. He had to see that I was actually serious. I wasn't about to let him play me. I wasn't going to play no man's fool or be his other woman. Even though I was only seventeen and never had a man before in my life, I wasn't dumb. I'd seen the shit most women went through with sharing the same man. Trust and believe, I wasn't trying to be like them, so I was making that shit known to him again.

After leaving the shop with Tracy, we decided to head to the mall to do a little shopping. Thanks to the money that Aqura had given me for doing his hair and the five hundred that Onijae had sent for me, I had enough to buy something for all of my siblings and myself. Once we were through with shopping, I headed straight home to get ready for work. I was happy that I didn't have to close the store that night because I was in no mood to stay late.

When I got to work, I was thankful that the place wasn't packed. There were a few people, and that was including staff. I spoke to everybody before I walked straight to the back to get myself together. I was ten minutes early, so I didn't have to worry about rushing.

I'd been sitting in the break room for five minutes when I heard the door open. My head was down, so I had no idea who it was.

"What's wrong, Delaney?" I heard someone ask. I looked up and saw Heather standing there. Heather was the other manager at the store. She and I were friends, but we weren't close friends.

"Nothing is wrong. I'm good," I told her before I placed my head back down. The truth of the matter was that I wasn't all right. My head was killing me, and I couldn't get Onijae off my brain, but I wasn't going to tell her that.

"You know if you need to go home, you can. I can always work myself. Besides, there's not too many people shopping here today," she suggested.

"Thank you, but I don't need to go home. I just needed a minute to get my thoughts together," I said, getting up from the table. She looked at me with questionable eyes, but before she could say anything, I did. "Honestly, Heather, I'm really okay. I've just been through a little bit, but I'm good now. Nothing is going to stop me from clocking in and making this money."

"Okay, but if you need to talk, or you need to go home, you can come and tell me. I'm always there for you if you need me to be," she said, grabbing me into a hug.

"Thanks, boo. I really appreciate it," I replied, hugging her back. "Now come on and let's get up out of here before people be looking for us."

"All right," she said, laughing.

Together, we made our way to the front of the store, which was a good thing, because just that fast, plenty of people were coming in. I walked over to the register to clock in before I placed my nametag on and began helping the customers. With any luck, that would keep my mind off everything that was going on.

I was helping this mother find her daughter a pair of shoes when my phone chimed. Ignoring it, I waited until I finished helping them to pull it out. To my surprise, I had a message from Onijae.

What time do you get off?

I looked at the message and read it before placing it back into my pocket. I wasn't about to entertain him. Then I remembered that I had my iMessage thing on, which let him know the exact time I had looked at his message. I knew he was going to feel some type of way about me not responding, but that was all on him. He needed to know that he wasn't going to be playing with me. If he wanted a toy to play with, they had too many toy stores around here for that. He could easily grab him up a few toys, and then sit around and play with them, because he most definitely wasn't going to be playing with me.

A few minutes later, my phone chimed again. I knew that it was Onijae, so I didn't even bother to pull out my phone this time. Instead, I continued to do my job.

It was around five in the evening when I finally decided to take my lunch break. I wasn't that hungry, but I needed a break, so I walked to the food court and found a table in the corner. I was pulling out my phone to call Tracy when it began ringing. I looked at the caller ID. It was none other than Onijae himself. Ignoring his call, I placed the phone on the table and sat with my head back.

Lord, why must he be so difficult? I thought as I sat at the table. I wanted him, but I didn't want the baggage that came along with him, nor was I trying to be a nigga's sideline forever. I mean, he had already made it clear that he loved Bianca. So why should I waste my damn time getting into something that was going to be hard to get out of? I'd rather just not get into it at all. Well, that was what I kept trying to tell myself.

"I know damn well you saw me calling and texting that phone, Lay Lay," I heard him say from behind me.

"Of course I did," I replied, not even bothering to turn around to acknowledge him.

"Don't go getting smart, Delaney. I'll turn this mall the fuck up."

"Do what you please, Onijae," I replied nonchalantly.

I knew he wanted me to be scared or worried, but I wasn't. He needed to be worried about his old lady, because if someone happened to see him sitting at this table talking to me, I was pretty sure she would flip her top on him.

"Why are you acting like this?" he had the nerve to ask me.

"Look, Onijae, I'm not trying to get into all of this right now. So, I would like it if you would just drop it, okay?"

"Delaney, I don't know what I did to you, but I'm honestly sorry. I didn't mean to make you feel the way that you're feeling right now," he explained, but all of that shit was going through one ear and out the other. He knew damn well what he did to make me feel like this, but since he wanted to act crazy, I was going to act crazy right along with him.

For a while, we didn't say anything to each other. We just sat there lost in each other's eyes. In my mind, we were together. This was the man of my dreams, but I knew it was only a figment of my imagination. This man was never going to fully be mine and mine only. No matter what he said, how he said it, what he did, or how he did it, he still belonged to someone else—which was what saddened me.

"Are you going to tell me what time you get off or not?" he asked, breaking the silence.

"I get off at eight. Why?"

"Because I want to come and pick you up, Delaney, that's why."

"Onijae, I don't need you to come and pick me up. I've been catching the bus all of my life, and I'll continue to catch it," I told him. His ass wasn't slick. He was not about to get me to be alone with him, nor was he about to get me in his car.

"I don't want to hear all of that shit," he said, raising his hand up at me. "I'll be out in the front of the mall at quarter to eight. Don't make me cause a scene, ma."

"I told you that I don't need you to give me a ride."

"You heard what I said," he said, getting up from the table. "I gotta go take care of some business. I'll see you later."

I opened my mouth to speak again, but I was hushed when he placed his lips on mine. I quickly pulled back and looked around to make sure that no one we knew was around. "You can't be doing that, Onijae," I told him.

"I'm not doing anything, Lay Lay," he said, flashing me a bright smile that warmed my heart. "Remember what I said. I'll be waiting on you outside at quarter to eight."

"Yeah, whatever." I waved a hand at him.

He smiled again before he walked off. I continued to sit there and watched him disappear. The minute he left, I pulled out my phone to call Tracy, but she didn't answer. I was about to call her again when she sent a message saying that she was with her boo. I understood but told her to call me when she had some time. After she replied, I got up and headed back to work, hoping that the rest of the day would fly by. I didn't want to admit it to myself, but I was excited about Onijae picking me up from work later.

Before I knew it, the next few hours had zoomed by. It was now dark outside, and I was just about done with my shift. All I had to do was fix the bins in the front, which

I did immediately, and I was out of there. Before fully leaving the store, I made sure that everything I had to do was complete. Once I was sure, I grabbed my purse and made my way outside of the mall.

As I made my way out the door, I spotted Onijae's truck waiting by the sidewalk. My heart started beating so fast that I thought I was going to have a panic attack for sure. I didn't know why, because I'd been alone with him before. Somehow, I knew this time was going to be different, though. I knew that him getting mad because I didn't want to answer him, but then turning around and picking me up, was just him trying to be territorial.

"Hey little lady," he said, getting out of the truck and opening my door for me. He moved in and placed a kiss on my cheek before he stepped back. I got in, and he closed the door behind me. Then he walked back over to his side and got in. I don't know what he had in here, but it smelled good as hell. We gazed at each other before I reached over and placed a kiss on his lips. I knew I had surprised him because I surprised myself. I pushed back, preparing to sit back in my seat, only to have him pull me back.

"Stop running from me, ma."

"I'm not running from you," I mumbled against his lips as we engaged in another kissing battle. He was kissing me so much that I almost couldn't catch my breath, and when he finally did pull back, I didn't want him to.

"You ready to go home, or you want to come with me?" he asked, looking at me with those gorgeous brown eyes of his. Of course, we both already knew the answer to that question, so I really didn't know why he even asked it.

"I'm coming with you, boo," I said, which caused him to smile a huge grin.

"Okay then," he said before he started the car and pulled off.

Since I was not going home, I texted Daija to let her know. I sat back in the seat and waited to arrive wherever it was that we were going. Honestly, I was nervous as shit, but I was excited as well. I could not wait to see what he had in store for me.

Onijae

I knew Delaney was probably wondering what I was doing. Shit, truth be told, I was wondering what I was doing my damn self. You see, after I had left the store earlier, I made it my business to come up with something to make it up to her. I was going to get her a gift or two, but then I thought about it. Gifts were not going to be enough. I really needed to show her that I wanted her. Therefore, I booked us a room, ordered some food, and still bought her a few gifts, so that I could make her feel special.

When we pulled up to the hotel an hour later, shorty was fast asleep. She looked so peaceful sleeping there that I hated to wake her up. I really hoped that she was not going to flip out on me because I took her so far, but I had to go somewhere where no one would notice us. Running into anyone and them going back to tell Bianca would probably fuck with my chance of being with Delaney, and I could not let that shit happen. I knew I probably had a lot of work to do, but I was going to try like hell to get it together.

After finding a parking spot, I pulled in and parked. Turning over, I lightly shook her, trying to get her to wake up. She did not wake up right away, so I shook her again. This time, she sat up and looked around. I noticed the confused look on her face, so I spoke.

"We're at a hotel in Austin," I slowly said, trying to gauge her reaction.

"Okay, well, why are we still sitting in the car then?" she asked, taking it much better than I thought she would.

"Because we just got here, ma," I said, smiling.

"Well, let's go," she said, taking her seatbelt off. "Hold up, wait. Damn, I don't even have any clothes to put on, and I desperately need to take a bath."

"Don't worry about all that," I said, reaching into the back seat and pulling out a purple and-pink night bag. I set it on her thighs, and she began to open it. "While you were at work, I asked Tracy to do a little shopping for you. I hope you don't mind, shorty."

"Aww, that's so sweet of you, Onijae," she replied, reaching over and kissing my lips. "Now come on and let's go inside. I need a bath and a few hours of sleep."

"All right, come on," I said, cutting the truck off. We got out. I opened up the back door to get my overnight bag and the food bag, along with two additional bags. When I had everything, I closed the door and activated the alarm behind me.

"You need some help, boo?" she asked. Before I could respond, she removed my bag from my hand.

"Thanks, ma."

"No problem," she said as we made our way into the hotel. We had to stop by the front desk to check in and get the keys to the room. Once we were done, we rode the elevator to the floor and headed to our room, where I placed the bags on the table and took a seat.

"I know your ass ain't tired," she joked.

"Shit, you can laugh all you want, but I'm tired like fuck, shorty," I said, lying back on the bed.

"Uh-huh, well, I'm about to go take a bath," she said, which made me sit up.

"You want me to come in there with you? I mean, do you need some help or something?"

"Nah, I don't need any help," she said, poking out her tongue and laughing. "Stay your hot ass out here. Besides, what I do need you to do is have me something to eat, because I'm starving."

"I'm two steps ahead of you, shorty," I said, getting up from the bed. I walked over to the table where the bags were and picked up the one that contained our food. "See, I thought about your hungry ass already."

"That's a good boy," she said, clapping her hands together. "Now, have that ready by the time I finish taking my shower, or we gon' be up in here fighting."

"I'd love to tangle with you, ma," I replied as she made her way toward the bathroom.

She stopped right in front the door, turned, and blew me a kiss before she proceeded into the bathroom, making sure that she closed and locked the door behind her.

An hour and some change later, I finally heard her coming out of the bathroom. She was lucky I wanted to be bothered with her because I almost fell asleep on her ass. I knew she probably did that shit on purpose, but I was going to make her ass pay for that.

"Damn, you feeling me like that?" she asked once she walked into the room.

There were a few teddy bears, candles, candies, flowers, food, and gifts hanging all around the room. I couldn't take credit for all of that, though. It was Tracy who helped me do all of this, and who deserved the praise. I had rented another room, which was next door. She had brought all of this when she went shopping for the clothes and stuff. She had left it in the other room on the bed, so all I had to do was lay it out and hope that Delaney would like it. I had spent almost a thousand dollars on her, and I hadn't even sniffed her pussy yet. So, yeah, she could definitely say that I was feeling her.

I gotta remember to thank my little sister for every-thing she's done for me today.

"Umm, hello, I'm talking to you, Onijae."

I chuckled a bit before looking around myself. I had been momentarily distracted by what she had on. Delaney stood there in a two-piece short Pink pajama set from Victoria's Secret.

"You can say that, shorty," I said, walking over to her. I wrapped my arms around her and placed a kiss on her forehead. "I'm not trying to do anything with you. I just want you to know that I'm serious about being with you. I didn't bring you here to have sex with you or anything, but if it happens, then it happens."

"I know, and I'm not worried about that. I'm just glad that we're actually spending time with each other. As I said before, I'm not into being that other woman, so don't make me feel like it. The minute I feel as if I'm being that, I will politely go about my business," she said, which made me squeeze her a little tighter.

I gave her a stern look before I placed a kiss on her lips. "You gon' make me hurt your little ass. Come on, so we can eat and get us some rest," I told her as I grabbed her hand.

My phone started ringing as we were walking over to the table. I waited until I had her seated at the table to go and check it. I already had an idea of who it was, but I wasn't too sure. The minute I picked up the phone, I saw that my guess was right. Bianca was calling, as if I didn't tell her that I was leaving. I knew she was only calling to try to ask me where I was, which was why I didn't bother answering the phone. I ignored her, placed the phone in my pocket, and went back over to the table.

"My bad, shorty," I said sincerely.

"It's cool, boo," she replied dryly. I knew she was lying, but I didn't push it. I wasn't going to let Bianca spoil our night.

"You want something to drink?" I asked her.

We'd been sitting there eating for all of fifteen minutes in silence. I had no idea what was going on inside her head, and Lord knew how bad I wanted to know.

"Nah, I'm straight." She continued to eat her food.

Placing my fork down, I got up and walked over to her. Grabbing her hand, I pulled her up from her seat, then sat down in the chair and pulled her on top of me.

"Don't act like that, shorty. If you got a problem, then speak on it. I don't need you around here acting like somebody done stole your last piece of cake and you faulting me for the shit," I told her.

I had said that last part to try to get a quick laugh out of her, but I didn't get anything. She just sat there staring at me without saying a thing. I turned her around, preparing to go in on her, but then my phone started to ring again. I felt her body stiffen before she got up from my lap.

"Answer your phone. It's quite obvious that she needs you or something," she said before I heard the bathroom door slam behind her.

I sat there with the ringing phone in my hand, contemplating whether I should answer it. I knew this was why Delaney was acting the way she was acting. I didn't know why I hadn't put the shit on vibrate. Better yet, I could've just cut the shit completely off, then everything would've been fine. Now I had to deal with this shit.

I started to answer the phone in the room, but I knew that wouldn't have been the best thing for me to do, so I decided to take the call outside in the hallway.

"Hello," I said, answering the phone, pissed.

"Oh, so *now* you want to answer the fucking phone. Where the fuck you at? Because we need to talk, Onijae," Bianca yelled so loud that I had to take the phone from my ear.

"First of all, you need to lower your muthafucking tone when you're talking to me, Bianca. I'm not your child, so remember that fucking shit," I spoke through gritted teeth. "Secondly, I want to know what the fuck are you calling me back to back for? I know damn well you ain't dead, so why the fuck you just blowing my damn phone up like this?"

"Like I said when you answered the phone, we need to talk. Now, where the fuck you at?" she asked, yelling again.

"Is that what you're calling me for, Bianca? I already told you that I had some business to take care of for my father, which was out of town. So tell me why the fuck you calling me with this bullshit now," I said, silently counting to ten in my head. I didn't know why she was acting like this. "Besides, it wasn't like I didn't ask you if you wanted to come. You said no, so I went about my business. What do you need to talk about?"

"Fuck you, Onijae. You know damn well you're not doing a damn thing for your father, but you'd better listen to me when I say this. If I find out that you're out there up to no good, I'm going to make you and whatever bitch's life a miserable one. You're not about to leave me, so you might as well get that shit up out of your head, because you're about to be stuck to me, whether you want to or not. So be sure you tell that bitch that wifey said hello and welcome to the muthafucking team, nigga," she said all in one breath.

I opened my mouth to blow her ear off, but I heard a beeping sound in my ear. I pulled the phone from my ear and noticed that the bitch had hung up.

"Ain't this about a bitch!" I said as I pulled up my messages and decided to send her a text. I didn't care about anything at this moment. I went straight duff on her stupid ass. I didn't know and didn't care to know why this bitch was acting the way she was acting, but she needed to get herself together and quick. What she didn't know was that she had one foot already out the door, with the other not too far behind it. All she had to do was keep acting the way she was acting, and she was going to make me being with Delaney easier.

Speaking of Delaney, I knew shorty was probably mad as fuck at that moment. Truth be told, I really couldn't blame her either. If that had been me, I would've been feeling the same way.

Once I was through going off on Bianca, I powered my phone off and placed it in my back pocket. Now that this shit was out of the way, it was time for me to go and apologize to Delaney. I was praying she would accept my apology and not treat a nigga like he wasn't shit, because everything I had planned would really be irrelevant. I needed to be on her good side. I didn't care if I had to beg and plead. I was going to do just that and then some. Then the next day, I would be satisfied knowing that I had put a smile on her face.

Entering the room, I noticed that the food was gone from the table. I didn't see Delaney anywhere, but I heard noise coming from the bathroom. I wanted to go and check on her, but I knew better. We weren't at that level yet, and I didn't want to overstep my boundaries. Instead, I took a seat on the bed and waited for her to come out.

I used that time to think about everything that was going on in my life. Financially, I was doing great. The shop was making money as usual, the garage wasn't doing badly, and the store that I was trying to put together was coming along great.

The only thing that was going wrong was my love life. As I had mentioned before, I still had love for Bianca, but I wasn't in love with her anymore. Lately, she'd been becoming this person that I didn't care to want anymore. She didn't know it, but she was the one who was pushing me to be with Delaney. That, and I still couldn't get over the fact that she had cheated on me. I knew some people would say that I was singing the same old tune, but it was what it was. That was something I couldn't get over or change. I thought that getting back together, we could get over it, but now I knew that we just couldn't. Now the only thing left for me to do was to break the news to her, hoping that she didn't flip out.

"What are you over there thinking about?" Delaney asked me.

I looked up and noticed her standing there, watching me. She now had on a pair of sweats and a T-shirt.

"What's going on? Where are you going? Are you leaving?" I asked one question after another. I got up from the bed and walked over to her. "Don't leave, ma. I promise that I'm going to make things better. I'm leaving her, but I just need some time to do so."

"You don't have to lie to me, Onijae. I'm not going anywhere. I just need to take a walk and get some fresh air," she said, rolling her eyes.

"But I'm not lying to you, Delaney. Whether or not it's with you or someone else, I can't be with Bianca anymore. I can't trust her anymore, and it's obvious that she can't trust me, even though I didn't give her a reason not to. She's only on my tail because of what she did to me. I can't be faulted for what she did, and I won't," I said, being honest. "I didn't know how tired I was until tonight. I didn't know why I kept trying to make up excuses and reasons for why I kept Bianca around, but I'm through with that."

I looked into her eyes, wishing that she would say something, but she didn't. Shorty stood there looking as though she didn't give a fuck about the shit I was saying.

I didn't mean to, but I laughed. Shit, that was all a nigga could do right now. Without saying a word to me, she walked right past my ass, heading for the door.

"I'll be back in a little bit. I'm just going for a little walk," she told me before she opened the door and left me standing there, looking like a hopeless fool. I hoped that when she got back, she'd be up for talking, because we most definitely needed to talk.

Chapter Eight

Delaney

I didn't know what to say when Onijae told me about leaving his girlfriend. I wanted to be happy. Hell, I wanted to jump for joy, but I didn't. I couldn't be getting happy and then the nigga turns around and goes back to her. That would make me look like a fool, and I was not about to be a fool for anyone. Y'all already know what I said about that.

I'd been walking the streets for the past thirty minutes when I finally decided to head back to the hotel. It was already hot outside, and I knew that Onijae was probably looking for me. Besides, I didn't know shit about being down there. Before somebody jumped out and grabbed my ass or shot me, I knew I'd better get back. After thinking about that, I damn near ran back to the hotel and up to the room.

When I entered the room, Onijae was now lying in the bed with the remote in his hand. He looked at me, and then turned back to the TV.

Oh, shit, I thought as I made my way into the bathroom. Turning the shower on, I began to undress. I hopped in and took a quick shower to wash the sweat and stench away from the walk. Once I was through, I got out, wrapped a towel around me, and headed back into the bedroom.

Onijae was now sitting on side of the bed with his head in his hands. I tried to walk past him, but he grabbed me before I could. For a few minutes, he sat there with his arms wrapped around my waist and his head lying against my stomach. I honestly didn't know what to say or what to do, so I just rubbed the back of his head as I'd seen people do on TV. My heart was beating so loud that I could literally hear it. It felt so awkward that I almost wanted to pull away.

"You don't have to say anything, Delaney. I just want you to listen to me," he said, breaking the silence. He then pulled back and looked deeply into my eyes. "I want to be with you so bad, but I have a few things I have to do before I can fully be with you. Now, I'm not asking you to wait or be nobody's other woman, as you say, but I do want you to give me credit. There are things that I have to do in order to let Bianca go peacefully, and knowing her like I do, she won't go like that.

"She's going to try to make my life a living hell, and I'm not trying to bring you into that, shorty. During that time, we'll still be kicking it, but only if you want to. Like I said before, it took me a while, but now I know that Bianca and I can't be together, and whether you wait on a nigga or not is clearly your choice. If you choose to go and be with someone else, I really won't be mad. Upset a little, but never mad, because it's your life, and how I came in it, the timing was completely off for me."

I just sat there listening to him. I heard what he said. In fact, I heard him loud and clear. I didn't know how to respond. On one hand, I wanted to be happy, but on the other hand, I couldn't. He kept saying that he wanted to leave Bianca, but how did I know that he would really do it? Then he was talking about how he was going to need time. I wanted to ask him how much time he really needed, but I left that alone. I was going to give him the benefit of the doubt, and I hoped that I wouldn't regret doing it.

"Okay," I said, nodding my head.

Before I could get another word out of my mouth, he stood up, and his lips came crashing onto mine. Almost immediately, our tongues began doing a dance of their own. His hands then began roaming my body beneath the towel. Not long after, the damn towel was on the floor, and I stood in front of him, dead-ass naked. I was nervous as he looked over my body, licking his tongue as if I were a meal he was about to devour.

"Come lay on the bed for me." He guided me over to the bed, where he laid me down.

I'd never done anything like this before, so I used one hand to cover my breasts and the other to cover my prized possession. Once he saw that, he laughed, which made me feel even more nervous.

"I see you acting shy, huh?"

"I'm shy when I'm doing something that I've never done before," I said, looking up at the ceiling.

"What do you mean, something that you've never done before?" he asked, standing straight up. He had this confused look on his face, which made me regret saying anything to him.

"I mean I've never done anything like this before," I said, repeating myself.

"Wait, shorty. You mean to tell me that you've never done *this* before?" he echoed, pointing back and forth between the both of us.

"Yes, that's what I'm telling you, but since you seem a little bit slow, I'll bring it all the way home for you," I said, now sitting up. I grabbed the sheet from the bed and wrapped it around me, and then I turned my attention back to him. "When I say I've never done this before, I mean just that. Like, all of this is still new to me. I haven't even so much as kissed a boy besides you," I said, explaining myself the best way that I could.

"So basically what you're saying is that you're a virgin? Am I right?" he bluntly asked.

"You don't have to say it like that, but yes, that is what I am saying," I said, feeling a hundred percent foolish. I was embarrassed even saying that I was a virgin.

I felt worse when he took a seat on the bed and started staring off into space. I got up and attempted to move, but then I felt the sheet being pulled from me.

"Where are you going now, Delaney?" he asked with a little attitude.

"Honestly, I don't know. I just feel like you don't want me around you right now."

"Did I tell you that, ma?" he asked.

"Well, you didn't exactly say it, but I assumed that since I told you what was up, you didn't."

"Never assume anything, shorty, because you'll definitely make an ass out of yourself. I didn't sit down because you told me that you were a virgin. Well, I did, but that was not what I was thinking, Lay Lay. I honestly couldn't believe that you're still one. I thought for sure that you would've been done, you know, but you didn't, and now I want to know, are you sure you want to give me something so special? I mean, I would love to have it, but I'm in no rush, ma. If you're not ready, then I won't push or hound you," he said calmly.

I stood there having a full-length conversation with myself. *No, I haven't had sex before. Truth be told, I don't know a damn thing about it. I'm as green as hell when it comes to that, but I still wonder. I know that one day I will have to have it. So why not let that day be today?*

"I'm sure," I said, nodding my head. That was all I had to say, because the next thing I knew, I was naked on the bed again.

"Since you've never done this before, I'm going to take this one step at a time. If anything hurts or feel uncomfortable to you, let me know and I will stop, okay?"

"Okay," I said, nodding my head.

He climbed on top of me and just lay there, staring in my eyes, which was making me feel so nervous that I started shaking.

"You can cool out and stop being scary. I won't do anything to harm you, baby," he said, placing his lips to mine yet again.

The kiss didn't last long at all. He began kissing my neck, which immediately began making me feel good. Making a trail from my neck, he traveled farther. I gasped when he took my left breast into his mouth while rolling my right nipple between his two fingers.

"Oooo . . ." I couldn't lie if I wanted to. This shit was feeling so good that I wished that I had done the shit sooner.

"You like that?" he asked with my nipple in his mouth.

"Yessssss . . ." I moaned as he began sucking a bit harder, but not too hard.

He then switched and started paying my right breast the same attention. I swear, this man had me wanting to scream to the heavens above. After paying attention to my girls, he began kissing a trail down my stomach, which also felt good as hell.

"Open your legs wider, Lay Lay," he said, looking up at me.

"For what?" I asked, covering myself up again. I had an idea of what he might do, but I wasn't sure if he was going to do it.

"Just do what I ask you to do and stop acting all scary. I told you if you want to stop, then we most definitely can," he said, sitting up again.

"No, I don't want to stop," I told him.

"Well, move your hands and open your legs like I asked you to," he said, going back down.

I removed my hands as he asked me to, but I took a few seconds longer to open my legs. When I did, I made sure that I closed my eyes at the same time. I wasn't trying to see anything. It was a good thing that I kept my pubic hair trimmed on the regular, or I really would've had something to be embarrassed about.

I was silently laying there with my legs wide open, waiting on him to do whatever he was about to do. Absolutely nothing could have prepared me for what happened next. He dove headfirst between my legs, kissing my lower lips. When he used his tongue to lick it, I almost caught an asthma attack. That's how irregular my breathing had become.

"Arch your back for me," he instructed as he used his hand to help me.

Once I was in the correct position, he dove back in, but this time he didn't play around. When I tell you he was licking and sucking as if his life depended on it, he really was, and he was doing one hell of a job.

"Oh, shit," I moaned as I felt a fuzzy feeling. A few seconds later, I began shaking. When I felt liquid between my legs, I became mortified.

"Oh my God. Did I just pee on myself?" I was feeling embarrassed again.

"Nah, you didn't pee on yourself," he answered, laughing.

I don't know what in the hell was funny to him. When he looked at me, I gave him a look and sat up.

"Stop being so sensitive, ma. You didn't pee on yourself. You just had an orgasm, and it tasted good, too."

"Shut up, fool," I said, feeling a little relieved. I then crawled over to him and began kissing him. Even though I was scared, I still grew a little courage.

"You gon' make me act a fool, shorty," he said in between kisses.

"Maybe that's what I want you to do, daddy," I replied boldly.

I busted out laughing at the look on his face once I said that. Without warning, he grabbed me and flipped me over so that he was lying on top of me.

"I'm going to ask you one more time. Are you sure that you want to give me something so precious and delicate?" he asked. His forehead was pressed against mine, and he was looking in my eyes.

I didn't open my mouth. Instead, I thrusted my pelvis in his direction, hoping that he would catch on. He nodded his head and got up again. This time when he stood up, he started undressing himself. Piece by piece, he removed every stitch of clothing until he was completely naked.

Once I saw what he was working with, I began having second thoughts. Not only was this man fine, but he was definitely packing, and I mean packing. I was almost damn sure that not all of that would fit into me.

"Lay down flat and be calm, but let me know if this hurts, okay?" he said softly as he lay on top of me.

"Okay, just take your time," I told him as I tried to calm my nerves.

I watched as he reached between his legs and began stroking himself. I watched in awe as he grew bigger by the second, and then he positioned himself at my opening. I held my breath as I anticipated what was to come next.

"I'm only going to do an inch at a time," he said as he began easing the tip inside of me.

At first things were just okay, but the more he entered me, the more the pain increased. I didn't know how females could even take this shit, because this wasn't all that it was cracked up to be.

"Oh God," I groaned, feeling like I was about to pass out.

"Are you okay?" he asked, looking down at me. I wanted to scream "hell no!" and for him to get the hell up off me, but I didn't. I wanted him to finish so that I wouldn't be a virgin anymore.

"I'm fine," I replied, taking a deep breath.

"Okay, I'm about to put the rest in," he told me, and before I could answer, he pushed all the way inside of me.

"Oh, shit!" I yelled out.

It felt as if he were ripping me in two. That's how painful it was. I knew his back had to be burning or hurting him, because that's how deep I was digging my fingernails in it. I felt him stop, which pissed me off.

"Don't come asking me shit. Just do what you have to do, Onijae!"

"Okay, damn," he said as he started back up.

After a few minutes, the pain subsided. It had been re-placed by an amazing and great feeling that I really didn't want to stop. I barely knew a thing about having sex, but I knew that I couldn't just lay there and do nothing, so as he was pumping into me, I thrust my hips back at him.

"Oh, shit," I heard him moan out. I didn't know if it was because I was bad or good, but he didn't stop, so I guessed it was the latter. "Slow down, Lay Lay, damn. As a matter of fact, come here."

"What? What are you doing?" I asked as he got off me and pulled me up.

"Don't be afraid. I promise I won't drop you," he said as he picked me up.

Immediately, I wrapped my arms around his neck and my legs around his waist, praying that he wouldn't drop me. He then lowered me onto his erection, which caused both of us to moan out in pleasure.

"All you have to do is bounce up and down," he panted as he helped me a bit.

After a while, he removed his hands, letting me do my thing. I'd be lying if I said that this didn't make me feel good, because it did. I'd finally had sex, and even though it was painful at first, I damn sure was glad that I had. I was no longer a virgin, even though I didn't know how to feel about that.

For the rest of the night, Onijae and I had sex on every surface of the hotel room. There wasn't a spot in there that we didn't touch. That's how much fun we had. When we did stop to lie down, it was almost five that morning, and I was beyond tired. Overall, it was a good day, and I could only imagine what the following days would bring.

I didn't wake up until that evening, and when I say that I was sore, I was just that. I looked over expecting to see Onijae, but I didn't. I sat up in the bed, hoping to see him, but he was gone.

"Onijae," I said, calling out his name, but he didn't answer. I threw back the covers and got out of the bed. He wasn't in the bedroom, so I headed to the bathroom to check there. He wasn't there either, but he had left a message on the bathroom mirror saying that he would be back at two o'clock. I walked back to the room and noticed that it was almost one o'clock already, so he wouldn't be that long.

Since I was up, I decided I'd take care of my hygiene while I was at it. As I went back into the room to grab my bag, my phone rang. Walking over to the nightstand, I picked it up and noticed that it was Tracy calling me. I had a mind to ignore her ass since she hadn't called me back, but I didn't.

"Well, look who finally decide to call me back," I said, answering the phone.

"Girl, bite me. I was busy, and I'm pretty damn sure you were too. You liked the things I picked up for you yesterday?" she asked, laughing.

"Bitch, fuck you. They were cute, and yes, I was indeed busy," I said, letting out a girlish giggle.

"So you really did it, huh?" she asked. I was sure if I could see her face, she'd have the biggest Kool-Aid smile.

"Yup, surely did, and it was fucking amazing. Now I see what all the fuss was about," I said as I thought about everything that had gone down the night before. I had to squeeze my legs tight together because I could feel myself getting wet.

"Okay, bitch, I don't want to know too much. That is still my brother," she said, making a gagging sound.

She always had to be overdramatic and shit, but I got where she was coming from. If that had been my brother, I probably would've felt the same way she was feeling.

"Anyway, where his ass at, though?"

"Girl, I don't know. All I know was that when I woke up, he wasn't here. Then when I walked into the bathroom, there was this note taped to the mirror, saying that he was going to be back at two."

"I wonder what his ass is up to," she said, taking the words right out of my mouth. I also wondered what he was doing, and why he hadn't woken me up when he left.

"Anyways, my man is here, so I got to go. I hope you have fun, bestie. Make sure you text or call me when you make it home, trick."

"Okay, don't do anything I won't do," I told her, laughing.

"Yeah, I should be telling you the same thing," she responded. "Don't go being too hot either."

"I won't, and you better not either," I said, hanging up the phone.

Grabbing the bag, I headed in the bathroom to take a shower. I placed my phone on the counter, along with the bag. I then walked over to the shower and turned on the water. I walked back over to the bag and removed the dress that I had seen in it the day before. There were a pair of sandals in another bag that would go great with it. I went back into the bag and removed a two-piece black bra and panty set and sat it on the counter as well.

Once I had everything out that I needed, I began to undress. After stripping out of everything, I grabbed the Dove soap that I loved to shower with and headed in the shower. I stood exactly underneath the shower head, letting the water run down my body. I don't know about other people, but a hot shower really does give me life.

After standing under the water for a few minutes longer, I grabbed the soap and washcloth and began to take a bath. I washed every inch of my body, making sure to be easy to my already sore kitty. Once I was finished, I rinsed off and repeated the process a few times. When I was through, I turned the water off and got out.

Wrapping a towel around my damp body, I grabbed my phone, the bag, and my clothes, and headed back into the room. I placed everything on the bed before removing the towel and drying off. Making sure that I was dried, I let the towel fall to the floor as I reached for the lotion that sat on the nightstand next to the bed. After putting lotion on my body, I slipped into my undergarments.

I was about to put on my dress when I heard the door open. I turned around to find Onijae and some other dude standing there. I stood there frozen as I used the dress to cover as much of my body as I could.

"As much as I'm enjoying the view, I would appreciate it if you put some clothes on, shorty. We have company," he said as he tried blocking dude's view.

I was ashamed, so I hurried my ass to the bathroom to finish getting dressed. Quickly, I slipped the dress over my head. I walked over to the mirror to see how it looked. As usual, Tracy always got my size right, but this one was a little tight. It showed off my figure a little too much.

Since I was already in the bathroom, I grabbed the comb, brush, and edge control out of the bag, along with a ponytail holder. Since I didn't have much to work with, I just placed my hair into a high ponytail. Once I was through, I cleaned up the mess, placed everything back in the bag, and headed back into the room.

"Now, that's much better," Onijae said, walking over to me. He wrapped his arms around me as he placed a kiss on my lips. "I missed you, Lay Lay."

"I missed you too. Where were you?" I asked him.

"I had some things to take care of before we leave. You were sleeping so peacefully that I didn't want to wake you up."

"What do you mean, before we leave?" I asked with a smile on my face.

"I'm taking you to Miami for the week, shorty," he replied, which made me scream. I couldn't believe that he was taking me on a trip.

"Are you serious?" I asked, jumping up and down. I was as excited as a kid in a candy store would be.

"Dead ass. If you hurry up, we can make our plane, which leaves in an hour," he said, looking at his phone.

"But I have to get my things together. You should've told me that earlier," I told him as I tried to move out of his embrace, but he pulled me back.

"Chill out. I already had my boy take your shit down to the car. The only thing that's left in here is us, so bring your ass on because if we miss our plane, I'm putting that on you."

"Boy, whatever! Let me grab my purse and stuff first," I told him.

He let me go. I went around the room collecting whatever I had left in there. I made sure to double check because I wasn't trying to leave anything behind. Once I had everything, I walked back over to the door, where

Onijae was standing, talking on the phone. I wasn't trying to be in his business, so I waited outside for him to wrap up his conversation.

Three minutes later, he was ending his call. He walked over to me and wrapped his arm around my waist. "You ready to have fun in the MIA?"

"Surely is."

"Well, come on," he said, grabbing the bag out of my hand. He then grabbed my hand as we made our way to the lobby.

I couldn't wait to call Tracy and tell her about this. She was going to be mad because we had always promised to hit MIA up together. Oh, well. She was with her nigga, and mine was taking me where I had always wanted to go. She was going to be all right, but if she wasn't, then that was on her. I was taking my country ass to Miami, and I hoped Onijae would be ready because I planned on having one hell of a time there.

Bianca

I don't know where the fuck Onijae done fell and bumped his head, but he had better get his shit together. If he knew like me, he'd do that fast, too.

I'd been sitting in the same spot for a while, staring at the three pregnancy tests that I had taken. Yup, I was pregnant, which meant that Onijae and I were going to be parents. What I had thought was just a stomach virus was actually a nine-month stomach virus. I couldn't believe it, so I went and purchased a few tests. They all came back positive.

I knew that Onijae might not be too happy about it when I told him, but that was his business, not mine. We spent so much time lately, arguing about any and everything. I didn't know why, but it felt like he was literally picking a fight with me. If he wasn't ready for a child, then he had better get ready, because if the Lord said the same, this baby was coming, and he had better be prepared for it.

Getting up from my seat, I headed into the kitchen. I threw the three tests in the garbage can before walking over to the sink to wash my hands. I then walked over to the refrigerator to find something to eat. I hadn't noticed I was hungry until then. I looked high and low and noticed that there really wasn't too much in there to eat, which meant that I would probably have to go grocery shopping, which was something I hated doing.

After grabbing my purse and keys, I headed out the door. As I was walking out the door, my phone rang. I fished it out of my purse, hoping that it was Onijae calling, but it was Carlos instead.

"Hello," I said, answering the phone.

"Hey, baby, what are you doing?" he asked.

"Nothing, I'm about to head to the grocery store. What's going on with you?"

"Waiting on this clock to move, so that I could get off. You busy tonight?" he asked as I made it to my car.

I unlocked the door and got in, starting the car immediately.

"No, I'm not actually. What do you have in mind?"

"I just want to chill, if that's all right with you," he said, shocking me. I couldn't believe he'd said that, especially since he loved having sex.

"That's cool with me, Carlos. Where do you want to meet up?" I asked as I backed out of the driveway and headed toward the grocery store.

"Our usual spot would be good enough. I'll pick up some snacks and food and meet you there around eight."

"Okay, I'll see you later," I said, hanging up the phone just as I pulled into the parking lot of the grocery store. That was the benefit of staying a few minutes away from the store. I was glad that it didn't take long to get there. Once I found a parking spot, I grabbed my purse, got out, and locked the door behind me.

As I headed inside the store, I decided to hit my sister up. I hadn't seen her in a while, which was normal for her. I wondered what kind of trouble she had been getting herself into. Anyways, I couldn't wait to tell her all about the baby and everything, hoping she would be just as happy as I was.

The phone rang a few times before going to voicemail. I hung up and proceeded to dial her again, but it did the same thing. I was going to leave her a message, but I decided against it. She would just call me back once she'd seen that I had called her.

I was happy when I noticed that the store was halfway empty, which meant that I wasn't going to be up in there long. All I needed were a few things to hold me over until Onijae got back from his business trip in Miami, assuming he wouldn't be gone too long. Grabbing a basket, I went around the store, getting everything I needed. I even picked myself some snacks too. I had to work the next day, so I most definitely would be needing that. Once I had everything I needed, I headed to the register to check out.

I was almost at the register when I spotted Onijae's little sister and the dude Devin, who worked in his shop, holding hands two registers down. *That little nasty bitch*, I thought as I pulled out my phone to snap a quick picture. I quickly turned my head so that they wouldn't see me, and I looked at the picture that I had taken. The shit was clear as day. I knew damn well her brother didn't know a damn thing about the two of them dating or whatever. I couldn't wait until that little bitch tried to play with me again. I was going to send that shit to Onijae's ass so quick that her ass was going to regret it.

After paying for the few groceries that I did have, I headed out of the store. I was glad that my car wasn't parked too far because I was tired. Once I made it to my car, I loaded the groceries in the car and hopped back in. I checked my phone to see if my sister had called me back, but she hadn't, so I tried calling her again. Just as before, she didn't answer, so I hung up the phone.

Even though I didn't want to, I headed back to my empty-ass house. I hated being there when Onijae wasn't there, but what else could I do? At least I had Carlos to keep me company that night, but until then, I was heading home to take me a much-needed nap.

A while later, I woke up to the sound of my phone ringing. Looking at the clock on the nightstand, I noticed that it was almost eight o'clock. I hurried and jumped up because I was going to be late meeting Carlos. Grabbing my phone, I saw that I had a few missed calls from him and two from my sister. Deciding to call her back later, I went ahead and called Carlos back.

"Hello," he answered on the first ring.

"I'm so sorry for not answering the phone for you," I said, immediately apologizing. "I had done fell asleep, and obviously I was tired, but I just woke up."

"It's cool. I was just calling to remind you about tonight and to ask you what kind of snacks and food you wanted."

"It really doesn't matter. Whatever you get is fine with me," I replied, yawning.

"Shit, it sounds like you're still tired," he said with a light chuckle.

"A little, but let me go hop in the shower right quick. I'll call you when I'm on my way," I told him.

"Okay," he replied.

We both hung up the phone. I took a seat on the side of the bed to get myself together. I was still a little bit tired, and I didn't feel like going anywhere, but I knew that I couldn't stand him up. After sitting there a few minutes longer, I got up and made my way inside the bathroom, where I headed straight for the shower. Turning the water on, I allowed it to run a few minutes to get it to a decent temperature. Once I had it where I wanted it to be, I undressed and climbed in. I stood directly under the faucet as I allowed the water to run down my body, thinking that the water would wake me up.

After standing there for what was probably ten minutes, I finally decided to take a bath. I grabbed my body wash and rag and quickly washed and rinsed every inch of my body. Wrapping a towel around my body, I headed into the bedroom.

"Damn!" I yelled out as I hit my toe on the dresser.

Once the pain had subsided, I opened the dresser drawer and grabbed my undergarments. I then walked over to the bed, dried off whatever water I had left on my body, and applied a little bit of lotion before I began putting my underwear on. Once I was finished, I headed to the closet, where I grabbed a simple sweat suit and threw it on with a pair of all-white J's.

Once I was dressed, I headed straight downstairs. I made sure that everything was locked and secure before I grabbed my keys and made my way to meet Carlos.

When I pulled up to the hotel, Carlos was waiting outside for me, as I had asked him to do when I called him a few minutes earlier. I quickly found a parking spot before cutting the car off. When I opened the door, he was standing there, smiling down at me.

"What you smiling for?" I asked, a bit curious.

"Do you know how beautiful you are?" he asked, making me blush. "And your skin is glowing."

"Thank you," I said, giggling. I handed him my bag before I got out.

Together, we walked hand in hand toward the entrance of the hotel. As we passed by, people were smiling and waving at us.

If only y'all knew, I thought.

Once we made it inside, we headed straight for our usual room. I was quite amused when I walked into the room and saw everything Carlos had laid out for me. He actually made me feel special, something I hadn't felt in a while.

"Take a seat on the bed and make yourself comfortable," he said, handing me a tray with fruits on it.

I was all too happy to do as I was told. When he walked over to the bed, grabbed my feet, and began giving me a massage, I almost fainted. This man was all too good to be true.

"You keep making me feel this good, and I'm going to have to hire you full-time," I said, in between bites of the pineapple I was eating.

"I'll happily quit my day job, too," he replied, which made the both of us laugh.

"I know you would. That's why I said it," I told him, laughing.

"You know I'd do anything for you," he said, getting up.

I tried to act as if I didn't hear that part.

"What do you have to eat?" I asked, changing the subject.

"I brought a little food my mother cooked, and I picked you up some Popeye's, since I know that's what you like to eat at work," he said, bringing the Popeye's bag over to me.

I went straight for the biscuit and red beans and rice that I knew he had in it. I opened the bag and pulled everything out. Just as I removed the top off the beans to eat it, I jumped off the bed, running full force to the bathroom. I almost knocked everything down.

"Are you okay, Bianca?" Carlos asked, running behind me.

I couldn't answer him because I was too busy trying to make it to the toilet. I made it just in time to empty out all of the fruit that I had just consumed.

"Oh my God, let me get you a bottle of water," he said, running back out of the bathroom.

I sat on my knees, throwing up everything, until I had nothing left, and then I kept dry heaving. After five minutes of sitting on the floor, I got up and flushed the toilet, and then walked over to the sink and rinsed my mouth. At the same time, Carlos came walking back into the bathroom with a bottle of water and a wet towel.

"Here," he said, handing me the towel and bottle.

I rinsed my mouth out first, then dabbed the towel over my head.

"Here, I brought you something to take," he said, handing me two pills.

"What are those?" I asked him.

"Aleve. That was the only thing I had in my bag," he explained.

"Thanks, but I can't take that," I told him as I opened the bottle of water and took a drink from it.

When I looked at him, he was looking at me with a confused look on his face. Then, as if a light bulb went off in his head, he got it.

"Oh my God, you're pregnant!" he yelled.

I looked at him, without saying a word. I then left the bathroom, heading back over to the bed.

"What's wrong with you?"

"Nothing," I said as I grabbed my things, preparing to leave.

"Well, where are you going?"

"Home. I don't feel good," I said, trying to put my shoes back on, but he stopped me.

"Don't go, Bianca. Stay here with me. I'll be your nurse for the night," he told me.

I stood there and thought about it. Either I could stay there with him or go back home to an empty house. Truth be told, I was only trying to leave because I was trying to avoid his questions. I didn't need him asking anything that I didn't want to answer.

"Okay, but could you just hold off on the questions right now?"

"You got it."

I placed my shoes back on the floor and took a seat on the bed. My head was spinning with questions of my own, but I refused to ask them—well, at least I didn't want to at that moment. Eventually, I would have to.

I lay down in the bed and silently thought about the next nine months. As excited as I was to become a mother, I was scared shitless as well.

Chapter Nine

Delaney

We'd been in Miami for five long days, and I must admit that Onijae was indeed showing me a great time—well, somewhat of a good time. Aside from his sex addiction, he'd been the perfect gentleman. Anything I wanted, he made sure that I got it. I didn't eat anything but the best, and when we weren't eating or shopping, we were partying. I wasn't even eighteen, and I was getting into clubs as if it were nothing. I guess for the right price, I could do anything I wanted to do.

I'd be lying if I said that I wasn't missing my friend, because I was. When I first called her and told her that I was in Miami, she cursed me out from dusk to dawn, talking about I knew how much she wanted to go there. Yes, I did, but she was all booed up, and I didn't want to interrupt her. She was fine, and so was I. Well, that was until Onijae started leaving me in the room for hours on end by myself. At first, I was cool with it, but by day number three, I became bored and decided to call in my best friend. I damn near had to beg her brother to pay her way, but after I threatened not to give him any, he happily obliged. Now, here we were, on our way to pick her up from the airport.

Once we made it to the airport, we parked in front so that she could see us easily.

"I sure hope she hurries her ass up," Onijae said, taking the steering wheel.

"You're going to get off my friend before we have a problem," I said, rolling my eyes at him.

"No, you're going to stop playing with me, Lay Lay. The only reason I did this was because you backed me into a corner."

"Threatening to stop fucking you was not backing you into a corner," I told his dramatic ass.

"It is when you got good pussy like the one that's sitting between your legs. I don't know what I would've done if you wouldn't have given me none. I think I would've started going through withdrawal and shit," he said, almost making me choke on my cold drink.

"Boy, if you don't go sit your little stupid ass down somewhere," I said, laughing.

"I'm already sitting down," he said smartly. "Come on. There her confused ass go right there."

I turned to see Tracy walking out of the airport. She didn't notice that we were there. That was probably because we hadn't told her what we were riding in. Without waiting another second, we got out of the car and walked over to her.

"Beeeeest!" I yelled, running over to her.

She turned in my direction when she heard my voice and practically knocked people over trying to get to me.

"I missed you so much."

"I missed you too. I'm so happy to be down here!" she yelled, pulling me into a big hug.

"I can't believe that we're in Miami. Bitch, you know I'm Snapchatting, Facebooking, and Instagramming all of this, right?"

"I wish y'all would come on with y'all dramatic asses. I'm not trying to be standing out here all day fooling around with y'all," Onijae said, fucking up our moment.

"You ain't nothing but a hater," Tracy told him. "Here, help me with my bags."

"I ain't helping you with shit. You ain't handicap," he said, scrunching up his face.

All I had to do was give him one look before he walked over and grabbed her bags.

"Damn, let me find out Delaney been beating on you and shit. Got you doing shit with one look and shit," Tracy joked.

"You can think that if you want. You already know how I gets down," he said before he picked up her bags and walked over to the car.

"I hope you ready to cut up, because tonight we're going clubbing," I said as we followed Onijae to the car. I couldn't wait until that night. We were going to cut up, and I hoped we could behave without anything bad going on.

"Come on, Tracy. I know Onijae's waiting on us," I called out to my slow-ass friend. I had been waiting on her for fifteen minutes, and I was beginning to get impatient. I was beyond ready to go out and have some much-needed fun. We'd been shopping and having fun all day long. Of course, we had put a dent into her brother's pocket, but he didn't seem to mind. As long as we were having fun and enjoying ourselves, he was happy.

"Girl, I'm not worried about him, but I'm ready," she said, walking out of the bathroom.

"Damn, it's about time," I said, getting up.

"You like?" she asked, turning around so that I could get a full view of her body.

"You know I do. You look cute, but you know your brother will probably trip," I told her as we grabbed our clutches and headed out the door.

"Again, I'm not worried about him. You're the one who needs to be worried about him, not me."

"Really?" I asked, becoming a little scared. I was wearing a three-quarter sleeve, black lace romper. I didn't find anything wrong with it, except the fact that it was the kind with shorts, and mine kept hiking up my thighs every once in a while.

"You look cute, though. Hopefully we can keep my brother from spazzing on the niggas that are going to be checking you out."

"Nothing like that will happen. We're going to have a good time, not to cause trouble."

"Yeah, you can think that if you want. Let my brother see too many people checking you out, and we're most definitely going to have problems."

"Girl, whatever," I said, shaking my head as we made our way to my room. We were almost an hour late, but I didn't think he would go off on us.

Using the key that I had, I opened the door. When we walked in the room, Onijae was sitting on the bed with his head in his hands. I immediately got the sinking feeling that something was most definitely wrong, so I walked over to him.

"What's wrong, babe?" I asked, rubbing his back.

He didn't say a thing, but simply looked up at me with sad eyes, then placed his head back down.

"Nijae, what's wrong?" Tracy asked him this time.

He looked up at her before looking back at me. It was then I noticed that he was holding my phone.

"Onijae, what's going on, and why do you have my phone?" I asked him. I didn't know what to expect. Hell, I had no idea what he was even doing with my phone.

He didn't say anything, but he did hand me the phone.

"Your sister said for you to call her immediately," he said in a small voice.

I grabbed my phone out of his hand and called my sister. Placing the phone to my ear, I looked up to find Onijae staring at me. I was beginning to get worried, especially when Daija's phone rolled over to voicemail. I hung up and dialed her number again.

"Hello," she answered, her voice sounding cracked up.

"Daija, what's going on? Is something wrong?" I asked her.

For a minute, she stayed on the phone in silence. I knew she was still there because the call timer was still rolling, and I could still hear her breathing.

"Hello?"

"Delaney, the house caught on fire," she said after a few minutes.

"What did you just say?" I asked, not believing her.

"I said that the house caught on fire. We lost everything!"

After she repeated it, I had to take a seat because I could feel myself getting a little lightheaded.

"What? How did that happen? And where y'all at now?"

"Honestly, I don't know. One minute we were laying down sleeping, and the next minute, we were being pulled out of the house by firefighters. We're at Parkland Hospital right now, getting checked out."

Nothing she was saying to me was making any sense to me.

"Daija, where were Mom and Dad? Were they in the house when the fire started?" I asked her.

"Yes, they were—"

"Well, let me talk to them. I don't understand how there was a fire and no one knows anything about it," I told her. I didn't understand what the hell was happening. "Just let me talk to Mom, Daija."

"I can't," she said, a little above a whisper.

"What you mean, you can't? Where the hell she at?" I screamed. I felt the bed move before Onijae appeared in front of me.

"Because Mom and Dad never came out of the house after the fire!" she yelled, breaking down. "They're dead, Delaney. Our parents are gone! The firefighters tried to get to them, but they couldn't. By the time they finished getting us out of there, the house was engulfed in flames."

"Oh my God, nooooo!" I yelled, screaming at the top of my lungs. The phone fell from my hands as I broke down crying.

"Delaney, baby, it's going to be all right," Onijae said, coming to my aid.

"They're gone, Onijae. I can't believe they're gone!" I kept repeating.

We sat on the floor as I cried my eyes out for the next hour or so. My parents had their flaws, but they were still my parents. I needed them just as much as my siblings did. Without them, I wouldn't be here, and now they were gone. I didn't know how I was going to get through this, but I knew I had to be strong for my siblings.

When we arrived back in Dallas four hours later, I headed straight to the hospital to check on my brothers and Daija. It was almost three o'clock in the morning, and I was nowhere near tired. I was happy Dallas was with Onijae's mom, so at least I didn't have to worry about her at that moment. All I had to focus on were Dedrick, Derrick, and Daija. I just hoped I didn't have to go through too much, because Lord knew I couldn't take it.

When we pulled up to the hospital, Onijae let Tracy and me out in front, while he went to find a parking spot. I didn't waste any time as I walked inside and headed straight to the nurse's station.

"Excuse me," I said to the nurse sitting behind the desk. She was talking on the phone while chewing a piece of gum. "I'm here for my brothers and sister."

"Hold on," she said to the person on the phone. "What are their names?"

I told her their names then waited for her to look them up.

"Okay, they're on the second floor. If you go down that hall, you're going to see a set of elevators. They'll take you right where you need to go," she told me.

"Okay, thank you," I said, walking off.

"You go. I'm going to stay here and wait for my brother, and then we'll come up," Tracy said.

"Okay," I said.

I found the elevator and rode it to the second floor. When I got off, I headed straight to the nurse's station there. After getting the room numbers, I headed to go and check on my siblings.

I decided to go and check on the boys first, since they were in the same room. When I walked into the room, the nurse was checking Dedrick, while Derrick was watching TV. I stood off in the corner and waited until she was finished, because I wanted to ask her a few questions about them.

"Hello, I'm Delaney. I'm their sister," I said, walking over to her.

"Hi, I'm Rayanne. I've been working on them since they got here."

"And what is wrong with them?"

"They're fine, actually. They were just treated for possible smoke inhalation. They're being discharged in a minute," she said, which made me happy.

"Okay, well, I'll be right back. I'm going to check on my little sister down the hall," I told her. I left her checking Derrick as I went to check on Daija.

When I entered her room, the doctors were in there.

"Umm, hello. I'm Delaney, her sister," I told them.

"Okay. I'm Dr. Gavin and this is Dr. Spencer. We treated her when she came in here."

"Okay, and what's going on with her?" I asked them.

"Well, she's fine. We just want to keep her for a few more hours. We need to run some tests and monitor her."

"Tests? Monitor her for what?" I asked them.

They both looked at each other before they looked at Daija. "Do you want to tell her, or do you want us to tell her?"

"It's fine. I don't care," she said, waving them along.

"Tell me what? What could possibly be going on now, Daija?" I asked her.

"Well, Ms. McGuff here is pregnant, and we need to monitor her and the baby to make sure that they're safe."

"Excuse me. You said what now?" I asked because obviously I had heard them wrong.

"I'm pregnant, Delaney. Damn," she said, putting her head down.

"And when were you going to tell me this?" I asked, walking over to the bed.

"I wanted to tell you the day you came home from Tracy's house, but I didn't know how to. I couldn't handle the possibility of the things you were going to say to me. It was bad enough that I was an outcast and doing everything in my power to get attention. I didn't expect to get pregnant, Delaney. I swear I never meant for this to happen!" She began crying.

I wanted to scream and go off on her, but I couldn't. She needed me, and I was going to be there for her. I walked over to her and pulled her into a big warm hug. Yes, she had made a mistake, but that wasn't my biggest concern at the moment. Right now, I had to be strong for my brothers and sisters.

"Okay, you all can continue," I said to the doctors.

For the next thirty minutes, we sat on the bed, listening to the doctor explain everything that was going on with Daija and the baby. For the most part, everything was good, but they wanted to keep her to make sure that it stayed that way.

"How are we going to get through all of this?" Daija asked me.

"Honestly, I don't know. We're just going to have to take it one day at a time, I guess," I said, staring at the walls. I didn't know how, but I was going to. I had to be strong for my babies.

Truth be told, I didn't know if I could, though. I was going to have to pray and ask God to give me the strength to get through these next few weeks. Only God knew how hard this was going to be, but I remembered someone telling me that God gave all of his hardest battles to his toughest soldiers. I'd lost my parents, my house, and found out my sixteen-year-old sister was pregnant. Lord have mercy, I hoped and prayed that I was one of those soldiers.

I walked through the church filled with so many emotions that were running through me. No matter how much I thought about it, how many times I remembered seeing their burnt remains in the morgue, or how many times I replayed the memories of that night, I still couldn't believe that my parents were gone. As I walked down the aisle of the church, I held on to Tracy's arm as tightly as I could. I was trying hard as hell to be army strong for my baby siblings, but I'd finally reached my breaking point. When I looked at the two caskets sitting in the front of the church, which contained both of my parents' bodies, I broke down. Everything that I had kept inside for the past few days came pouring out like a running faucet.

"Come on, Dee baby. It's going to be all right," Tracy said, rubbing my back.

I didn't move. I couldn't. I was momentarily stuck. Just knowing that I was never going to see their faces again made me cry even harder. I always remembered my grandmother telling me to never question God and his plans, but it was one of those times when all I wanted to do was ask him why. Why did he have to take my parents? Why did he leave us with that burden? Don't get me wrong, my parents weren't saints. In fact, they were far from it, but they still were my parents. I loved them. They were all that my siblings and I had, and now we were left all alone.

"Delaney," Dallas said, running over to me.

It was only then that I decided to get out of the funk that I was in. Remembering that I was the oldest and needed to be there for them, I dried my tears and headed over to the front pew. I sat Dallas on my lap and stroked her curly hair. I was so happy that she had been with Ms. Lillian when everything went down with the fire at the house, because only the Lord knew how much I would've died on the spot if something had happened to her. She really didn't have any idea about what was going on right now. All she knew was that Mommy and Daddy were in the sky with the angels watching over us.

"You good, boo?" Onijae asked from the pew behind me, where he and his family were sitting.

I turned and gave him a slight smile before nodding my head. I thanked God for him and his family. They'd been there for me and my siblings since everything happened and assured us that if we needed anything, we could count on them. Ms. Lillian was also a great help with the kids. Of course, she didn't know that I had any dealings with her son, and it was best to keep it that way for now. I couldn't have her looking at me funny and thinking I was some kind of slut, especially since I was seventeen and her son was twenty-four.

"Good morning, everyone," Pastor Nelson said, interrupting my thoughts. He was another person I was thankful for. According to Ms. Lillian, he and the rest of the members of the church had paid for our parents' funeral. We didn't have to come up with a dime for anything. I needed to make sure that my siblings and I thanked him and his congregation dearly for doing so much for us. Truth be told, I didn't know one single thing about planning a funeral, and I sure didn't have the money to pay for it. So again, I needed to let him know how thankful I was for that.

I looked around the church and had to admit that I was surprised by the turnout. Almost everyone in the state of Texas knew about my parents and the demons that they'd battled on a daily basis, but that didn't stop them from coming out and paying their respects. I was glad that they never held that against them because my parents were actually great people before they got strung out. I just wished they would have stayed that way. I wished I had pushed harder for them to go to rehab. Maybe if I had, things would've turned out differently, but now it was too late.

As I sat there listening to the choir singing "Goin' Up Yonder," which happened to be my mother's favorite gospel song, I started boo-hooing. I cried not only because my parents were gone, but because I hadn't really known them. I cried for the many nights I'd lain in bed at night without any lights or water, wishing that my mother would just get herself together. I cried for the times we went hungry and dirty. I cried because from now on, I was the only role model that my siblings had, and I cried because I was now responsible for the little kids all by myself. I mean, I had been taking care of them before, but now I really didn't have a choice.

"Oh God, not my sister!" I heard a woman scream, breaking me out of my thoughts.

I turned around to see my mother's sister, Aunt Sharon, being helped up from the floor. When I looked closely, I noticed that both of my uncles were with her, which made me tense up. I rolled my eyes because after all these years, she chose now to show up. After the many times that my mother went to her family for help, none of them cared. They turned their backs on her and on us as if we were nothing and no one. Now they wanted to miss her and act a fool. Where was all this loving and caring bullshit when she really needed it?

"Lord, please don't let them come over here with this foolishness," I said to no one in particular. I was trying to mourn the loss of my parents in peace, but if they came over on some other shit, I was going to let them have it.

"Who's that, Laney?" Dallas asked me.

"That's nobody, honey," I said, turning back around. I was kind of hoping that Sharon would walk right back out the door.

"Do you want me to get my parents to escort them out of here?" Tracy asked me.

I hadn't noticed that my leg was shaking until Daija grabbed it and gave it a gentle squeeze. When I looked up at her, she nodded her head at me. I smiled a small one before laying my head on her shoulder. Even though the past week had been a trying one, that moment gave me a sense of peace. Right now, nothing else was on my mind. Nothing else mattered. As long as my siblings and I were together, I was fine.

"Delaney."

I heard my name being called. I turned only to find my aunt standing right in front of me.

"I'm so sorry, niece. I should've been there for y'all."

"It's okay," I replied nonchalantly.

"If there's anything we can do, please call us," my uncle had the nerve to say.

I couldn't help but roll my eyes. Where was all of this when my mother was living, though? Where was this caring family and shit? Maybe they could've pushed her to go to rehab or something, but instead, they turned their backs on her, and now they showed up acting like they were really hurt. I didn't understand how they could show their faces and speak those words when they had a chance to do all of that but didn't. All those questions I wanted to ask, but I decided to keep my mouth closed. I simply nodded and watched as they walked along. I really hoped they would leave after the service because I surely didn't want them at the repast.

The rest of the service was beautiful. Everything that I had asked the pastor to do, he did. I had a poem that I'd written and wanted to recite out loud, but because I was so emotional, I couldn't. Just like the best friend that she was, Tracy decided to do it for me. As I wished I could, she did it beautifully. She did choke up at the end, but I thanked her for doing what I couldn't do.

Once the service was over, we followed the pallbearers out to the cemetery, where my parents were buried in the same plot. We placed more than two dozen roses on my parents' graves before we watched each casket be lowered into the ground. Again, my aunt decided to act a fool, which only pissed me off. I mean, I didn't say a thing about the shit she did in the church. I didn't understand why she wanted to try it again at the cemetery. Again, I bit my tongue because it was not the time or the place. If she kept that shit up, I didn't know how long I was going to be able to bite my tongue.

We were leaving the cemetery, about to head to the repast, when someone called my name from behind. I turned to see Pastor Nelson heading our way. I removed my hand from Daija's and went to meet him halfway.

"Morning, Pastor Nelson," I said to him. "Again, I want to thank you for doing all of this for my siblings and me. I don't know what we would've done if you and your congregation hadn't helped us out."

"Like I said before, you really don't have to thank me. I was just doing what God wanted me to do. Which reminds me." He passed me an envelope.

I gave him a questioning look before taking the envelope out of his hands.

"The church did a collection for you and your siblings. Now, I know this may not be much, but it's enough to get you all a few things."

"I really don't know what more I can say," I said, getting teary eyed. "You all have done so much for me and my family, Pastor, and I just want to truly thank you from the bottom of my heart. I don't know what we would've done if it wasn't for you and your church's generosity."

"You're so very much welcome. Just continue to do what you've been doing for you and your siblings. The Lord will be with you every step of the way. Take care."

He pulled me into a warm hug. I hugged him back so tight I thought I was going to break him or something. "I hope everything goes well for you all, and hopefully we'll be seeing you guys soon."

"Yes, sir, you will. Have a great day. And thanks again."

"You too," he said and walked off.

I waited until he was a few feet away before I walked back over to Daija and everyone else. I could see the puzzled look that she had on her face. I ignored it and gave her a warm smile before I wrapped my arms around her waist.

"Come on, Dee. Let's get on out of here."

I didn't want a repast after my parents' funeral, but Ms. Lillian had insisted on it. She said it was best that we celebrated them now. We didn't think that many people would come, which was why we ended up having it at this small banquet hall, but boy were we wrong. The minute we arrived, my face dropped. The place was full. It was so full that some people had to wait to even get in the building.

As before, we had help with the repast. The place was decorated by someone that Ms. Lillian knew, and she offered her services to us for free. She had a gold-and-white theme, with pictures of my parents and me and my siblings all over. I was very pleased with how everything had turned out. I was sure that my parents were smiling down on us as well.

"You sure you don't want to get out of here?" I asked Daija as we entered the hall. On our way there, she had started feeling bad. I didn't know if everything was way too overwhelming for her, or if there was something wrong with the baby. Either way, I didn't want her to be there if she didn't want to be.

"I'm good, Delaney." She flashed me a reassuring smile.

I heard what she said, but I also noticed the way her face looked. Knowing that she would continue to say that she was fine, I decided to leave her be for the moment.

"Okay," I said as we headed to the banquet hall's kitchen area. I looked back to see both Derrick and Dedrick following us,with Onijae, who had a half-asleep Dallas in his arms. I didn't understand why he insisted on holding her. I knew that she was heavy because when I picked her up, I had to immediately put her back down. I smiled, though, because he, along with Tracy, was by my side every step of the way. I didn't know how I was going to repay them, but I was going to probably be spending the rest of my life trying.

Ms. Lillian and I both agreed that it would be much better if we had someone cater the event. That way, we wouldn't have to worry about the hassle of picking everything up from different places and then having to take it to the banquet hall.

"Y'all want something to eat?" I asked my siblings.

Dedrick and Derrick shook their heads no, and I didn't even try to wake Dallas, which only left Daija.

"Yes, please. I'm starving." She was rubbing her little pudgy belly.

I still couldn't believe that my little sister was having a baby. I smiled at her then walked over to the table where the food was. I grabbed a plate for myself, Daija, and Onijae, as well as a fork. I headed back over to them, and we began walking back into the hall.

It was kind of hard, but I found us a table in the far right, almost in a corner. I was kind of glad that it was a distance away from people because I really wasn't in the mood to be talking to anyone. Once we were seated, I placed everyone's plate in front of them. Since the boys didn't want to eat, they felt no need to sit at the table. So, they left and went somewhere else.

"How are you feeling, shorty?" Onijae asked me once he sat down. Dallas was now sitting on his left leg, with her head resting on his shoulder. That left his right hand free for him to eat with.

"I'm as good as I can be," I answered truthfully. My emotions were all over the place. I didn't want to cry because that would've made my siblings cry, so I held everything in. Now that the hardest part was over, I really didn't know how I was feeling. I knew that I'd just buried my parents and I was now responsible for five people, with myself included.

"Lay Lay, you know it's okay. You honestly can talk to me. I would never judge you." He scooted a little closer to me.

"I know, Nijae. I just don't feel like talking right now," I replied as I noticed Ms. Lillian walking toward us. I didn't miss the look she had on her face either. I guess she saw how close her son was sitting to me and she wanted to know why.

"Can we please talk about this later? You know people have no idea that we even have any dealings. I don't need them looking at me funny. Especially not right now," I said.

"Okay, but I want to talk to you later," he said just as she reached the table.

"Delaney, darling, I need you to come with me right quick. Your aunt is out here acting a fool, and she's about to make me lose the little bit of religion that I have left." She dropped the smile that was once on her face.

Looking at Onijae, I gave him a knowing look before I got up and followed her. We headed to the parking lot, where I spotted both of my brothers crying. Now, if anyone knew me, they knew for a fact that I didn't play about them. So, seeing them crying instantly pissed me off. Two feet away from them were my aunt and uncle. My aunt's clothes were messed up, and she was breathing very hard. To be honest, she looked like she had been running a marathon the way she was sweating.

"What the hell is going on here?" I asked the minute I reached them.

"She's trying to take them," Ms. Lillian replied.

I looked at my aunt and uncle, who both put their heads down in shame.

"Take them and go where?" I asked them directly, but they just stood there quietly like a couple of church mice. "I know y'all heard me ask y'all a question."

"Delaney, we were only trying to help you out," my uncle replied softly.

"I didn't ask not one of you for your help!" I yelled, shutting him up instantly. Their asses shouldn't have been there in the first place, and now they wanted to try to call themselves helping me. I didn't ask their asses for shit, which was why I was still a little confused right now. "Where the fuck was y'all trying to take them?"

"Look, little girl." My aunt stepped a little closer in my direction.

I honestly hoped she didn't do too much of that name calling and neck rolling, because this little girl was not about to take any of that shit.

"You better watch your mouth when you're talking to us. Don't forget that we're still your aunt and uncle. Now, we were only trying to help your ungrateful ass out. After all, we're still family."

"Help me out? How do you think that was helping me out?" I asked her because right now, she was really confusing the hell out of me. I knew damn well that I didn't ask them for their help, so I didn't know why they were even offering it. "As for us being family, that shit ain't no more true now than it was when my mother was alive."

"We all know that you don't have the means or money to take care of your brothers and sister. Hell, you're just a child your damn self, so how do you feel you can take care of them?" she had the nerve to say.

I knew that bitch was losing her fucking mind if she was saying what I thought she was saying. "I have the means. I go to work every day that I can. I've been the one keeping a roof over our heads, water for us to bathe in, clothes on our backs, and food for us to eat. I'm not saying none of this to brag about it, but I've been taking care of them since you all turned my mother down when she came to y'all for help. Now y'all want to wait until my parents are dead to pull some bullshit like this?" I replied, reading that bitch her rights.

"All of that is fine and dandy, but who's going to be there for them when you're off to college? What will you do then? Or maybe when one of them gets sick and needs to go to the doctor, who's going to take them? You don't have a car, let alone a driver's license. You can't take care of those children, and the state won't let you, because you're not even eighteen years old yet," she responded, sounding even more stupid. "I'll take your little ass to court if I have to. You don't have the funds or a house to take care of a family of five. Don't test me, Delaney. I'll see to it that all of your siblings are with me and the rest of the family."

"Obviously, you must have forgotten all about us since you moved out of the hood into ya fancy-ass palace. I'll be eighteen in two more weeks, so I'll be old enough then. Take me to court. We all know you ain't fooling nobody but ya damn self. You're just after the check that you know they'll get," I said, busting the bitch's bubble.

Yeah, I already knew about that shit. She wasn't fooling any damn body. My mother had worked all her life before she got hooked on drugs, and she had a damn good job at that. The bitch thought I was slow, but I was far from it. Not only that, but my father was also drawing his social security. I didn't know why she thought she could fool me.

"What money? In case you have forgotten, your parents were crackheads. They didn't have any money."

Before she could get another word out of her mouth, my hand went flying across her makeup-plastered face. I didn't give a fuck who she was or where I was. That bitch had just disrespected my parents in front of everyone at their repast, and for that, she deserved that slap across her face.

I knew she was shocked because she only stood there with her hand stuck to her cheek.

"Don't you ever in your bougie-ass life speak about my parents that way again. You don't know a fucking thing about them. And while you're airing out people's dirty laundry, let's talk about the real reason why you wear so much makeup. When was the last time ya husband whooped your ass?" I yelled as a pair of hot fresh tears began streaming down my face. I couldn't believe that she would actually talk about her own damn sister like that. "Get them the hell out of here."

"You little stupid bitch. I'm going to whoop your ass," she said, trying to get at me, but Ms. Lillian jumped right in front of her.

"I'm sorry, but we're going to ask that you all leave," she told her.

"Leave? Who the fuck are you to be asking me to leave? I'm not going any damn where. Especially since this little bitch done put her damn hands on me."

She tried to get at me again, but she made the mistake of pushing Ms. Lillian. Next thing I knew, Ms. Lillian had punched her dead in the face, drawing blood instantly. I was pretty sure that she had broken a bone, because her nose was lopsided.

"Bitch, you must have lost ya fucking mind putting your fucking hands on me. Now, I tried to ask you nicely to leave, but you just had to stay and mess everything up," Ms. Lillian said, hitting her again. Now, I knew I'd just seen her ready to slap my ass back, but she didn't dare pick her hand up to hit Ms. Lillian back.

"Ma, you all right?" Onijae came out of nowhere and asked.

I looked around, noticing that everyone who had been in the hall was outside, and they had a front row seat to the drama that was unfolding.

"I'm good. Y'all get this bitch up out of here before I go back to my old ways on her stupid ass," she told him, then turned to me and said, "Delaney, I'm so sorry for doing all of this at your parents' repast. I didn't mean for this to happen. Your aunt just brought that up out of me, and again, I'm sorry."

"It's okay Ms. Lillian. Sometimes people gotta do what they gotta do," I replied.

I honestly wasn't mad at her. Sharon deserved just what she got. I was actually glad that Ms. Lillian did what she did. The only thing I had to worry about now, on top of everything else, was her possibly calling the state on me and them taking my brothers and sisters away. Lord knew I didn't need that to happen. I guessed I was going to have to be prepared, just in case.

"Tracy!" I yelled and walked over to my friend.

"Yes, Dee," she said, looking at me with concern in her eyes.

"Can you please make sure that everything gets done here? I'm not feeling too well, and besides that, I want to get my brothers and sisters up out of here. People are staring, and I'm not in the mood," I said, feeling a headache coming on.

"You know I got you, boo. Go ahead and get some rest. I'll make sure that everything is handled just the way you would want it." She gave me a hug then tried giving me her car keys, but I shook my head.

"Well, how are you going to get back to the hotel?" she asked.

"You know your parents are here, and I don't have a driver's license. I'm just going to ask Onijae to take us," I said as I spotted him walking in our direction.

"Okay, but remember what I told you about him. Just because he's my brother don't mean that I'll always side with him. I'll come by to see you later. Take care of the kids, especially Daija and the baby." She gave me another hug.

Tracy was the only one that I had told about Daija having a baby for right now. I decided not to let everyone else know because I didn't want them to pass judgment on her or do what my aunt Sharon was trying to do. I had made Tracy promise that she wasn't going to tell anyone, and she agreed to help in any way that she could.

"What would I do without you?" I asked, hugging her a little tighter. "I love you, my baby."

"The same thing I would be able to do without you. Nothing," she replied as we pulled apart. "I love you too, best."

"You need to go ahead with that dike shit," Onijae said as he reached us. "The way y'all be around each other, out here hugging and shit. Y'all would make people think y'all are lovers instead of best friends."

"Fuck you, Onijae. What you need to be worrying about is why ya broad even showed up here, as if she and Delaney are cool," she said, rolling her eyes so hard at him I thought they were going to pop out of their sockets.

"Stop lying, Tracy. Bianca ain't even here," he replied, laughing.

"Yeah, well, I guess that's her twin walking this way, right?" she said, pointing her finger.

We looked in the direction that she was pointing and sure enough, Onijae's girlfriend was walking our way.

"Now, what was it that you just said?" Tracy asked.

"Shut up, Tracy. Damn," he said, turning back to us. "Delaney, let me see what she wants. I'll find you after."

"Huh?" I asked, confused. I knew that nigga was not asking me to leave. Shit, it was my parents' repast. Her ass shouldn't have been there in the first place.

"Please, I'm not trying to cause any more drama."

"Well, ask her to leave then," I told him.

"I will once I see what she wants."

"Fuck you, Onijae. Don't even worry about me. I'll be just fine. Come on, Tee," I said just as Bianca placed her arms around his waist and kissed his lips. I didn't know if he'd heard what I said, but I didn't care either. I wasn't mad that she did that because technically, she was his woman. What I was upset about was the fact that he seemed to be kissing her ass back. I mean, why try to be all lovey dovey with me and you're doing this shit?

"Come on, girl. Let's get out of here," Tracy said, grabbing my hand.

Pulling my eyes away from Onijae and his bird, I followed her. I didn't know what made me, but somehow, I found myself turning around to look at them again. When I did, I spotted Bianca standing there with a smirk on her face. I knew that she was enjoying this, and that was cool, because Onijae wasn't my concern. Yes, I had been foolish enough to believe that he actually wanted me, but I had bigger problems to be worrying about now. I was just going to take Tracy's advice and do what I thought was right for me.

Since the night of the fire, we'd been staying at a hotel. It wasn't all extravagant, but it was somewhere for us to lay our heads until I could come up with a better solution. I had begun filling out applications for a few three-bedroom apartments. Hopefully, I could get an answer sooner rather than later. I still had my job, but they had given me a whole month off with pay. I guess I did all right working there for them to be so generous. It was either that, or they truly felt sorry for me. Either way, I was happy for the extra time off. I only had one week left of school, and then I'd be graduating. I really didn't know how to feel, since my parents weren't going to be there to see me walk across that stage.

"You all right?" Daija asked, walking over to the chair I was sitting in.

"Huh?" I asked, quickly wiping the tears that had fallen down my cheeks. I had no idea that she was even up. The other kids were knocked out already. I guess she couldn't sleep either.

"You wanna talk about it, Dee?" she asked, sitting in the other chair beside me.

"I'm fine, Dai. What's going on with you?" I asked, ignoring her question. She didn't need to worry about any of it. I was the big sister, so I was supposed to be strong for them.

"I know you're trying to be strong for us, Delaney, but you're human. They were your parents too. It's okay for you to cry. I'm here, sis, and I know I haven't been lately, but I am now." She took my hand into hers.

I looked at her face and noticed that tears were falling. There was nothing left for me to do, so I began crying with her.

"It's going to be okay, sis," she said, laying her head on my shoulder.

I leaned my head on the top of hers and rubbed up and down her left arm.

"We're going to get through this together, sis."

"I know," I replied as I continued to cry on her shoulder. As much as I had tried to stay strong for them, they were only trying to be there for me. "I promise that I will do my best to try and give y'all a comfortable life. I know I don't have much, but with love and a plan, I have a lot. You just continue to go to school and graduate next year. Give your child someone he or she can look up to, Dai."

"My child, as well as myself, already have someone to look up to. We have you, and as much as I should've been saying this, I want to start now. Thank you for breaking your back to provide for us. Your childhood is gone because Mama forced you to be an adult before your time. I'm not trying to bash or talk bad about her, but you're more of a mother to me than she ever was, Delaney. God rest her soul. And yes, I did love her, but my love for her was limited. She was only the woman who gave birth to me. As for raising me, you did that."

"Daija, you shouldn't feel that way. Mama was a mother to us. She just got caught up," I told her. I didn't want her to feel that way about Mama. Even if what she was saying had truth to it, Mama had given her life, and for that, she should be grateful.

"I know you're for the right thing, Delaney, and while you might try to get me to see what Mama might or might not have done, my mind is already made up." She placed a kiss on my forehead. I knew that meant the conversation was already over to her. "Oh, and I think you deserve a man who's worthy of you. Now, I don't know what may or may not be the extent of you and Onijae's relationship, but you don't need a man who already got enough on his plate. You're too good to come second place to anyone."

"I already know that, sis," I replied, kind of feeling ashamed of myself. I'd had no idea that anyone besides Tracy knew that Onijae and I were fooling around. "Have you made a doctor's appointment yet?

"No. You were already busy with the funeral and the rest of our problems. I was just going to wait until later," she said, hunching her shoulders.

"Dai, there's a baby growing inside of you. Whether we have enough problems or not, you still need to check up on it. All that other shit isn't as important as this," I told her. I knew that we were going through enough, but the safety and wellbeing of her child needed to come first. "As soon as the doctor's office opens Monday, call and schedule an appointment, Daija. I'll handle everything else."

"Okay, I will," she said, heading to the bathroom.

"Oh, and Daija!" I called out to her.

"Yes?" She turned around.

"The father of that baby needs to be there when it's time for your appointment."

I could tell that she hadn't been expecting me to say that, but hell, I did. There was no way in hell he was about to leave her while she was pregnant. He was just as much responsible for the pregnancy as she was. They had lain down and made it together, and they were going to take care of the baby—*together*.

"Okay, cool," she said, then turned and headed to the bathroom.

I sat there shaking my head, not at her, but the predicament that we were in. Grabbing my purse, I reached for the envelope that Pastor Nelson had given me. I was going to take two thousand out to take the kids shopping for new clothes the next day. On Monday, I was going to add the rest of the money to my savings account. That was the only little bit of money I did have besides the check I was still getting from my job, but that wasn't much. It was time for me to go back to work and grind. I would take all the overtime that I could get. I just hoped that Daija was ready to act right because I was going to need her to watch the kids for me. Hopefully, everything would go as I planned it out in my head because only the Lord knew how much I was tired of everything going south.

"Delaney!" I heard Daija yell my name.

"Why are you screaming?" I asked, looking to see if she had awakened the kids. Once I saw that they were still sleeping, I turned back around.

"I've been calling your name for about five minutes. You were completely zoned out, sis," she said, laughing.

"Shut up." I laughed with her. It felt good to be able to laugh after everything we'd been through. "What's up, though?"

"Your phone has been vibrating for the past few minutes. Whoever it is must really need to talk to you. I think you should get it," she told me as she climbed into the bed that she and Dallas slept in. I always made a pallet on the floor because they needed the rest more than I did.

Getting up from the chair, I walked over to the table where my phone was. Picking it up, I noticed that I had a few missed called from Onijae. Shaking my head, I was about to place it back down when it started vibrating again. Yup, it was him again. I didn't see why he was trying to call me. Hell, he didn't seem to worry about me when he was all booed up with his old lady. Just to be petty, I sent him one of those pre-made texts that always pop up on the screen. I then turned off my phone and headed to the bathroom to take a shower.

Onijae was the least of my worries right now. I had too much already going on in my life. I was not about to add a man who came with drama. The best thing he could do was go back to Bianca because I wasn't trying to hear that. I was going to listen to what Tracy said. After all, she was his sister, so she was probably better fit to judge him than I was. Tracy looking out for me was probably God telling me to let that shit go. So, that was what I was going to do. The only thing I was going to focus on now was making a better future for me and my siblings. Anything else was bullshit.

Chapter Ten

Tracy

The weekend went by faster than I wanted it to, and it was Monday again. I was happy that it was our last day of school and we were only going to turn in our books and stuff. Honestly, I really didn't feel like being there, especially with Dee not being there and knowing everything that she was going through. I could only imagine how she felt now. I just wished there was something I could do for her in her time of need.

What most people didn't know was that I'd die for my friend. Our friendship was so real that I'd pick her over my own brother. I knew that most people probably called me disloyal, but Delaney was more like my sister than my friend. She had done things for me that we'd never spoken of to anyone, which was why I'd forever remain loyal to her, no matter who or what it may be.

Pulling up to the school, I parked in my usual spot and got out of the car. Since Dee wasn't going to be at school, there was no reason for me to even be going to breakfast. Not that we ate anyways. We would just meet up there instead. Heading straight for my home room class, I decided to stop by my locker to get my books. That way, I wouldn't have to be walking backward and forward to get books. Grabbing my school bag, which I never used, I placed it on my shoulder and closed my locker.

"You look so funny carrying a school bag, girl," I heard a voice say behind me.

"Oh my God, Dee!" I yelled, turning around once I recognized her voice. "I thought you wasn't coming to school today."

"I wasn't, but since today was the last day, I decided to come. I mean, I've gone to school all my life, waiting for this day to come. I just couldn't miss it." She laughed. It was good to see her smile after what she'd been through.

"Right," I agreed as we began walking toward our class. "So, have you thought about what I asked you?"

"Tee, I don't know. Like, I can't just up and leave them here for a whole week," she answered.

"Delaney, I already told you that my mother is willing to watch them until we come back, girl."

"And I appreciate that, I really do, but like I said before, I'ma have to think about it. Truth of the matter is, I can't keep going to your mother to watch my siblings. That'll make me seem irresponsible and shit."

"Come on, Dee. We've been planning this trip since the beginning of our senior year." I was practically begging her. It wasn't that I couldn't go. I just didn't want to go without her. Like I'd said, we had been planning the trip together, so it made sense for us to go together. Besides, it was going to be a graduation present from me to her.

"Tracy, I don't even have the money to be going any- where, so that is out of the question."

She tried to walk off, but I stopped her. "Delaney, you know money is never a problem with me. No matter how much something is, I will always have your back. I don't understand why you're tripping," I told her.

"Tee, you know I love you. I appreciate everything you've done for me throughout the years, but I'm tired of letting people pay my way. I want to be able to pay my own way sometimes, but since I have to take care of my siblings, I can't. Not only do I have to find somewhere for us to stay, but I have other things to worry about. I can't make the trip, Tee. I'm sorry."

"Delaney, I've already paid for everything. Are you going to make me waste my money?" I asked her. Even though I was lying, she didn't need to know that. Shit, if that was what I had to do to get her to come, then, oh well. I just couldn't go all the way to Miami and not have my best friend there with me.

"Well, you're going to have to take someone else with you because I won't be able to go, Tracy," she said, shocking me. That wasn't the response that I was looking for.

"Delaney, please. I promise I won't ask you to go anywhere else that you don't want to go. Just go with me this one time," I begged.

She stood there looking as if she wasn't worrying about me or what I was saying, so I was prepared for her to say no.

"All right, Tee, but this is going to be the last time. I have to get my life together for the kids." She brightened up my day. "When do we leave?"

"Oh, thank you, Dee. We leave the day after graduation, which is Saturday," I replied, squeezing my eyes together because I knew she was about to pop off for the short notice.

"I see you pushing it, huh, Tee?" She laughed one of those "I can't believe this shit" laughs.

"Don't do that, Dee. I already told you that my mother will keep an eye on the kids. They'll be staying with her until we get back."

"And what did your father say about that?"

"He's cool too. You know he loves Dallas, Derrick, and Dedrick," I said, which made her smile, but only briefly.

"I know your family took to me, my brothers, and sisters like their own, but I don't want to be a burden on somebody else," she said.

"Don't do that, Delaney. You know my parents don't have a problem keeping them."

"What am I doing, Tee?" she asked, but she already knew the answer.

"You're looking for a reason. You're trying to find anything to be wrong, so you won't have to go."

"No, I'm not. I'm really not trying to do anything to be wrong."

"Come on, Dee. We've been friends forever. I know you, but you have nothing to worry about, baby girl. Let's just get through graduation and enjoy our vacation."

"All right, Tee," she replied.

She didn't sound like her normal self, but that was okay. I had a lot of things planned for my friend. Hopefully, she would like each surprise that I had lined up because she deserved them all.

Once school was over that afternoon, Dee and I decided to drop by the shop. Well, I did, because I hadn't seen Devin in days, and I truly missed him. Delaney wanted to pass, and I knew it was because of my stupid-ass brother, but I talked her into it. I also told her that if he tried to start some shit, we'd run up on his dumb ass and have everybody in the damn shop looking at us. She laughed, but I knew that was what she really wanted to do to him.

Delaney wasn't the fighting type. Now, don't get me wrong. I didn't say that she couldn't fight. I clearly remembered her beating this bitch down our sophomore year, but she hadn't provoked it. Delaney was the quiet type. You'd really have to push her buttons for her to react stupidly, but once you did, that was your ass. She was a mini Laila Ali. She had them hands, and when she had to, she wasn't afraid to use them.

Before getting out of the car, I made sure that I looked good. It wasn't like I was going to be able to talk to him like I wanted to anyway, but I damn sure wanted him to notice me. I then applied a little bit of Nude by MAC to my lips. Turning to Delaney, I noticed her staring out of the window.

"Are you okay? Do you want to go?" I asked her. I mean, if she didn't want to be there, I wasn't going to make her stay.

"I'm good. I was just thinking, that's all." She forced a smile on her face.

"Dee, if this is about the trip, you don't have to come. I'll just get somebody else to go with me."

"Nah, it's not about that either. I told you that I'm going, and I am. You better not try to give somebody else my spot, Tracy." She was finally beginning to act like her normal self.

"Damn, don't try to kill me. I won't give nobody your spot, girl," I replied, acting like I was hurt.

"Oh, girl, please. You were always a drama queen," she said, laughing. "Now, come on and let's go. The faster you see Devin, the faster I get to leave here."

"Okay," I replied as we both got out of the car.

When we walked in the shop, it was packed as usual. There were dudes all over, trying to either get their hair cut, dreads retwisted, or hair braided. I was truly happy that I didn't know how to do hair because I was sure that my brother would have been bothering my nerves to help him out. Thankfully, I didn't have to worry about that.

"Aye, what are y'all doing here?" I heard Devin ask. I didn't miss that loving look he gave me when he asked, either. I honestly thought I was the only one who noticed his face before he turned, so that no one else could see him.

"We're minding our own damn business. Something that you should be doing," I said, putting on my normal act for everyone around the shop. I always talked to him like that when people were around. I didn't need anyone knowing that we were an item, at least not yet, which meant that I had to act like his boss/best friend's annoying little sister.

"Jae, you better come get her little ass before she make me sit her in this chair and cut all of her pretty hair off," he said, making everyone laugh.

"You do that, and you'll regret the day you met me," I replied as I walked over to my brother, who still had his back turned to me. He was so busy putting the finishing touches on someone's haircut that he didn't bother to look our way.

"D, you better leave my little sister alone, man," he responded as he removed the barber's cape from around dude's neck. The dude then stood up, removed his money from his pocket, and handed it to Onijae. They then dapped each other up before he waved and went about his business. "What you want, Tee? You see that we're busy up in here. If you ain't trying to help, you need to be leaving."

"You know damn well that I can't do no got damn hair. How the hell am I supposed to help you out?" I asked him. I couldn't believe he had the nerve to try to play me like that.

"Try picking up a broom and maybe sweeping the floor then," he replied, laughing his little stupid-ass laugh that I hated so much.

"Yeah, that's really fucking funny, stupid ass," I said, pushing him in his chest. "I'm telling Dad, too."

"You were always a drama queen," he said, finally looking up at me. "I know you didn't come all this way to aggravate me. So, what's up?"

"Tee, come on. I have to go see about the kids," Delaney said as she walked up to me.

It was as if I was somehow invisible or something the minute she did. He had completely forgotten about me.

The minute she opened her mouth to speak, his focus went straight to her.

"Okay, give me two minutes while I talk to my brother right quick," I told her.

She looked at him, but she didn't say a word. She turned and began walking away.

"What's up with your girl, Tee?" he asked me.

"I don't know what you're talking about, Onijae. Will you be able to help them with the house once we leave?" I asked. I knew him, and sometimes when he didn't get his way, he'd quickly change his mind.

"I already said that I was. Why you keep asking me that?" he asked, catching an attitude.

"Because I want this for her. She needs this, Onijae, and the way you're acting right now is kind of making me regret asking you," I whispered to him.

"I'm good. I just want to know why she's acting the way she's acting," he had the nerve to say.

"We've already had this conversation, Onijae. Leave my friend alone and worry about your girlfriend," I said before I turned around and spotted Delaney talking to the little cutie whose hair she had braided the last time she was there.

"See, that shit there is going to get her fucked up. Watch. Let her keep playing with me if she wants," he said, attempting to walk to the front of the shop where Delaney was.

"She's single, unlike you." I stopped him before he could move one muscle. "I'm pretty sure that you don't want to make a show in front of all these people. I'm more than sure you don't want Bianca to find out about your growing feelings for Delaney."

"You do know that you're my sister, right?" he asked, looking at me sideways.

"Yeah, I do. That still doesn't mean that I'm going to let you play my best friend," I said. As a matter of fact, I didn't know why he thought playing that card was going to make it any better.

"I'm just saying we came from the same people, you know."

"And ya point is?" I asked because he was really working on my nerves. If that had been Bianca and someone else he was trying to two time, then I probably wouldn't be acting like that. Since the chick he was after was my best friend, that was a different story. "You've already made up your mind. It's time for you to let her be. It's good to let things end before they even begin, though. I'll talk to you later."

I knew that my brother was probably cursing me out in his head, but that was his problem, not mine. Delaney was a sweet girl, and yes, Onijae was my brother, but I was not about to let him bring her any drama. She'd been through enough already, and she was not about to add a man and his stupid-ass girlfriend to the list.

"Come on, Dee. Let's bounce," I said, walking up to her. I didn't speak, but I did give dude a simple wave. Shit, I wasn't trying to be all in his grill. That was her li'l boo, not mine. My nigga was only a few feet away.

Speaking of him, I turned around, and just like I thought they'd be, his eyes were dead on me. I wanted to blow him a kiss, but I knew that was going to draw some attention. Instead, I flashed him a quick smile before I turned back to my friend and her new friend.

"So, will you call me tonight?" I heard him ask her.

"Umm," she began to say, but I answered for her.

"Yes, she will call you tonight," I replied, giving her the eye. I didn't know why she was acting that way. Last time I heard, she actually thought he was cute or whatever, but there she was acting like the dude was ugly or something.

"Thank you, Tracy, but I have my own mouth." She playfully rolled her eyes. Turning to him, she then said, "Yes, I'll call you, and I'll most definitely braid that head of yours also."

"Uh-huh, that's how you do it," I said with a laugh, referring to her flirting with him.

"All right, shorty, gimme a hug." He opened his arms and wrapped them around her before she could object or reply.

I didn't know why, but I felt a pair of eyes on us. When I turned around, my brother was in the back, looking at us with the hardest look ever. I'd seen that look on more than one occasion, and it usually led to him losing his cool. When I spotted him walking our way, I knew it was time for us to exit the building.

"Bitch, come on. Here comes my brother," I said, grabbing her by her arm.

She looked back and hauled ass when she saw him. "I'll talk to you later, Aqura!" she yelled right before we made a dash for my car.

I was thankful that it wasn't far and that it was push start, because I hopped right on in, started it up, and pulled off right as my brother was walking out the door.

"The fuck we running for, and what was his problem?" she asked once we both calmed down.

"We were running for our damn lives. His ass was pissed because he saw you talking to dude from the other night," I said just as my phone dinged. I looked at the screen and noticed that I had a message from him. Shaking my head, I showed her the message.

"You need to tell him that I'm grown, and he doesn't own me. As a matter of fact, tell him to kiss my ass and worry about that bitch Bianca. I'm not trying to live my life pleasing a man who ain't my man," she replied.

I was happy that she knew how to stand up for herself, because I would've hated to see her settle for anything less than what she deserved.

"All right now, Delaney. You go, girl. But tell me what's going on with you and the dude from the shop." I changed the subject. I wasn't trying to depress my friend by talking about my no-good-ass brother. Hopefully, she'd keep that backbone that she had because I was really rooting for her to find love and a man of her own.

Bianca

Everything between Onijae and me had been going great lately. He'd been staying home a lot, and he texted me all day, every day. I had yet to tell him about the pregnancy because I was afraid that it would push him away. Not only that, but I was not sure if I wanted to keep it. I still didn't know exactly who I was pregnant by yet, which was probably the main reason I hadn't told him.

What I didn't have to worry about was Tracy's little ho-ass friend. Ever since her crackhead-ass parents died, I hadn't seen much of the bitch. I was glad because she was really starting to piss me off. I'd noticed the way that Onijae looked at her. I also noticed the way he cared for her and her snotty-nose-ass siblings.

I couldn't believe what I saw the day of her parents' repast. He didn't know I was there because I stayed in the back of the church the entire time. I didn't see a reason to be anywhere near the front. I wasn't a part of the family, and I couldn't stand her ass. I didn't care that her parents were dead, either. I only went because my woman's intuition told me to, and obviously, I needed to be there. I almost lost it when I saw my man and that little bitch who was in high school hugged up like they were a family.

Hell, his family had taken to her faster than they took to me. I mean, I was aware of what I had done to him, but they didn't treat that bitch any type of way. They welcomed her and her little bitch-ass sisters and brothers in like it was nothing.

I knew it had everything to do with that little girl Tracy, but I was going to see her, too. She couldn't have thought I forgot about her and her bullshit. All in due time, though. Her ass was going to wish she had been nice to me.

"Bianca!" I heard Onijae yell my name.

"I'm in the living room," I replied, refusing to move from my spot. I'd just started watching the new show *Power,* and I couldn't believe the shit Ghost, Tasha, and Tommy were going through.

"What you up in here doing?" he asked, sitting down next to me.

"I'm watching *Power*. What's up with you?" I asked, pausing the TV. I looked up at him to see a look of frustration on his face. "What's wrong?"

"Just aggravated, that's all," he replied, pulling his phone out of his pocket. I watched as he texted somebody, and then he hopped on Facebook.

"What you cook?" he asked.

"I didn't cook anything. I've been sitting here all day," I said, but then I regretted it.

He cocked his head to the side and looked at me like I was crazy. "And you're happy to be saying that shit." He jumped up.

"Where are you going?" I asked, getting up too. I followed him as he headed for the door.

"I'm going to my mother's house to get something to eat." He opened the door and closed it before I could say I was coming with him.

I had no idea what was on his mind, but something was there. Onijae had just been acting like that lately. Something or someone had caused it, and I wanted to know who or what.

Grabbing my phone from the sofa, I dialed his number as I headed for the door. Placing the phone to my ear, I opened the door just in time to see him backing out of the driveway. I watched as he picked up his phone and put it back down, which only angered me. I hated when he did that shit and he was clearly doing it to piss me off.

I hung the phone up and tried calling him again. That time it didn't even ring, but the voicemail automatically picked up. So, I went to the house and tried calling him from there, but it also went to voicemail. That made me figure that he had powered it off on me. Pissed, I went back to the living room and sat down. After a few minutes of pouting, I decided to say fuck it. Grabbing my phone, I called on the one person who I knew wasn't going to ignore me.

"Hello," he answered on the second ring.

"What are you doing?" I asked in my sweetest voice.

"Nothing. Getting some rest before I go to work. What's up with you?" he replied in between yawns.

"I was trying to see what was up with you, but since you're getting rest for work, I'll let you rest," I said, knowing that he wasn't going to even allow that.

"Now, you know I always have time for you," he said, biting the bait just like I knew he would. "You wanna come over, or do you want to go to our usual spot?"

I didn't know why, but I found myself thinking boldly. Since my boyfriend was ignoring me and doing God knows what, I wanted to do the same. "I'm coming over," I replied, figuring it wouldn't hurt me since Onijae wasn't home. He most likely wasn't going to be looking for me, so I might as well go have fun. Besides, I thought it was time that I tell someone about the pregnancy.

"Okay, I'll be waiting for you," he replied.

I hung up the phone, got up, and headed to my room. I threw on a shirt and a pair of pants, grabbed my keys and purse, and walked back to the living room. Before leaving, I turned the television off, then I locked up and left.

When I pulled up to Carlos's house, my stomach started to hurt. I didn't know why, but I suddenly became nervous. Maybe it was because I had finally decided to tell him about the baby, or maybe it was because the last time I was there, things had gone bad. Hopefully, that wouldn't happen this time. Pulling into the garage, I got out of the car, and there he was, waiting on me with open arms.

"How are you doing, beautiful?" he asked, pulling me in for a hug.

"I'm good. And you?" I replied as I hugged him back. I stood there in his arms a few seconds longer than usual, as I enjoyed the feel of his touch.

"Are you okay?" he asked once he noticed that I didn't pull back.

"Yeah, I'm good. I just needed that hug. That's all," I said, finally prying myself from his loving arms.

Yeah, I know what most people would think of me, but I didn't give a damn. Carlos was my rock when Onijae was my headache and heartache. He would drop everything no matter what was going on. Even though I was in a relationship with someone else, that didn't matter to him. His love for me was real and out of this world.

I kept on telling him that he needed to find himself a girl who was going to be there for him and give him her all. He wasn't trying to hear me, though. He was convinced that one day we were going to be together, get married, and start a family. What he didn't know was that shit wasn't going to happen. I loved Onijae too much to even consider leaving him for someone else. Of course,

I didn't tell him that, though. I just let him believe that one day his wish was going to come true.

"Come on. Let's head inside the house," he said, opening the door for me.

I walked in the house before him as he locked the door behind us.

"You hungry? There's food and fruit in the refrigerator."

"Nah, I'm good. Come on and follow me to the bedroom. We have to talk about something," I replied as I began walking to the room. I smiled when I noticed that the place looked exactly the way I'd left it. Well, except for a bigger bed and a different comforter set. Other than that, it looked the same.

"What's up?" he asked, entering the room with a bowl of fruit.

Even though I said I wasn't hungry, I couldn't help but to eat a few grapes. Popping them all in my mouth, I looked over, and he was staring straight at me.

"What?" I asked, feeling a little awkward.

"I thought you said you didn't want any," he said, feeding me a piece of pineapple. It was so good and juicy that I couldn't even answer him. "Yeah, I thought so."

"Shut up and leave me alone," I replied, fake pouting like I was mad.

"Aww, nah, why do you have to be like that?"

"I'm good." I flashed him a bright smile.

"Okay, well, what did you want to talk about?" he asked, handing me the whole bowl.

"Thank you," I said, popping a few more grapes into my mouth. "Carlos, I have to tell you something, and I really don't know how to."

"Just say it, Bianca. I'm pretty sure it's not that hard to say," he replied, giving me a smile.

I closed my eyes and tried to force the words out. "Okay, well, I'm pregnant," I blurted out.

When I opened my eyes, he was sitting there staring at me. He didn't say anything. He just sat there continuously staring at me. I hadn't expected him to do that. Hell, he was the one who had always wanted a family—but I guess not.

"Umm, I have to go." I suddenly jumped up from the bed and grabbed my purse and keys. I began walking to the door, but he stopped me before I could reach it.

"Where are you going? Why are you leaving?" he asked, rubbing up and down my arm.

"I'm about to head home, since you obviously need a little time to process this whole thing."

"No, you don't have to leave. I was just shocked, that's all." He pulled me back toward the bed. "Sit back down so we can discuss this."

"Okay," I replied, sitting down like he told me to.

"Now, how far along are you?" he asked.

I probably should've thought about that before I decided to tell him.

"I don't know. I haven't been to the doctor yet," I replied, feeling a little sad. I knew that he was disappointed in me from the way his face dropped.

"What do you mean? Why haven't you gone to the doctor yet? How do you know you're pregnant then?" he asked.

"I haven't gone to the doctor because I'm not ready. I know that I'm pregnant because I took three tests," I said, rolling my eyes. I knew his damn ass wasn't trying to play with me on the slick. I wasn't that type of girl, though.

"Oh, okay. So, what are you going to do?"

"What do you mean?" I asked, a bit confused.

"I mean, do you plan on keeping it?" he asked.

"What the fuck you think? I'm not one of those bitches who'll lay their asses down and let some doctor scrape my insides out just because I didn't want to the deal with the consequences of my actions. I'm a big girl, and I intend to do just what a big girl would do when she gets pregnant!" I spat, blowing my top. I couldn't believe his ass even let the thought of me getting an abortion cross his mind.

"You didn't have to go off like that. I wasn't saying that you were one of those girls." His voice was soft. I knew his ass wasn't about to act like a child, though.

"You didn't have to because your choice of words did," I said, getting up.

I was getting my ass up out of there before I said or did something I would regret later. Grabbing all my belongings, I damn near ran all the way to the door. My hand was on the knob, and I was about to turn it when he asked a question that damn near knocked all the wind out of me.

"So, whose baby is it?"

"Huh?" I asked, pretending as if I hadn't heard him. I turned to see his head cocked to the side as he just stared at me.

"You don't even have to play those games. Remember, you're not one of those females," he replied, excluding the word *bitch*.

I didn't know why, but something inside of me told me to lie to him. I mean, that was what I wanted to do, but I couldn't. The truth of the matter was that I didn't know which one of them was the father. I was screwing them both. So, I guess that did make me one of those bitches. Crazy thing was, he knew that I was screwing two people, which was one of the reasons I didn't want to take him too seriously. Let Onijae find out that I was still fucking with Carlos while still fucking him, and he would have a fit and then some. Carlos was different. It was like he wasn't trying to fight for my love like most of the movies I had seen, and that wasn't what I wanted. Instead of lying, I told him the truth.

"Honestly, I don't know which one of you is the father."

"Okay, cool. So, does he know? And if not, when and what are you actually going to tell him?"

"As of now, he doesn't, but I do plan on telling him. I just have to find the perfect time and a way to do it," I said as I suddenly realized the position that I was in. I was pregnant, and I didn't even know who the father of my child was. Onijae didn't know about it, but Carlos did, and I was not sure how he felt about it.

"You know you're going to have to tell him sooner rather than later. I honestly don't know how you plan to, and I don't care, but you have to."

"I know, and I will, but I'm going to wait until after I go to the doctor and get everything situated," I said, hoping that he would just let it go because the shit was really pissing me off. As always, though, shit didn't go my way.

"And when do you plan on telling him about us? I mean, I really hope you don't try to wait until after the baby is born and all to actually do so," he said.

"Look, I'm going to leave before you continue to piss me off and have me up in here causing all kind of hell," I said.

That time, I didn't even give his ass the opportunity to stop me. I speed-walked my ass back to the garage. I opened it before I headed to my car and got in.

I had started the car when he came walking out the door.

"Wait, Bianca. Let's talk. You don't have to go!" he yelled as he began walking toward the car.

As far as I was concerned, there was nothing left for us to talk about. His ass wasn't going to do shit but bring that stuff up again, and honestly, I was just over it all. Completely ignoring his ass, I put the car in reverse and backed out onto the street. I turned back around and noticed him standing in the garage, looking like a lost puppy. I almost felt bad, until I thought about what his ass had said. Putting the car in drive, I pulled off like someone was coming after me.

There was no damn way I was going to tell Onijae that I was cheating on him. Telling him that I was pregnant and it was possible that he wasn't the father was really out of the question. If he hadn't left me before, he was surely going to leave me then. I loved him too much to let him leave me, so the truth was going to have to wait. Hopefully, the baby would turn out to be Onijae's because I absolutely could not live without him. That man was my all, and there was no way I was going to give him up that easily.

Onijae

I knew that I probably shouldn't have gone off on Bianca and stormed out on her the way that I had, but I couldn't help it. We'd been in such a good place lately that I didn't want to ruin it, but then again, I couldn't help it. I was still heated about the fact that Delaney had come to my shop and didn't speak one word to me. It was bad enough that she'd been ignoring me, but then she went and did that. To make matters worse, she was flirting with some nigga in my face. I mean, she already knew that I wanted her, and doing that was disrespectful as fuck. She was lucky I hadn't shown my ass out in the shop because I didn't want anyone in my business, and most of all, I didn't want Bianca to find out.

Unlike what most people may have thought, I actually loved my girl, even though she aggravated the hell out of me. I knew it might not seem like it, seeing as how I was after Delany, but I did. I just liked Delaney and wanted her too.

Unlike Bianca, Delaney was different in age and in maturity. Where Bianca was a grown woman, she still had the mind frame of a child. Delaney was young, but she had her mind and thoughts together. Like most older people would say, she had an old soul. From what I understood and what my sister had told me, she'd been the caregiver to her siblings since she first started high school. She was smart, loving, caring, and pure. Something about her demeanor drew me to her. I couldn't shake the feeling, and my sister knew it.

Like right now, even though I had said that I was going to my mother's house, there I was standing at the door of Delaney's hotel room. I'd be lying if I said I didn't feel like a fool. I did. There I was, a 24-year-old man, practically stalking a 17-year-old. I guess Cupid's little dude ass was still out or some shit.

Knowing that she shared a room with her siblings and they had school in the morning, I decided to call her cell phone instead of knocking. The phone rang a few times, and then it went to voicemail. Now, I already knew she was up because she had just been on Facebook liking and commenting on shit. Yup, she was my Facebook friend also. Hanging the phone up, I dialed her number again, getting the same results. That's when I decided to text her.

Come talk to me. I'm standing outside of the door.

I sent the message and waited until she texted me back. Hell, I thought she wasn't going to, but as usual, shorty surprised me by texting me back.

I don't know why. Bianca's not anywhere in here.

I had already had a feeling that she was mad about that, but I just didn't know if I was right or not.

I texted her again. You need to cut all of that out man. Come outside so we can talk.

She replied: I'm not cutting shit out. Leave me alone. I don't want to be bothered with you. Go home to your girlfriend because what we were trying to start ended before it even began.

She sent the next text before I could even answer her. I'm really not in the mood. Please do me this solid favor and just leave.

Delaney, come outside so we can talk about this please, I texted.

Honestly, there's absolutely nothing for us to talk about. I'm just glad I got to see you for the person you truly are. I already know that you won't stop texting me. Therefore, I'll stop replying all together. Goodbye, Onijae."

Not trying to hear that, I tried calling her. The phone didn't even ring that time but went straight to voicemail. I didn't know if she had truly turned her phone off, or if she had just placed my phone on the block list. I decided to call her private the next time. It did go to voicemail, but that didn't make me feel any better. Putting the phone in my pocket, I was about to knock on the door, but then I decided against it. I wasn't going to push her, so if she didn't want to be bothered with me, that was fine. Well, for now it was. I wasn't giving up, though. She was going to get over it. I'd just have to give her time to, that's all.

I ended up going to my mother's house after all. I still needed to eat, and I was pretty sure that she had cooked. Pulling up in the driveway, I spotted my brother's car and wondered what he was doing there. I was hoping that we weren't supposed to be having dinner as a family, because if so, I had totally missed the memo.

Walking up to the door, I started to knock, but I decided to use my key instead. Entering the house, I heard laughter.

The hell is going on here? I thought as I headed in the direction that it was coming from.

"What's going on here?" I asked, walking into the kitchen.

Sitting at the table were my mother, my little big-head-ed-ass sister, and my father, who all seemed to be having the time of their lives. There were papers and all types of things scattered on top of it.

"Hey, son, what are you doing here?" My father was the first person to ask.

"Well, I was coming here to see what you all were doing, and I walked into this. What's going on? Is there something I need to know?" I asked, looking straight at Tracy. I wasn't sure if she had told them about what had happened earlier.

"Well, your sister has done it again. I'm convinced that the good Lord placed my baby here to do great things for people," my mother said, looking at her one and only daughter while smiling the biggest smile I'd ever seen.

"Well, don't keep me in the dark any longer. Let me in on what the brat did," I said.

"You can kiss where the sun doesn't shine, Onijae," she replied, shocking everyone at the table.

"Tracy!" my parents yelled simultaneously while giving her the evil eye.

"Ma and Da, I'm truly sorry, but he's been asking for this all day. Which is why he didn't come when Omari came earlier. I didn't call him."

"What?" my mother yelled. "I thought you said you called him but he didn't answer."

"Nope, I lied. I didn't want to see his stupid face while we were planning everything out," she said, rolling her eyes at me.

Hell, I wasn't worried about shit she was saying. All I wanted to know was what they were planning.

"Why the hell would you do that?" my father asked, clearly upset.

She looked up at me and rolled her eyes before she turned back to them. Before she even opened her mouth, I already knew that she was going to rat me out.

"Well, we got into an argument earlier today when she asked me for my card to pay for something really important," I lied before she could even open her mouth.

She looked at me with her head cocked to the side and gave me a sinister smile. I'd clearly fucked myself, and honestly, I felt that I deserved it.

"Yeah, what he said," she replied, hunching her shoulders. When no one was looking at her, she mouthed, "You. Owe. Me," one word at a time, adding a dramatic pause between each word.

I thought the shit was funny, but I played it cool.

"Y'all made her like that," Omari said, cracking a joke to lighten the mood.

"Hell, that was Mama and Daddy's doing," I said, throwing my hands up in defense.

"And you added fuel to the already burning fire," my father said, joining in. "Oh, and Junior, you need not to forget about the times she batted those eyes of hers and had you eating out the palms of her hand."

"How can I forget? I bought a lot of toys in my days," Omari replied, making everyone laugh.

"Okay, now, y'all leave my baby alone," my mother told us.

"Thanks, Ma," Tracy replied, sticking her tongue out at us.

"Don't 'thanks, Ma' me. I'm trying not to slap your ass for lying to me!" she yelled, pushing her away. "Now, let's talk about the surprise for Delaney. I'm just so excited and proud of my baby for stepping up and being a true friend to that girl. Oh, that reminds me. Onijae, make sure we talk before you leave, okay."

"All right, Ma," I replied.

My eyes immediately shot to Tracy. I needed to know if she had said anything to her. She shook her head no, which kind of relieved me a bit, but it still had me wondering what Ma wanted to talk to me about.

"All right now. Tracy, fill your brother in on the plan," she said, happily clapping her hands together. I didn't know what the plan was, but apparently my mother was happy about it.

"Okay, listen. And you better pay attention." She picked up a few of the papers that were on the table. She then began to tell me about everything she had going on for Delaney.

To say that I was shocked wasn't quite how I was feeling. I was actually proud of my little sister for sacrificing so much for her friend. I mean, I knew the extent of their friendship and how cool they were before, but this meant their friendship was way more solid than I thought before. I finally got to see the Tracy that Delaney talked about all the time. Hell, I was just now learning that she had a heart made of gold, and I'd known the girl for eighteen whole years.

"So, when do you plan on giving all of this to her?" I asked, super excited. Just like them, I couldn't wait to see the look on Delaney's face when she saw everything Tee and my parents had done for her. Hell, they were kind of making me jealous by the way they were treating her.

"So, you're cool with your part, right?" Tracy asked once everything was laid out flat on the table.

"Yes, I got it. I'ma even get some of my crew down at the shop to pitch whatever they can in too," I said, wanting to do everything I could.

"You don't have to do that, Onijae. We have all of that under control already."

"I know, Tee, but it would help to have extra hands," I told her.

"Yeah, you're right, but make sure that no one says a thing to her. I don't need anyone spoiling the surprise." She pointed her finger at me. "Or else I'ma come down there and beat them all up."

"Yeah, right, but I got you. I'ma just tell them that it's for a family member that's in need, or some shit like that," I said, trying to think of something.

"Cool. And I'll get a few of the dudes at the office to pitch in too," Omari added. "I like home girl, and she most definitely deserves this."

"Yes, she does, and I'm going to make sure that she gets it," Tracy said, smiling so hard I knew her cheeks were hurting.

"All right, well, I'm about to head out," I said once I noticed what time it was.

"Let me walk y'all to the door," my mother said to both me and Omari.

"Y'all?" he asked, looking at her like she was crazy. "I didn't say that I was going anywhere. As a matter of fact, I'm about to head upstairs to my room right now. I'm sleeping at the crib tonight. There's no way that I'm even attempting to leave knowing how sleepy I am right now. If anyone wants or needs me, I'll be in my room."

"You ain't shit but a big-ass mama's boy anyway," my father told him. He got up from the table, said good night, and headed to bed himself.

"Oh, Onijae," Tracy said, walking up to me. "You owe me. I need a dress to wear for graduation, so pay up."

"You make me sick, girl," I said, pulling my wallet out of my back pocket. Pulling five bills out, I handed them to her and shoved the wallet back in my pocket. It was a good thing that the shop wasn't my only means of income because dealing with Tracy would've had me broke.

"Thank you very much," she replied before she bounced her happy ass down the hall.

Shaking my head, I turned back to my mother, who was smiling hard. We then continued to walk to the door.

"So, Ma, what is it that you want to talk to me about?" I asked.

"Are you happy in your relationship, son?" she asked out of the blue.

"Yes, I am. If I wasn't, I would've left already," I answered, shocked. Her question had thrown me off a little bit, though. "Where is this coming from?"

"Okay, then," she replied, nodding her head. "What's going on with you and Tracy's friend Delaney?"

"What?" I yelled, trying to play it off as best as I could. "There's nothing going on between me and that girl, Ma. Where did you get that from?"

"Onijae, I'm your mother. You should never lie to me."

"I'm not lying to you, Ma. There's absolutely nothing going on between me and that girl."

"Well, explain to me why the two of you looked like y'all were a couple the day of her parents' funeral. I watched you the whole time, Onijae. You didn't leave her side until I called her when her aunt was trying to take the kids. You stayed by her side the whole time. Hell, if I saw it, I know everyone else did," she said, clocking me.

I couldn't believe that she had actually been watching us the whole time.

"Oh, and let's not mention how your face lights up and your whole mood changes when she enters the room. Hell, it doesn't even light up like that when Bianca's old, tired ass enters the room. So, I'm going to ask you again. What's going on between the two of you? And you better not lie to me."

"Like I said, there's nothing going on between us. I only stuck by her side the day of her parents' funeral because she needed someone to be there for her. Not to mention that her little sister stuck to me like glue. Like I told you a few minutes ago, I love Bianca, and I'm happy in my relationship."

"If you say so, Onijae. I just don't want no bullshit out of this. If you're not willing to be there wholeheartedly for either one of them, then don't try to have your cake and eat it too," she said with a raised eyebrow.

"I'm going to give you the benefit of the doubt, though. Don't forget that we have to go shopping this week when Tracy and Delaney leave to go on their trip. I don't want any shit out of you, so it's probably best if you leave your little girlfriend at home. As a matter of fact, you don't even have to tell her about what's going on. I'm not trying to deal with her when we already have so much to do. Knowing her, all she'll do is cause drama and have us behind. We all know how important this is for Tracy, and I'm not trying to disappoint her."

"All right, Ma," I replied, laughing at how dramatic she was being, but I halfway agreed with her on that. Bianca was known to always complain about things when they were not going her way or were not all about her. "I'll see y'all this weekend. Good night."

"Good night, babe. Call me when you make it home, so I'll know that you've made it there safely. Love you."

"Okay, and I love you too, Ma," I said as I made my way to my car.

Once I was inside, I started it up and backed out of the driveway. I laughed once I noticed my mother still standing there in the doorway. I guess no matter how old we got, she was always going to treat us like babies. Once I was on the road in front of the house, I blew the horn at her a few times.

Checking the time, I noticed that it was almost eleven o'clock. I was pretty sure that I already had a million missed calls from Bianca, and I knew that she was going to flip once I entered the door. All I knew was that she better not work on my nerves because I had no problem going back to my parents' house and sleeping there.

Since I only stayed thirty minutes away from my parents' house, it didn't take me long to get home. Pulling up to the house, I opened the garage door and spotted Bianca's car in there. I decided to just leave my car in the driveway in case I had to leave quickly.

Turning the car off, I grabbed my phone and headed inside. Entering the house, I noticed that the television in the living room was on. I thought maybe Bianca was still in there, but she wasn't. Turning off the TV, I headed upstairs and found her in the bed, sleeping peacefully. I stood there looking at her for a while.

When I had first met Bianca, we were still in high school. We didn't have anything other than the things that our parents had given to us. On our own, we had nothing. Aside from her being strong, smart, and beautiful, she had an independent vibe that drove me to her. She was also cool, laid back, loyal, and faithful, which had all changed lately. I knew that I told her that I was going to try, and honestly, I really wanted to. I just didn't want to end up in the same situation that she'd put me through before. I honestly didn't think I'd be able to take it if it did happen again.

After a few minutes of watching her sleep, I decided to head to the shower. I still had hair all over me from earlier. Besides that, I wanted to see if I could call Delaney again. Powering my phone back on, I placed it on the counter as I headed to the shower to turn the water on. Making sure that the water was at the right temperature, I turned and headed back over to the counter.

My phone began buzzing from the missed notifications that I had, but not one of them were from Delaney. Going straight to her number, I pressed CALL and then placed the phone to my ear. Of course, it still went to voicemail, which made me a little upset. Placing the phone back down, I didn't bother texting her. I undressed and hopped in the shower. She was going to come around. If nothing made her, the surprise that Tracy had, which we all were pitching in for, would. Once she opened her eyes, I was going to be right there waiting for her.

Chapter Eleven

Tracy

The day of graduation had finally come, and I was excited, but also nervous. Basically, my whole family was there to help me celebrate my day. Hell, I had even invited Devin, and I really hoped that he would show up. He said that he would, but we all know how men like to change their minds. Plus, my brother was going to be there, and Devin didn't want to seem a little suspicious by being there alone. I told him just to come with my brother, but to make sure that he brought a gift for me and Delaney. That way, he could play it off as if he was just there to show his little annoying play sisters some love.

Honestly, I'd be glad when all of it was over and done with. I was so tired of having to creep around. I didn't care that he was twenty-three and I was just eighteen. I was tired of hiding my love and affection for a man that I adored. I couldn't wait until we could go public with our relationship. My brothers were probably going to kill us both, but my Dev was worth it.

On the other hand, I was concerned about Delaney. Even though today was supposed to be one of the best days of our lives, her parents weren't there to celebrate it with her. It was a good thing she had her siblings, because without them, this day wouldn't be one to celebrate. I honestly hoped she enjoyed her day because I had planned some interesting things for her. Right now, I was just hoping she was ready to leave.

"Are you ready?" I asked, walking into the bathroom of the hotel room that my mother had booked for us. She had hired a freelance makeup artist, a hair stylist, and someone to do our manis and pedis. I had to say that we looked stunning.

"Yes, I'm ready. I just have to grab my cap and gown. Everything else is a go," she said, turning off the lights in the bathroom.

"Well, come on before you make us late for our high school graduation," I said, following her.

We grabbed our things, making sure that we weren't leaving anything behind. Once we were sure, we grabbed our caps and gowns and headed out of the room.

"Your mother is still going to pick the kids up for me, right?" she asked as we walked through the lobby, heading for the door. "I don't want her to forget them."

"I already told you yes, but I'll call and remind her," I said, rolling my eyes upward. Delaney was such a Susie homemaker that it could be annoying. Pulling my phone out, I dialed my mother's number and waited as it rang.

"Good morning, darling. Did you gals like everything?" she asked. I was guessing she was referring to the spa treatment. "Please don't tell me that I have to call and curse someone out."

"Ma, no," I replied, laughing. "Everything was wonderful. We enjoyed it so much. Thanks, by the way, but I was calling to make sure that you didn't forget Delaney's sisters and brothers at the hotel."

"Tell Delaney to calm her little self down. I've already picked them up. In fact, we're heading to the school as we speak," she said, making me feel much better. I mean, I already knew that she wasn't going to forget them, but knowing that they actually had them was a relief for both me and Delaney.

"Okay, Ma, we'll meet you all at the school," I told her as we arrived at my car.

Placing our things in the back seat, we hopped in the front. I started the car, and we were on our way.

"Hey, where's Daddy?" I asked.

"He's in the car with your brothers," she replied, making me smile.

"One more thing, Mom," I said before we hung up.

"Make it quick. You know I don't like to be bothered when I'm driving." She sounded a little annoyed.

"Girl, bye. But please tell me that Onijae did not bring his Chihuahua with him," I replied, hoping that she would say he didn't.

"Well, I won't tell you then. I'll see you when you walk across that stage. Bye, Tracy. I love you." She said it all in one breath before she hung up in my face.

"I can't believe she hung up on me," I said out loud. "Okay, well, the good news is that my mother already has the kids."

"And what's the bad news?" she asked, laughing her ass off.

"Well, the bad news is that I think we might go to jail for cruelty to an animal today, because if Bianca says one thing that I don't like, I'ma pound her eyes out right then and there."

"You will not. Today is our day, and I'll be damned if we let that stupid bitch fuck it up," she said, suddenly getting a boost of energy from out of nowhere.

"So, you're not mad that they're going to be there together?" I asked, hoping that she had finally come to her senses.

"Girl, fuck them. And no, I'm not mad. I can't be mad if that man wants to bring his girl to his sister's graduation.

After all, she's his woman, Tee. I'm not. Therefore, I have no right to even think about being upset when I see them," she said, making me proud.

I was so happy that she had found her backbone that I wanted to celebrate before the celebration.

"Bitch, I can't wait until we hit those Miami streets. I'ma party so hard that I may regret it the next day," I said, excited that she had agreed to go on the trip with me.

"Yo, bitch, try me. I'ma let my hair down and turn the fuck up. Who knows? I might even get laid while I'm there too," she replied, almost causing me to wreck.

"Bitch, you better stop talking like that while I'm driving. Fuck around and make me hit something or someone," I said, busting into a giggling fit.

"I'm serious. I just might," she replied with a straight face.

"We'll talk about that shit later," I said as we pulled up to the school. "First, let's go receive the diplomas we've worked so hard for all these years," I said, finding a parking spot.

I couldn't help but to get excited all over again. We were graduating high school together after everything that we'd been through. Some friends didn't even last that long, and yet we had. Like I said before, I couldn't wait until we were in Miami because a vacation was long overdue for both of us. Hopefully, Delaney would be able to relax and not worry about her siblings every hour on the hour.

Delaney

It was the day of graduation, and surprisingly, I was happy. Although my parents weren't there to celebrate such a special day with me, I had my siblings and my best friend in the whole wide world. Besides, Ms. Lillian had been a great mother figure in my life. Now, in no way, shape, form, or fashion was I trying to replace my mother because there was no one on the Earth who could do that. However, Ms. Lillian had been very helpful throughout the past few weeks. For that, I was very thankful.

As I sat there looking at all the people who had come out to help our class celebrate, a lone tear fell from my eye. My parents weren't there physically, but they were there mentally. I then looked at my siblings, who were seated with Tracy's family, and I smiled. My support system wasn't as big as hers, but at least they were there.

"Are you okay?" Tracy whispered, pulling me from my thoughts. Even though we weren't supposed to be sitting next to each other, there we were anyway.

"I'm good. A little nervous, but good. What about you?"

"Bitch, I'm happy as fuck. All my childhood I've waited for this day, and now that's it's here, I can't stop smiling. I'm especially happy that I don't have to see this school ever again." She was laughing so loud that people were beginning to look at us. It was times like those that I wished I was in the back row.

"Girl, calm down. Shit. You got all these people looking at us crazy," I said, looking around.

"Girl, fuck them people. I bet they don't want to fight," she said, looking back at them while rolling her eyes. It was a good thing that the ceremony was almost over because I didn't think she would be able to sit there quietly any longer.

"You better chill out," I replied just as they called her name.

"I am, girl."

"Go ahead, my baby," I said, pulling her in for a hug. "Congratulations, Tee."

I watched as she got up, making sure to put extra pep in her step. She wasn't fooling me. I saw Devin out there in the audience. I honestly thought they made a wonderful couple. I just couldn't wait until everyone got to see it.

Again, I found my mind wandering off, but I was pulled back by Tracy's family's loud screams. I looked over, and every last one of them, including my sisters and brothers, were on their feet, cheering her on. When I looked at her, she had the biggest smile I'd ever seen on her face. She posed for a few pictures before she walked off the stage.

Four names later, and it was finally my turn. When they called my name, I got up slowly. My heart was beating so fast that it was beginning to scare me. As I walked toward the principal, who was holding my diploma, I looked out into the audience at the same people cheering me on. I smiled, knowing that they supported me just as much as they supported Tracy.

I noticed Onijae clapping, which made me happy, but when I saw his girlfriend sitting down in her seat beside him, that quickly vanished. It didn't matter if I wanted Onijae or not. There was always going to be a reminder of why I couldn't have him for myself, which was why I'd pulled back.

Once I receive my diploma, I posed for a few pictures, and then I was on my way back to my seat.

"You do know how fine you are in that cap and gown, huh?" Tracy asked once I resumed my previous seat next to her.

"Same goes for you, bitch," I replied, cheesing hard as hell.

"I know, and I can't wait for them to see us once we change up out of these caps and gowns. If their mouths weren't open now, they'll definitely be open then," she said, smiling a sneaky grin.

"Bitch, you sad, but yes, they will," I cosigned with her.

I looked up on stage and noticed that the superintendent was giving the closing remarks, which meant that the ceremony was coming to an end. I was glad because I was more than ready to get on out of there.

Once the ceremony was over, we headed back to the hotel to get ready for our little get together that Ms. Lillian was throwing for us in their back yard. We decided that was all that we needed since we were leaving for Miami the next day. Now, I actually couldn't wait for that. I was even good with leaving the kids with Ms. Lillian.

"Come on, Delaney. My mother has been blowing my phone up wondering where we are!" Tracy yelled from somewhere in the suite.

"I'm coming now!" I yelled as I placed the last coat of lipstick on my lips. I then began to check myself out in the mirror. Once I was pleased with everything, I grabbed my clutch and headed out of the bathroom to meet up with her.

"Damn, bitch. You giving me a run for my money," she said as she walked around me. I was wearing a yellow two-piece lace casual maxi dress with a long split on the side of the skirt. I had on the earrings and bracelet that Tracy had given me that morning as a graduation present, with a pair of silver wedge heels and my silver clutch. She had on the exact same thing, but her outfit was red, and she had on a pair of gold wedges with her gold clutch. I swear we were banging from our heads to our toes. We were definitely going to turn heads the minute we stepped in that yard, and that was what I wanted to do. If Onijae hadn't been sweating me before, he was damn sure going to be sweating me now.

"Oh, shit. It's damn packed," Tracy said when we pulled up to her parents' house. There were so many cars all over the place that there wasn't even a place for us to park.

"Damn, where are we going to park at?" I asked her. We'd already circled the block, and everything was taken. Just as we were pulling back up, a few people came walking away from the yard and got in their cars and left.

"Bingo," she said, whipping into one of the spots like she was a race car driver. "Come on, bitch. Let's get out before we miss the party."

"Lord, I don't know what they're going to do with you today." I laughed as I got out of the car.

Right as we were about to walk around to the back yard, Tracy's phone rang. She answered it and said a few things before she walked off back toward her car. A few seconds later, a black Camaro pulled up. She then directed the car to pull up beside her in the empty spot, which it did. Once it was secured in the spot, whoever it was turned off the car. I watched as the door opened, and Aqura's sexy ass stepped out with two gift bags in his hand. I looked from him to Tracy, then back to him, and smiled.

"Don't be smiling. You better come over here and get his sexy ass before some thirsty bitch out here tries to!" she yelled, giving me that *Bitch, you better come on* look. Shaking my head at her, I walked over to where they were.

"You could've told me that you had invited him," I said to her once I reached them.

"Well, I didn't," she replied, poking her tongue out like a child.

Ignoring her, I turned to him. "Hey, you," I said, pulling him in for a hug.

"Hey, yourself. You look good as fuck," he replied, hugging me a bit tighter.

I didn't know why I suddenly began to feel shy, but I could feel the butterflies churning in my stomach. He then reached down and placed a kiss on my lips. That only made my stomach churn more.

"Hell no. We don't have time for that shit right now. Let's go," Tracy said, walking over and breaking us up.

"You're such a hater," I said, laughing as I wiped my lips and fixed my clothes.

"Here you go," Aqura said, handing her one of the two bags he had in his hand.

"Oh, he's a keeper," she said, accepting it. "Thank you, but really, y'all need to come on before my mother start blowing my phone up again."

"All right then, come on," I said as I grabbed Aqura's hand and followed her.

When we entered the back yard, just like Tracy had said, it was packed. We didn't predict that so many people would be there. Like always, Ms. Lillian did a wonderful job with the decorations. Everything was laid out beautifully, and the cake was wonderful.

"Girl, your momma did the damn thing once again," I told Tracy.

"Don't she always," she said, looking amused. "I'll be right back. Let me go holler at everyone."

"All right, cool," I said as I spotted my siblings heading our way. I wanted to laugh at Daija as I noticed her wobbling. She tried so hard to hide her pregnancy from people, but it was becoming harder and harder by the day. I swear, it was like she was almost to the end, and she was just beginning—which was why I couldn't wait for her to go to the doctor. Once I knew that she and the baby were safe, I was going to be even happier.

"This is for you," Aqura said, handing me the other bag.

"Thank you so much," I replied as I removed the bag from his hand. Leaning in, I gave him a kiss on his lips.

"You better stop that," he said, laughing.

"Only if ya want me to," I said just as Dallas jumped on top of me.

"I missed you too." I laughed, grabbing her into my arms.

"We've been waiting for you," she said, looking at Aqura.

"Hey, Delaney," Derrick and Dedrick said, giving me a hug. "You look pretty."

"Thanks y'all," I said, kissing the tops of their foreheads. "Y'all were being good for Ms. Lillian, right?"

"Yes, they were," Daija answered. "Hey, sis. You look pretty."

"So do you. You're glowing, by the way." I pulled her in for a hug. I hugged her a little longer because I wanted her to know that I loved her.

"I suppose this belly is the reason behind that," she whispered in my ear before she pulled back.

"I suppose so," I said with a smile. "Did you make a doctor's appointment yet?"

"As a matter of fact, I did, and my appointment is two weeks after the week y'all come back home. It's on a Wednesday," she replied, rolling her neck a little.

I excused that because I knew she was playing.

"And before you start with your shenanigans, I tried getting something a little earlier, but that was all they had," she said.

"All right, cool. Go get yourself something to eat and have a seat," I told her. "You don't need to be walking around and not eating in your predicament. Don't make me have to baby you up your whole pregnancy because you know I will. I won't think twice about it."

"Okay, enjoy your day, and congratulations, sis. We're so proud of you," she said as we hugged again. "All right, let me get out of here before we both start crying. You know how emotional I've been lately."

"Yes, I do, and thank you so much. All of this, plus my future accomplishments, will be for you all," I told her, meaning every word.

"I know, and I'll make you proud also. Just don't give up on me."

"You know I won't," I told her. "Now, go."

"All right now. You don't have to be so bossy. Come on, y'all," she said, smiling as they walked off toward the food tables.

Turning back to Aqura, I noticed that he looked a little uncomfortable. "Are you all right?" I asked him.

"Yes, I'm good. Just not used to being around so many people I don't know." He let out a nervous chuckle.

"You don't have a thing to be worried about. The Loves are the sweetest people in town. They're like my second family," I said, looking around at everyone in the yard.

My eyes just so happened to lock with Onijae's as he stood there talking to his friend and a few other people. I would have thought he was happy if it weren't for the mug that he had on his face. Dude looked pissed, and honestly, I kind of figured out why. I didn't know why he was mad when he had all that he needed right in front of him.

Pulling my eyes away from his, I decided that it would probably be best if I stayed clear of him. "You want something to eat or something?" I asked Aqura.

"Sure, and how about a drink too," he said, blowing air out of his mouth.

"Okay, I can do that, but first let me introduce you to Ms. Lillian," I replied as I spotted her, Tracy, Devin, Mr. Love, and Omari standing in a huddle. Before he could object, I grabbed his hand and began pulling him their way.

"Hello, everyone," I said once I reached them.

"Oh, hey, darling," Ms. Lillian said, hugging me. "Congratulations also."

"Thank you." I was smiling so hard my cheeks were hurting. I then went through a round of congratulations before I got to introduce Aqura. "Okay, everyone. I'd like for y'all to meet my friend, Aqura."

"Hello, darling," Ms. Lillian replied, shaking his hand.

I then watched as both Mr. Love and Omari sized him up before they welcomed him.

"What do we have here?" I heard Bianca's voice before I even saw her. Turning around, I saw her standing there attached so tight to Onijae's arm that she looked like she was cutting off his blood circulation.

"I know you better not start no drama because I have no problem putting you in your place in front of all these people," Tracy said before I could even open my mouth.

"All right now, there won't be none of that here," Mr. Love said to the both of them.

"Well, y'all better tell her to chill out. I don't even know why she's here in the first place."

"I'm here because my boyfriend asked me to come, that's why," she said smartly.

"All right, all right. Cut that shit out," Omari said, stepping in the middle of everyone. "Tee, you're not about to mess up your day. It's supposed to be a day of celebration, and that's what y'all two are going to do. Onijae, get ya girl, man, because if they jump her ass, that'll be good for her."

"I ain't scared of nobody," Bianca continued.

"Nobody said you was scared, but you're going to respect this day," Ms. Lillian said matter of factly. "Now, if you got a problem with that, you already know how to escort yourself from here."

"Come on, bae. Let's go get something to eat," Onijae said with his eyes focused on me.

I laughed because he was being the king of all petty people right now. I really hoped that he didn't think for one minute that I was bothered by any of it.

"Boy bye," Tracy said, laughing. "Come on, Dee. Grab ya boo and let's enjoy our day. We don't need these vultures ruining it."

"Come on, Aqura," I said, grabbing his hand.

I was trying to walk away, but Onijae and his pet were in my way.

"Can y'all please move."

"Y'all need to cut all of that attitude shit out. I'm getting tired of the both of y'all asses," he fussed as he moved to the side.

Ignoring him, I pushed past him, making sure that I rolled my eyes at his bitch in the process.

"Damn, what was all of that shit about?" Aqura asked me.

"Nothing. Let's just forget about it," I told him.

"Okay, fine by me," he replied as we made it to the food table.

I grabbed two plates and began putting food on one of them. I didn't even bother to ask him what he wanted because by the way he was eyeing the whole table, I knew that whatever I put on the plate would be good enough for him.

Once I was done, I handed him his plate and began fixing my own. I was hungry as hell, but I didn't fix a mountain plate. I wasn't the type to actually eat in front of people, especially not a man.

"What kind of drink you want?" I asked after we found an empty table.

"Just give me a beer while I eat this. Once I'm done, you can fix me a drink." He laughed.

"All right, cool. I'll be right back," I replied and headed inside where the drinks were. Once I located the drinks, I grabbed a beer for Aqura and a soda for me.

"You really brought that nigga up to my parents' house?" I heard Onijae ask behind me.

"Your parents don't have a problem with it, so I don't know why you're even speaking on it," I said, giving him major attitude.

"Well, I do," he had the nerve to say.

"That's none of my concern. Now, move out of my way, so I can go back to my date." I was trying to walk past him, but he blocked me.

"Why are you doing this?" he asked, grabbing my arm.

"What are you talking about?" I asked him.

"You know you want me, Delaney. Why are you playing hard to get? Most of all, why the hell are you here with him?"

"First of all, I'm not playing hard to get. I just know my worth and know what I deserve. It sure as hell ain't a man who's already got a woman with enough problems. I'm not meant to be nobody's side piece, and I'll be damned if I'll be some man's other woman. Okay, yes, I do want you. I want you more than anything, but I can't be that other woman. I just can't, which is why I'm choosing the man with none, so that I can be his only woman. Excuse me for having a little bit of dignity, but I have to go," I said, damn near in tears.

I wanted him to be my man, but like I said, I wasn't fit to be any man's other woman. I'd watched women play second to men who would never be with them. I refused to put myself in that same predicament. I was a queen, and if that meant being alone, then so be it.

"Let me go, Onijae," I pleaded, but he only tightened the hold he had on my arm.

Before I knew it, his lips were covering mine. Somehow, I found myself kissing him back. I didn't mean to, but my body had a mind of its own.

"Y'all gon' need to stop that shit before y'all get busted," a voice said from somewhere in the room.

Pulling back, I saw Omari standing there, shaking his head.

"Correct me if I'm wrong, but didn't the both of you come here with someone else?"

"Yes," I answered shamefully. I couldn't believe that I had let Onijae get to me again. "I'm sorry."

"You don't have to apologize," he said, walking over to me. "I see that my little brother has gotten his claws into you. However, the question is, are you ready to be someone's side chick? Because honestly, I don't think he's going to leave Bianca. I mean, after everything she's put him through, he's still there, which is something that I don't get, but that's on him. Now, I look at you as if you were my little sister, and I just think this right here is not what ya want or need."

"O, man, chill out," Onijae said, but Omari gave him this crazy look.

"I'm down for you, little brother, but I just can't let you ruin this girl's life. I mean, she's been through enough already," he told him. He then turned back to me. "You are a queen. You deserve a man who's going to love you and only you. I can see that you have a few issues that you need to solve, but you gotta respect yaself, Delaney. Do you want to be someone's side chick?"

"No," I answered sadly.

"Well, you already know what you have to do then," he said, moving to the side.

Nodding my head, I pulled my arm from Onijae's hold and headed back to the party. I didn't even bother looking back because I was too embarrassed.

On my way out, I noticed Bianca giving me the evil eye. The bitch was really starting to get on my nerves, but still, I decided not to address her. She wasn't even worth my time, and quite frankly, she was mad with the wrong person. Who she needed to be mad with was her nigga. He was the man who didn't want to leave me alone, the man she shared history with, the man who was obligated to her, not me. I could be petty and let her know a thing or two, but she didn't need to. Instead, I blew her a kiss as I headed back to the table where Aqura was seated, talking to my little brothers.

"Hey," I said, setting the beer down in front of him. I took a few bites of my food as I watched them play. "Are they giving you a hard time?"

"Who? These little dudes?" he asked, tickling them. "Nah, they're cool. What's up, though? You good?"

"I'm fine, actually," I said as I turned to look around. I noticed Bianca and Onijae having what looked to be a heated conversation about whatever. I was pretty sure that I was the topic, but again, that was their problem.

"Do they always fight like that?" he asked.

"Who?" I asked, turning back around to face him.

"Them." He nodded his head toward Onijae and Bianca.

"I have no idea," I replied just as Tracy appeared.

"Oh, no, girl. Get your ass up and let's party. We just graduated from high school, and you're over here being a prude," she said, pulling my arm.

"Tracy—"

I tried to object, but she hushed me.

"I don't want to hear that shit. Get up and let's go." She pulled me to the middle of the yard.

"Hey, y'all, it's our graduation day!" she yelled as she began to dance. "Come on, Dee. Don't leave me hanging. Everybody come and get on the dance floor with us."

Just like that, the middle of the yard was packed with people dancing. I even saw Mr. and Mrs. Love dancing, and boy, was that hilarious. I wasn't doing anything until Dallas came and grabbed my hands and began dancing. Everyone knew that I couldn't turn my baby down, which was how I ended up moving to the beat as well. Even Aqura and Daija came and danced.

The party didn't stop until ten that night, which was way too late for the kids. It was a good thing that they didn't have school the next day, because all of them would've been dragging. Even though my parents weren't there to celebrate one of the biggest days of my life, I was happy to be surrounded by people who loved and cared for us.

Now that it was over, it was time for me to get back to being the big sister my siblings needed me to be. Well, after our trip to Miami.

"Bitch, come on," Tracy screamed as she continuously blew the horn of her car. I looked around frantically as I tried to see if people were looking at us. "You been with that nigga all night. It's time for y'all to say goodbye to each other."

I know what y'all may think, but y'all are wrong. Yes, I did go home with Aqura, but I didn't go to bed with him. Well, yes, we slept in the same bed, but we didn't do anything besides cuddle and kiss. We practically lay there all night, getting to know each other. It felt natural to talk about each other and our families. Of course, I broke down when I told him about my parents and how they'd died. Lucky for me, he was there to comfort me. He held me in his arms as I cried. He didn't speak a word. He just sat there and listened, and I was happy for that.

When the morning came, he went back with me to the hotel and stayed with me until Tracy pulled up. The kids had been at Ms. Lillian's since the night before, so I didn't have to worry about them. However, I did call to make sure that they were straight and behaving correctly. I also thanked Ms. Lillian, but she tried to hang up on me. She told me that it wasn't a problem for her and that I should enjoy my trip. She promised me that if anything was to happen, she would call me, and other than that, she didn't want me ringing her phone line for anything. I laughed but agreed. I mean, she said that I couldn't ring her line. She didn't say anything about me ringing Daija's phone.

"You are such a damn hater. Let me live a little. Do I tell you anything when you and your boo be all lovey dovey," I replied, giving her the finger. I then turned back to Aqura.

"I'm going to miss you," I said, feeling this giddy feeling in the pit of my stomach. I felt so comfortable around him, and he made me feel so special. He respected me, and he didn't push up on me. He was willing to be patient, and for that I was happy.

"I'm going to miss you too." He gave me a kiss. "Make sure you text me when y'all make it there."

"I will. Be safe, boo," I said as I attempted to pull away, but he pulled me back and kissed me again.

"I swear, if you don't come ya ass on, I'ma leave your ass here and enjoy this vacation by my damn self," Tracy said, getting back in the car.

Rolling my eyes, I pulled myself away from Aqura.

"Damn, shorty's mean as hell," he replied.

"Actually, she's not. It's just that we've been talking about this trip for four years, and now that it's finally here, she don't want to miss it, and neither do I," I corrected him. "I'll talk to you when I get back, okay?"

"All right. I'll see ya later, ma," he said, giving me a quick peck on the lips.

Letting go of his hands, I turned around and headed over to Tracy's car. Opening the door, I turned back and waved before finally getting in.

"Bitch, you know you're wrong for that shit," I said as she pulled off, heading straight for the airport.

"I'm not wrong for shit. Y'all was getting on my damn nerves anyway." All of a sudden, she burst into a fit of laughter. "Don't be mad with me, Dee. I wasn't able to see my man this morning, so I'm a little jealous. Charge it to my head and not my heart."

"Yeah, yeah, whatever," I said, waving her off.

The rest of the ride to the airport was quiet, not because we were beefing, but because I was lost in my thoughts, and she was lost in hers.

"Come on, Dee," Tracy said pulling me out of my thoughts.

When I looked around, we were sitting in the airport's parking lot.

"Your ass must have flown here, huh?" I asked as she parked the car and we got out.

Walking around to the trunk, we grabbed our bags and headed inside of the airport. I didn't want to admit it, but my heart was beating fast as hell. I'd never in my seventeen years of life been on an airplane, which was why I was standing in line scared as hell. The line ended up moving faster than I thought it would, and just like that, we were boarding the plane and headed to Miami. I only hoped that this trip would be as exciting as we hoped it was going to be.

Chapter Twelve

Tracey

"What up, Tee?"

I felt someone tapping on my shoulder. I moved my shoulder, hoping that they would just leave me alone.

"Tracy, wake up!"

"Hell, what?" I asked, opening my eyes. For a split second, I had forgotten where we were until I looked over at Delaney and saw here sitting there with her lips poked out. "Why are you looking at me like that?

"Because I've been trying to wake your ass up for the past five or so minutes, that's damn why," she answered as she stood up. "I'm guessing you want to go back home, since you're still sitting there."

"Ha ha, funny. All ya had to say was that we were here," I said, getting up and stretching. I then grabbed my purse and headed to the exit.

"So, what's the first thing you plan on doing while we're here?" she asked as we headed to get the rest of our bags.

"Bitch, do you really have to ask? We're definitely about to go party," she said, doing a quick little one-two step.

"I know you better not try and dance like that," I joked.

"Girl, please. Then my nigga hit me up with a couple of fake IDs, so ya know it's about to be on and popping."

"Uh-huh, you better not be getting us into no damn trouble." She sounded like a grandma.

"Bitch, I don't want to hear that shit. We're about to live these five days up like they're going to be our last," I said, heading to find the exit and the nearest cab. I'd waited four years for this trip, and I was damn sure going to enjoy it.

"Delaney, are you ready?" I yelled as I walked around, making sure everything was straight for when we left in the next few minutes.

"Here I come!" she yelled. A few seconds later, she appeared, and as always, baby girl was killing it.

"I see why my brother be going crazy over you."

"Girl, shut up and come on," she responded, smiling so hard. "You're not so bad yourself."

"All right, come on. Let's go," I said, picking up her phone, which had rung. "Our ride is here, and we can't be late."

"Do I have to be scared or concerned or something?" she joked, laughing.

"No, boo, because just like Allstate, we're going to be in good hands. Now, come the hell on," I said, heading for the door.

We left the room and headed for the elevator. We spent the whole ride down to the lobby trying to make sure we were both straight. We even stood in the elevator's mirror and snapped a few pictures. Once the elevator reached the first floor, we got out.

"Come on. They're parked out front waiting for us," I told her. I couldn't wait to see her face when she got in the car and saw exactly who it was that we were meeting. She was going to be shocked, but all too thrilled at the same time.

"Where?" she asked as we stood out front. Just then, a stretch Cadillac pulled up. The door opened, and she stepped back.

"Come on, girl," I said, grabbing her hand, pulling her toward the car.

"Bitch, I know this ain't for us," she said, all too happy.

"Would I be getting in it if it wasn't for us?" I replied, leaving her standing out there.

"Bitch, I could just kiss you. This is the best graduation gift ever!" I heard her yell. She then hopped in, acting all girly and happy like she normally did when I would do something to make her happy.

"How about you just kiss me instead?" a voice said to her.

I swear, she looked up so fast. Hell, someone would've thought her neck was broken.

"Aqura?" she asked like she didn't see him sitting there. Before he could even reply, she jumped into his arms, placing kisses on his lips.

"Damn, shorty. You missed a nigga that much?"

"Yup," she replied, grinning like a schoolgirl. "Why? You don't miss me?"

"You know a nigga missed you, shorty," he told her.

"Uh, y'all really work on my damn nerves," I told them both. "I'm over here trying to have a good time. A nigga ain't tryna see y'all asses kissing all damn night."

"Anyways," she said, giving me the hand. She then stuck up her middle finger before turning her attention back to Aqura. "How did you get here?"

"Actually, we were on the same plane. I had first class tickets, though," he said, winking his eye at me.

"Shit, you balling, not me. I got what my money could afford. Next time your ass will be paying for our tickets, and we do want to ride in first class, baby," I told him as a matter of fact. I was playing, but I was serious at the same time.

"You got that, shorty," he said just as the limo came to a stop.

Looking out of the window, I noticed that we were in front of a club. I didn't believe it, but I became nervous as I noticed all the people standing outside.

"Are you going to get out, or do you plan to sit there?" he asked.

"Oh, my bad," I said getting out. No lie, I wanted to jump right back in there. From the moment that I stepped out of the limo, all eyes were on me. I was happy that I looked fly as fuck because the way they were looking had me scared to even walk.

"Come on. Follow me," he said, walking toward the entrance.

"Umm, you're forgetting something," I said, stopping him before he could go any farther. "We can't go in there."

"Why not?"

"Because we're not old enough, and apparently, you don't have the IDs I asked ya for," I said, looking at him sideways.

"Chill out, shorty. I got this. Now, come on," he said as he continued to the door.

I'd gone to clubs a few times back home, but being in a new environment had me a little afraid. What if they found out that we weren't old enough? What if they called the police and we got arrested? There were a lot of questions that were flowing through my mind.

"What's up, boss man?" I heard one of the bouncers say. I looked around, trying to see where he was, but I didn't see anyone. When I noticed him and Aqura dapping each other up, I was shocked.

"How's shit been going, Gust?" Aqura asked him.

I noticed how Delaney looked at me with a questioning look. I knew she probably wanted to know if I knew anything about him being a club owner, but I was just as clueless as she was at that point.

"I had no idea," I mouthed to her as we continued to stand there looking like fools.

"Everything's been cool. The crowd keeps getting bigger and bigger, but me and my boys got it."

"All right, good. Where that nigga Alfred at?"

"He's up there in his office," Gust replied as he removed the rope and let Aqura walk through. Delaney and I tried to walk behind him, but dude stopped us. "And where do y'all think y'all going?"

"It's cool, Gust. They're with me. Let them through, big dog," Aqura turned around and told him.

Of course, we heard the bitches in line sucking their teeth, but that was to be expected. Hell, if I would've been standing in that line damn near all night, I would've done the same damn thing.

"Remember their faces, Gust, because I think you'll be seeing them a lot."

"You got it, boss." He nodded as we headed inside of the club.

Now, I'd been to about two hands full of clubs, and none of them topped this one. It was huge on the inside, and just like the many people that were outside waiting to get in, there were more inside. I honestly didn't know how everyone was even going to fit in there. That's how packed it already was.

"Aye, y'all follow me to the VIP area!" he screamed over the loud music.

Nodding our heads, we followed him up the stairs. When we made it to the VIP area, I kind of felt a little self-conscious. I mean, every bitch in there was bad from her head to her fucking feet. Most of all, I saw big butts and pretty smiles. There wasn't a female in there that was half stepping, and I meant that literally.

"Y'all have a seat in that section over there." He pointed toward an empty section. "I'll send a waiter with something for y'all to drink. I'ma go run up to the office. I'll be back in a minute."

"Okay, cool," we both replied.

He kissed Delaney yet again before he disappeared.

"Bitch, I thought that nigga was off the chain before, but this shit right here is on a whole 'nother level," I said once he was gone. "That nigga ain't tell you about this shit?"

"Girl, hell no, and I'm kind of pissed, too," she had the nerve to say.

"The hell? Why are you pissed?"

"Because he ain't tell me 'bout this shit." She sounded like someone I know all too well.

"All right, Bianca," I deliberately said to her because that was just who she was acting like. I mean, she just met the dude, and she expected him to tell her his life story. Shit, she better not say shit to him when he came back, or we'd be having a few words of our own.

"Bitch, fuck you. That bitch could never be me, not even on my worst fucking day," she replied angrily, just like I had expected her to.

I was about to respond when the server appeared with a tray with four drinks on it.

"Mr. Coleman asked that I bring these to you ladies."

"I'm guessing he told you to go with something fruity, right?" I asked sarcastically because they were treating us like some children.

"Nah, actually he just told me to fix what I want. Now, don't let this drink fool you. It may be fruity, but this shit will sneak up on you and put you on ya ass in a heartbeat," she said as she began unloading the glasses on the table.

"Well, in that case, thanks," I replied as I grabbed my purse and removed a twenty-dollar bill. I tried handing it to her, but she stopped me.

"Thanks, but you don't have to give me no tip. I'm only doing my job, boo. Besides, Mr. Coleman pays me enough," she said, sounding a little too happy for me.

"Umm, okay. Thanks again," I told her once more. I waited until she was gone to turn my attention to Delaney. "You thinking what I'm thinking?"

"If you're thinking that Aqura and ol' girl have something going on, then yes, we're thinking the same thing."

"Yesss, bitch," I said, agreeing with her. "That bitch was a little too happy when she said that shit. Did he mention anything about having an ol' lady or something?"

"Bitch, please. If he would've said anything about that, I wouldn't have continued to be bothered with him," she said, grabbing her drink and taking a few sips from it.

I watched as her face did a twist before it relaxed.

"What the hell is wrong with you, girl?" I asked, looking at her closely.

"Bitch, this drink is off the fucking map." She took a few more sips.

"I should slap the shit out of you for acting like that behind a damn drink," I told her just as the DJ spun Rihanna and Drake's song, "Work." It just so happened to be one of my and Delaney's favorite songs. Oh, how many days we spent winding our bodies in the mirror like the chicks from Africa.

"Oh, shit," she said, moving in her seat.

"Hell no, bitch! Come on. Let's get up and head over there by the railings to watch," I said, rising to my feet. Before I made a move, I placed a napkin over my other drink. Hell, I couldn't have nobody spiking my drinky drink.

"Come on, Dee," I yelled as I began winding my hips in a circular motion.

Together we got the attention of everyone in the VIP area. There wasn't an eye that wasn't trained on us. That just boosted our egos up some more. I did notice the bitches turning their noses up because their niggas were looking. So, I thought I'd give them a little more to be mad about. Grabbing Delaney's hand, I spun her around so that her back was turned to me. Being that we were best friends and were not gay, she didn't move. Hell, she knew what I was about to do because we had practiced that dance for times like those.

The minute we started bumping and grinding on each other, it was a wrap. Every man in the section was basically drooling, and some females were too. We didn't stop dancing on each other until the song was over. By that time, Aqura and some unknown man was sitting at the table, waiting on us. When I tell you dude was fine, that couldn't quite describe him. Just like Aqura, he was dark skinned, and oh, how I loved me some dark men. He had to weight about 220 or something like that, and it was pure muscle. He sported a goatee and a head full of shoulder-length dreads. He was dressed in some blue jeans, a black V-neck, and some black Air Max 98s. He topped that off with a chain and watch that screamed money. Now, I wasn't money hungry, because a bitch has had her own since the day I was born, but I found myself kind of turned on.

"Y'all doing it like that?" dude asked with a raised eyebrow.

"If that's what ya say," I said with a hint of an attitude.

"Whoa nah, shorty. You don't have to be like that," he said, throwing his hands up in defense. All of a sudden, he burst out laughing.

"I see what you was saying, man," he said to Aqura.

"And what did he say?" Delaney answered, looking at him.

"All right, all right. I'm done. Y'all got me," he replied as he stood up.

I didn't miss the way he kept looking at me as he bit his bottom lip.

"I told you they were feisty, bruh," Aqura said, also standing up.

"Shit, I can see that. Especially shorty right there," he said, pointing at me.

"I got a name, and it damn sure ain't shorty," I said, rolling my neck at him.

"This here is Tracy, and this is Delaney," he said, pointing at me, then Dee. "Y'all, this is my man Fred."

"Pleased to meet you, Delaney," he said, giving her a hug. He then turned to me and stared.

"What?" I asked, turning my nose up.

"I like how you trying to play hard to get. I'ma break you out of that before you leave, li'l mama."

"Uh-huh," I said, waving him off.

He walked closer to me, which made my heart start to beat fast.

"You got a man?"

"Why?"

"Because I'm trying to make you mine, that's why," he said, inching even closer to me.

"Where your old lady at?"

"I don't have one," he said.

"Yeah, tell me anything." I took a much-needed step back. I don't know how and why, but that man had me feeling shy, and I never was one to be shy.

"I'm serious, boo." He pulled his phone out of his pocket. "Put ya number in my phone. I'd love to call you sometimes."

My heart was telling me to exit the stage left, but my mind was singing a different tune. I knew that I was with Devin, but somehow, I found this dude intriguing. Going against everything my heart was screaming, I grabbed his phone and programmed my number in his contacts. I then handed it back to him as he stood there continuing to stare at me.

"Stop staring at me like that," I told him

"I can't help it. You're so beautiful, shorty," he said, causing me to blush. "I'll see ya later. Make sure you're still here."

"I-I will be," I stuttered, barely able to get my words out. *Lord, please help me.* I closed my eyes as I tried to calm my racing heart rate.

"All right, shorty," he said, grabbing my hand.

When his lips connected with my skin, I thought I was going to pass out. My body was on fire, and normally that feeling was a good thing, but he was a total stranger. I watched him as he dapped Aqura up and left the room, taking my ability to breathe with him.

"Bitch, what the hell just happened?" Delaney asked, grabbing my shoulder. "I know damn well you didn't just give dude your number."

"I don't even know my damn self, and yes I did," I answered shamefully.

"I don't mean to knock you off your high horse, but what about Devin?"

"What are you talking about? We're good," I said, launching a nervous laugh.

"Shit, from the way that you were just cheesed up in ol' boy's face, I could've sworn that you were single and shit. I hope like hell you know what you're doing, girl, because love is definitely a dangerous drug," she responded. "Come on. Let's go sit back down."

I followed her as she headed back to the table. I didn't say a word because I knew I was wrong. If Devin found out, he was going to kill me, which was why I was going to do everything in my power for him not to find out. Lord knows I didn't want to hurt him, but still, that man had piqued my interest. Would we start something? I really didn't know, but I'd be honest and say that I was scared a little bit.

Delaney

Miami had been nothing but nice to us. We'd been down there for three days, with two days left, and I must say, I was enjoying my trip. The guys made sure that we experienced nothing but the very best. We didn't have to spend a dime of our money, so whatever we wanted, they paid for. They even moved us from our hotel room and booked us a suite at the Four Seasons. Yes, it was that serious. They wanted to make sure that we were comfortable and safe, even though they barely left us alone. However, I thought it was cute, and I was more than glad that I didn't have to worry about hiding or being caught, like I had with Onijae. I was happy and free to do what I wanted with Aqura, and it felt so damn good.

"Delaney, you like this?" Tracy asked me.

We'd been shopping for the past two hours, and I was ready to go. The guys planned on taking us to dinner on a boat, and that looney tune was trying to make sure everything was perfect. I'd already found a nice black dress to wear. Unlike her, I wasn't picky. I mean, I was going to look hooked up either way, but I didn't take shit to the extreme. She was a perfectionist who always made sure to cross her T's and dot her I's. She was a showstopper nevertheless, which was why she always took forever and a day when she went shopping.

"Tracy, please! The last few outfits you picked out were a hit, and I told you that, but you don't want to listen to me. So, pick whatever you feel is good enough for you. Just hurry up because we still have to go to the nail shop and then go get our hair done," I said, grabbing my ringing phone from my purse.

Looking at the screen, I noticed that it was Onijae calling me. I stood there deciding if I should answer the phone. He'd been calling me for the past three days, and I had yet to answer him. I just couldn't seem to get why he was calling me when he had Bianca by his side.

"Girl, your brother is blowing my phone up again."

"Man, see what the fuck he wants because he's starting to get on my damn nerves with his stalking ass." She rolled her eyes so hard I thought they were going to pop out of their sockets.

I laughed because although he was her brother, she was acting like she couldn't stand the ground he walked on.

"How may I help out?" I asked, answering the phone after what seemed like the tenth ring. I didn't forget to add a hint of an attitude either.

"Damn, that's how you answering the phone for me now?" he asked, sounding a little hurt. "I guess that nigga must be got ya feeling that way, huh?"

"Onijae, I don't have time to be going back and forth with you. Now, tell me how I can help you," I said, ignoring what he'd said. I knew he was just trying to get a reaction out of me, so I wasn't trying to fall for that.

"I miss you, Delaney. I miss the conversations we had late at night, and I miss the feeling of your body wrapped in my arms," he said, causing my stomach to churn.

I hoped he didn't think for one second that I was trying to listen to any of that bullshit he was spitting out of his mouth. I mean, a man would do and say anything when he wanted something.

"You can miss me with that bullshit, Onijae, because I'm not trying to hear it. I've already told you that there won't be a you and me because I'm not going to be the other woman to any man," I preached to him.

"But what if I leave her for you?" he replied.

I stopped and stood there for a moment. Would he really leave his longtime girlfriend for me? Was I making the right choice here? That was the million-dollar question that I needed an answer to. Then Omari's words came playing through my mind as if he was saying them for the first time again. *Are you ready to be someone's side chick? Because, honestly, I don't think he's going to leave Bianca. I mean, after everything she's put him through, he's still there, which is something that I don't get, but that's on him.* The minute I heard the words, I knew in my mind that I was making the right choice.

"You're not about to leave your longtime girlfriend for me, Onijae, so let's not even play like that, okay," I said just as I spotted Tracy at the register, purchasing whatever it was that she was getting to wear on our double date that night.

"Look, shorty, I'm not playing any games here. I want to be with you. Just let me come see you." He tried again, but I was already over it.

"No, thank you. Now, if you don't want anything else that's not impossible to get, I have to go," I said without giving him a chance to respond. I placed my phone back in my purse, grabbed my bags, and walked over to Tracy.

"What the hell did he want?" she asked with the screwface.

"Do you even have to ask?" I rolled my eyes. "He just won't quit it. Talking 'bout he was going to leave his girlfriend for me. I wish I was close to him, so that I could slap the dog shit out of his ass."

"The fuck he will. He's only saying that because he sees you entertaining someone else. Trust me, if he hadn't, he'd still be the same Onijae he was before Aqura came back around," she said, taking her bag from the cashier. She grabbed her change, then we turned and headed for the exit.

"Trust me, girl, that boy is selfish as fuck to try and pull some shit like that on you. Don't you go falling for that okie-doke."

"Bitch, how do you know so much about this?" I asked curiously.

"Besides my mother putting me up on game, I've had my heart broken a time or two. I learned from that shit and kept my game tight ever since. Not to mention, I noticed the way my brothers treat their women. So, you can say I learned the game from them too."

"Girl, your ass," I said, laughing at how much of an old lady she sounded like.

"Say what you want, but take my advice and you'll never have to worry about a nigga trying to run game on you and you taking the shit like a dumb-ass bitch. Don't go around here allowing no man to make you his side woman," she advised. "Now, come on. Let's go get ready for our date. I'm tryna use a rubber tonight."

"You are such a dog," I told her, laughing at her choice of words.

"Call me what you want, but just know I ain't no nigga's side chick," she responded.

"Uh-huh. You just better not let Devin find out that you got a side piece," I reminded her.

She didn't say anything. She only winked her eye at me.

I couldn't do anything but shake my head at her. Tracy was my girl for life, but I also knew that she was playing with fire. Hopefully, she wouldn't be the one getting burned.

"You look yummy," Aqura said, rubbing his hands together.

"Thank you so much," I said, pulling my dress down. I had no idea why it kept moving up my thighs, but it was beginning to get on my nerves.

Besides that, I was a little worried about Daija. She had called me earlier talking about a fight that she and her boyfriend—well, her baby daddy—had gotten into. She said she caught him at school hugged up with some other female, and then one thing led to another. I was happy school would be over for them the next day because the summer break was just what they needed.

"What's wrong?" he asked once he noticed that my mind had drifted off.

"Nothing," I said, deciding not to talk about it.

"Come on, Delaney. Don't give me that. I know something is bothering you. You can talk to me, shorty." He grabbed my hand.

"I'm just thinking about my sister, that's all," I said just to ease his mind.

"Is everything okay with her?"

"Yes, she just been a little bit stressed, that's all," I replied, hoping he would get the hint and leave the subject alone.

"Well, I hope everything gets better for her," he replied as we headed for the car.

We were unable to go on the boat ride because the captain of the boat got ill at the last minute. So, a simple dinner date was what we decided to do.

"Thank you, boo," I said, rubbing the back of his hand.

"Always," I replied as we arrived at Red Lobster. Yup, that was just what I wanted to eat. I heard that the lobster tails and shrimp were to die for, so I wanted to go.

Tracy didn't care one way or another since she was too busy flirting and whatever else her ass was doing with Fred's finessing ass. I really hoped she knew what she was doing. I mean, just a few days ago, she was madly in love with Devin and she wanted nothing but to be publicly involved with him. Now, there she was in Miami, being seen publicly with someone else.

I wasn't judging her at all. Hell, I was in a predicament with a man who was trying to make me a side chick, so there was no way I could talk about her. I just wanted her to be careful. Hell, I needed her to be.

As we were entering the restaurant, Fred's phone began ringing. Now, there was nothing wrong with a person's phone ringing, but when it was constantly ringing back to back, it was a problem. Then I already knew that Tracy was aggravated by the way her face was screwed up. I knew she wanted so badly to say something, but she didn't.

"Hello, and welcome to Red Lobster. How many people will be sitting with you all tonight?" the hostess asked.

"The four people you see right in front of you," Tracy said to her with an attitude. I already knew why she was mad, but she didn't have to take it out on the poor girl, though.

"Okay, ma'am. Let me go check and see if a table is ready. I'll be right back," she answered, not really worried too much about Tracy or her attitude. I guess she was used to people talking to her like that.

I was glad it was her and not me, because I didn't know if I would be able to take someone being that rude to me, especially when I knew that I didn't do a damn thing wrong.

"Thank you," I said in an apologetic tone. When she left, I shot my eyes over at Tracy. She looked at me and hunched her shoulders. I couldn't do anything but shake my head at her and the way she was acting.

"Okay, I found you all a table in the back." The hostess reappeared. She then grabbed four menus from the post. "Follow me right this way."

We followed her as she led us to a table in the middle of the restaurant. I wanted to tell her that I wanted one by the window, but I didn't want to be a pain to her. Once we reached the table, we all took seats as the hostess placed a menu in front of each of us. Since we obviously weren't ready to order any food, she took our drink orders instead.

Once she was gone, we began studying the menu, trying to figure out what we wanted. For the first five minutes, everything was great, until Fred's phone started ringing once again. Even I was beginning to get frustrated by the fact that he wasn't answering it. He would just peek to see who it was. I guessed it was someone he didn't want to be bothered with because he would just put the phone back in his pocket.

"Come walk with me to the bathroom right quick, Delaney," Tracy said as she stood up. She didn't even wait for me as she walked off toward the bathroom.

I looked at Aqura, who was sitting there looking as if he already knew what was up. I then looked at Fred, who was sitting there looking unbothered by it all. Shaking my head, I got up from the table as I headed to the bathroom. The whole way, I was fuming inside.

"What the hell is your problem?" I asked once I entered the bathroom and saw her standing in front of the mirror.

"Really, Delaney?" she asked. "I don't have a problem, and I know damn well you see Fred out there disrespecting me and shit."

"Tracy, you've had a problem since we first got here, and you know it. Bad thing is, you out there catching an attitude with the wrong damn person. Fred is the person you're mad with, and yet you're taking it out on that poor girl. Tracy, I've never seen you act like this. What's wrong with you?"

"Because that nigga got me fucked up. He has no idea who I am. I went out of my way to get cute for this date, and he pulls this kind of bullshit," she said as she continued to rant. "It's obvious that the nigga got a woman, but he's asking me if I got a man and shit. Like, really, dude?"

"I'm not even trying to hear that shit, Tracy," I said, waving her off. "I told you from the beginning not to get involved with a man you don't know, but you ain't want to hear that shit. You thought you had everything in the bag, but I guess you didn't. You tryna fall in love with a man you only knew for two damn days?"

"Bitch, don't get this shit confused. That nigga is cute, and I'm here in Miami on my dream vacation since ninth grade with my best fucking friend. I ain't trying to fall in love. I was, however, trying to get my pussy wet and maybe wined and dined a bit too." She flashed me a smile.

"Bitch, please. You ain't fooling nobody. You was big mad."

"To be honest, yeah, I was mad, bitch, and all that shit I just said was a front. I did want that nigga, even though I just met him. Crazy thing is, I was never planning on giving Devin up. Hell, they live in two different states. Why can't I have fun like men do all the time?" she foolishly asked.

"Bitch, whatever. Come on. Let's get back to those fools. I really can't take you right now," I said, heading for the door.

"I don't know why you think I'm playing, but I'm not," she said, following me. "I truly hope this nigga answers his phone, or powers it the hell off, because if it rings again, I'ma flip the hell out."

"Uh-huh," was all I said as we left the bathroom.

The minute we stepped out, we heard fussing coming from somewhere inside the restaurant. I didn't know who it was, but whoever it was, their girlfriend was going off on them about playing with other females and shit. That shit instantly made me think about Onijae and Bianca. That could've been me, but I was happy that I'd dodged that bullshit.

"Girl, home girl is going off. If I was her nigga, I'd be ashamed," Tracy said as we rounded the corner.

"You ain't lying. She's airing all of that nigga's dirty laundry and shit," I said, shaking my head. That shit was too embarrassing—add the fact that it was in front of a restaurant full of people.

As we continued to walk, my phone rang. Pulling it out of my pocket, I saw I had a message from Aqura.

"Bitch, I know you lying!" Tracy yelled all of a sudden.

"What?" I asked, looking at her.

She didn't reply, but she had this sour look on her face as she stared at whatever. I followed the line of her vision and couldn't believe it. My mouth instantly dropped when I noticed that the loud-talking woman, along with some other woman, was standing at our table. What was crazy was the fact that both Aqura and Fred were sitting there looking at the one who was yelling, which didn't give me a clue of who she was talking to.

"Ain't this some fucking bullshit," I said.

"Dee, you know I'm not scared, and if either one of them bitches say something to me, I'm going to jail for whooping her ass," Tracy said as she headed straight for the table.

Instead of sitting down back in her seat, she stood there, and I did the same. I knew that stance. We'd stood in it a few times before when we had to mess someone up.

"Oh, I guess y'all the bitches they fucking with, huh?" the woman said once she noticed us standing there. I could tell from by the way she was rolling her neck and eyes that she was trying to start some shit.

Her little friend didn't say anything. She just stood there looking at us with her arms folded across her chest. I noticed how she kept looking at Aqura, but I didn't say anything.

"Bitch, let me tell you something," Tracy told her. "First of all, I'm not the fucking one to play with. You're out here embarrassing yaself and shit when you could've handled that shit differently, and—"

Before Tracy could continue saying what she wanted, that chick cut her off. "I'm not even trying to hear none of that shit. Y'all don't even look old enough. Hell, look like y'all still in high school. Can y'all even buy a fucking drink? So, what, Fred? You're robbing the cradle and shit now?" she asked, looking at him.

So, we knew who she was there for after that. He didn't say anything, though. He just looked at her as she continued to make an ass out of herself.

"Know what, Tee? Let's go. We're not even about to give this bitch what she wants," I said, grabbing our purses off the table.

"Girl, fuck this shit," she said as we walked off.

"Delaney." I heard my name being called, but I didn't even bother to look back. I didn't have any words to say. That shit was ridiculous, and I didn't have time for it.

"How are we going to get back to the hotel?" she asked. "We rode with them, girl."

"We can call a cab or something," I replied as I pulled my phone out.

I got on the Internet to find the number for a cab service. Once I found it, I dialed it and ordered a cab to come and get us. I was happy when they said that there was a cab already in the area because I didn't think I would be able to last another ten minutes out here. I told them that we were going to be walking up the street before I hung up.

"Come on, Tee."

"Delaney!" I heard my name again. Ignoring him, I continued to walk up the street.

"I can't believe this shit," Tracy said, laughing. "We came here to have fun and get away from drama, and drama found us way in a whole 'nother state."

"Shit, tell me about it," I responded as I began laughing with her.

Right then, a car pulled up behind us. Turning, I saw the cab, along with the car Aqura and Fred had come to pick us up in. Not really up to talk to any of them, we headed for the cab just as the car door opened and they got out.

"Delaney," Aqura said, doing a light jog toward the cab.

I opened the door and got in. Just when I was about to close the door, he stopped me.

"What's your problem?" he had the nerve to ask me.

"Hell, if you got to ask that, something is wrong with you." I tried to close the door again. By then, I looked over and noticed that Fred had pulled Tracy up out of the car. Rolling my eyes, I turned back to Aqura. "Y'all made us look like damn fools up in there."

"Man, that didn't have a thing to do with me. That was Fred's baby mama, not mine," he replied as he ran his hand over his face.

"I told him to get her ass in check, but he didn't want to listen." He said that last part loud enough for Fred to hear.

"That's all good and shit, but don't put all that shit on Fred. I saw homegirl looking at you as if she was hurt as well. Who's she to you?" I asked.

He looked at me, but he didn't say anything, which was all the answer I needed.

"Yeah, I thought so. Now, can you please move, so I can go? Tracy, come on."

"Delaney, don't leave," he pleaded.

Just like I was before, I remained silent as I looked straight ahead.

"Tracy!" I yelled once more. Two seconds later, she was getting in the cab.

The cab driver was ready to go, but Aqura was still blocking the door.

"I mean, really?" I said.

"All right, shorty," he said, throwing his hands up. He looked at me one more time before he stepped back, allowing me to close the door. I didn't even tell him goodbye as I told the driver to pull off.

"You good?" Tracy asked me.

"Yeah," I replied. "How about you?"

"Girl, do you know this nigga tried to give me some lame-ass excuse? Come to find out the chick was his baby mama," she said. "I'm happy I never gave that nigga no punanny. Hell, from the way she was cutting up, I knew they were still fucking around, and that wasn't going to sit too well with me. I was trying to make him my side nigga, I wasn't trying to be his side bitch."

"Girl, you're too damn much," I said, laughing. "You wanna head back to the hotel?"

"Yes, please. I've had enough drama for tonight, and I'm tired," she replied with a yawn, which made me yawn.

I was actually glad that she had said that because I was tired as well. To be honest, I couldn't wait until the trip was over because it was becoming too much. Besides, I missed my siblings like crazy also. I couldn't wait to get home to see them, as well as give them all the gifts that I'd bought for them. A small part of me couldn't wait to see Onijae as well.

When we pulled up to the hotel, we paid the cab driver and got out. We then headed straight to our suite. We didn't waste any time hopping in the shower. Of course, Aqura had been blowing my phone up, but I didn't bother answering a call, nor a text.

Once I was finished in the bathroom, I powered my phone off and hopped in the bed. It was definitely an eventful day. Hopefully, the next day would be better.